TAKE ME SLOWLY PART 1

AURORA HOLLOW DUET

MAGGIE ALABASTER

Trigger warnings for mentions of child death and chronic illness.

Content advisory. This book contains MM.

This book is set in the fictional town of Aurora Hollow, Canada. British English spelling is used throughout, because the author is Australian. Any use of — is because I like them and is not an indicator of AI use. I do not use AI in my writing.

1

LEAH

"He's a goddamn motherfucker who needs to stay up on the mountain."

"Yeah he does. We'll make sure…"

I kept my eyes on my phone, ignoring the men who strode into Snowdrop Café, talking loudly, like they owned the place.

"What'll it be?"

I glanced up at the server who stopped beside my table.

Her wild curls were peppered with grey, warm blue eyes and a worn t-shirt with 'Carly' embroidered on the breast.

"Just a coffee, please," I said. "Nothing fancy."

Carly smiled. "That's good, because we don't do

much fancy around here." She gave me a wink before bustling away to make my coffee.

"Right. Thanks." I dropped my gaze back toward my phone, not really paying attention to anything on the screen.

Instead, I absorbed my surroundings. The smell of coffee, bacon and waffles with a hint of syrup. The muted sound of people sharing breakfast at tables around me. A quiet huff of laughter, followed by a louder giggle. A mother having breakfast with her child at the next table over. Sharing a moment of togetherness.

My gaze rose, traced the exposed beams that stretched the length of the ceiling. Live edged and raw, they'd probably hung there for over a hundred years. I bet they had some stories to tell.

"You think he'd get the message by now." Still talking loudly, the two men settled into stools at the bar top that ran across the front of the window, from beside the door, to the corner wall.

"Some people take a bit more…encouragement." One of them turned around, his deep hazel eyes settling on me for a moment before looking toward Carly. "Can we get a couple of coffees and full breakfasts over here?" He glanced at me again before swivelling around and returning to his conversation.

Carly placed my coffee down in front of me and rolled her eyes at his back before disappearing in the direction of the kitchen.

I forced back a smile, curled my hands around my cup and lifted it to inhale the smell. Maybe Aurora Hollow *wasn't* fancy, but the coffee smelled good. For a while I let it take me away from here, soothe my jangled nerves and let me remember a time before.

A childish peal of laughter dragged me back into the present. The reminder wasn't entirely unwelcome. Who could resist a laughing kid, after all? And reality wasn't too bad.

Today.

I looked over to see the kid holding a piece of bacon in her hand, grinning.

"Hey," her mother protested. "That's my bacon." But she didn't seem to mind, even when her daughter popped it into her mouth with a cheeky grin and chewed vigourously. She caught my eye and shook her head while smiling.

"I can't take my eyes off my bacon for a moment."

"It *is* bacon." I returned her smile. "Who can resist?"

"Not Sarah." She nodded towards her daughter. "You new in town?"

"Is it that obvious?" I winced.

"We don't get so many visitors this time of year," she said. "Especially in the middle of the week. Mostly folks come during the summer and winter. Right after school goes back, things get real quiet. For a little while. I'm Fiona Jameson." She leaned over and offered her hand. "This ratbag is my daughter Sarah."

I shook her hand. "Leah."

"Are you staying long?" Fiona asked.

"I don't know," I admitted. "Right now, I'm playing things by ear."

"If you need a place to stay, the cottage beside mine is vacant," she said. "Sarah and me, we're pretty quiet."

"What are you doing, Fiona?"

I glanced up to see the hazel-eyed man looming over both of us.

"I'm being friendly, Connor Ferguson," Fiona said tartly. "Something you and Riley could do with a lesson in."

"We're friendly," Connor protested. "We just don't go offering accommodation to blow-ins."

"Bullshit," Fiona scoffed. "Your whole livelihoods depend on people visiting Aurora Hollow."

"Tourists who don't stick around," Connor said.

He gave me a look that suggested I'd fit into that category if he had his way.

I decided right then to stay for longer. Just to show him Leah Kent wasn't going to be pushed around.

"What makes you think I'm not a tourist?" I asked easily.

He leaned back, regarded me before raising his finger and moving it around in a circle in the air. "You have that look about you. Like you're not here for zip lining or white water rafting."

"Him and Riley run the adventure tourism around these parts," Fiona said. "Mostly people don't die doing stuff with them."

I looked back in time to catch her smile. She was clearly trying to get a rise out of him.

"Mostly?" Connor sounded disbelieving. "No one has ever died on any of our tours."

"Yet," I said. I couldn't help getting in on the shit disturbing. That would teach him to be more welcoming.

"Right." Connor's voice was tight. "There's a first time for everything. How about a freebie, city girl?"

I let my gaze slowly slide back to him and smiled. "No thanks."

"Chicken?" he asked. He raised his stubbled chin in challenge.

"Sensible," I retorted. "I don't want to be your first fatality. Besides, think about what that would do for your reputation. Not to mention the potential lawsuit from my family." He didn't have to know that wouldn't come.

He leaned in closer, letting me smell the coffee on his breath. "Honey, that's what waivers are for." He straightened up, his smile all smug, as if somehow he'd won this round.

"It's still a no," I said. "So, Fiona, you were telling me about a cottage? I think I might stick around town for a while."

Connor grunted in annoyance before turning around and stalking back to his seat.

"Don't worry about him," Fiona said, flapping a hand in his direction. "Those guys always get restless at this time of year. When everything slows down, they take it personally. Like somehow it's their fault no one is coming. The truth is, folks are getting kids back to school. And you know, a lull never hurt anyone."

"It's good to have a break sometimes," I agreed, not quite meeting her gaze.

"Exactly," Fiona said. "Sarah, finish up your

breakfast. We have time to show Leah to the cottage before I have to get you to school."

Sarah groaned. "Do I have to go to school?"

"Yes, you do," Fiona told her firmly. "The law says so and so do I."

"The law sucks," Sarah declared. "I'd rather go fishing."

"She'd fish all day every day if she could," Fiona told me. "She's really good at it too. I hope you like fish, because we always have much more than we need."

"I love fish," I said. "Maybe you could teach me how to catch one."

"Right now?" Sarah looked hopeful.

"School," Fiona reminded her. "Then homework. Then fishing. Maybe Leah could come along with us on the weekend. We know a few places only the locals know."

I glanced in the direction of Connor and his friend Riley. Both watched me with matching expressions. Not quite hostile, but just this side of it.

"Are you allowed to take people there?" I asked pointedly.

"I don't need their permission," she said, giving them both scowls until they turned away to eat their breakfasts. "Don't let them get to you. They'll lighten up in a few weeks when the weather gets colder. Especially when the snow starts to fall."

I decided to take her advice and not let their attitudes bother me. So far, everyone else I met in Aurora Hollow was more welcoming. If a couple of guys had their heads up their asses, that was their problem.

"If I'll still be here then," I said. I meant it when I said I was playing it by ear. I might decide the next day that I wanted to go back to the city. Except I didn't. I needed this break. I needed to be somewhere else for a while.

"I hope you'll stick around," Fiona said. "This place needs shaking up and I have a feeling you're the person to do it."

"I have a feeling some people would object to me shaking up anything." I didn't look in Connor's direction; no doubt my meaning was clear enough.

"Those are the people who need shaking up most of all," Fiona said with a laugh. "Don't get me wrong, most people in town are wonderful. It's nice to meet someone new, is all." She swallowed down the last of her coffee and gestured at Sarah, who hopped up out of her chair before carefully pushing it back in under the table.

I dropped a couple of bills on the table to pay for

my coffee and followed them out the door, barely glancing at Connor before I passed. Just enough to see him curl his lip at me. I didn't even humour him with an eye roll.

"The best thing about Aurora Hollow, apart from the views of the mountains, is the fact you can walk everywhere," Fiona said.

I realised both of those things when I arrived yesterday. The town was compact, and the view over the Rockies was stunning. We weren't even at the highest point of the mountain, but rather nestled into a literal hollow about half way up. The view was still incredible. It must be even more stunning up at the peak.

"It's beautiful here." The air tasted clean and fresh. The town itself smelled of pine and maple, with a hint of water from the falls just out of town. If I listened closely, I could imagine hearing the rush of water pouring over rocks and gushing down the side of the mountain. All I really heard was the whisper of the wind and the crunch of our shoes on the road.

"It really is," Fiona said. "We're lucky to live here. I grew up here. Most of my friends left for the city, but you couldn't drag me away. And it's the perfect place to raise a kid. Even a precocious seven-year-old who has skinned knees more often than not." She looked fondly at her daughter.

"Dylan says precocious means I'm a smartass," Sarah declared.

"Dylan Fielding is as precocious as you are," Fiona told her. To me she said, "She's in her class at school. Some days, they're best friends. And some days they aren't."

I held back a laugh. "I remember those days. For me it was Emerald Garcia. Sometimes we shared our crayons and sometimes we didn't." I hadn't thought about her in years. I wondered where she was now. We lost touch when we went to different high schools. That seemed like a thousand years ago now.

Fiona laughed. "For me it was Connor's older sister, Whitney. We used to do everything together. Connor and Riley would always try to tag along, but mostly they'd pull our hair and be dickheads."

"So you've known them for a long time," I said.

"Practically forever," she agreed. "I could tell you some stories about those two."

We stopped in front of a pair of small cottages, both stucco, cedar shakes and double glazed windows. She pulled a set of keys out of her handbag and unlocked the door of the cottage on the right.

"I'm friends with the owner, so I'm the one who

lets in anyone who rents the place," she explained. "It's small, but it's fully furnished and close to the restaurants and cafés. And the grocery store and all that too."

"And us," Sarah said.

"That too," Fiona said. She handed me the keys. "I have to get her to school and me to work. Make yourself comfortable."

It seemed she decided I was going to rent the place. I decided she was probably right. This would do perfectly, for now.

2

———

LEAH

THE KEY TURNED EASILY in the lock, the solid wooden door opening with barely a sound. I stepped past a series of hooks hanging from a plank of wood attached to the wall, and into a small kitchen with butcher block countertops and a huge farm sink. A wide window let in a ton of light. I'd be able to wash vegetables and look out into the street.

The small dishwasher beside the sink looked relatively new.

I peered through a doorway that led off the kitchen. A neat bedroom held a queen size bed and a small wardrobe. It shared a bathroom with another bedroom the same size as the first.

"Wow," I whispered to myself. A clawfoot tub sat under the window, allowing a view of the forest of trees beside the hollow. I could see myself admiring that view while enjoying a glass of wine.

I stepped past a small, cosy living room, to a sliding glass door which led out to an equally small patio. A couple of Adirondack chairs surrounded a fire pit which looked well used. Was that a hot tub beside the patio? It was.

I'd definitely find my way in there at some point.

I took the short walk back to the hotel I spent the night at before, checked out and got my car. The drive back to the cottage was no more than two minutes. Moving the rest of my belongings into the cottage took only a little longer than that.

I tossed my drawing pad and pencils onto the dining table before setting up my easel near the back door, where the light was best. I placed my paints down beside it. I hadn't painted in years, but having everything set up was a nice start.

I dragged my suitcase into one of the bedrooms to unpack my clothes into the wardrobe. Fortunately I hadn't brought much with me, because it was a tight fit once everything was hung on hangers. A couple of things, including my snowboots and jacket were relegated to the wardrobe in the spare room.

I pushed my suitcase under the bed and was about to step out onto the patio when someone tapped at the front door. After startling half out of my skin, I hurried over to open it.

I half expected to see Connor or Riley glaring at me, maybe insisting I pack up and leave.

Instead, I was greeted by an older woman, her grey hair tied back in a braid that fell to her waist. In one hand, she held a pie, in the other a bottle of wine.

"I heard through the grapevine that someone would be living here." She pressed the wine to me before stepping inside. "Figured I'd offer a welcome."

"That's...very nice of you," I said. I heard the grapevine worked fast in towns like this, but I hadn't expected it to be quite this quick.

She placed the pie on the kitchen counter. "It's how we are around here. We take care of each other and welcome strangers." She nodded as though she was hoping to pick up some juicy gossip to share with that grapevine.

"Most people have been very welcoming," I said. Connor and his friend were spending too much time rent free in my head already.

"I'm Louisa Hill," she said. "Mayor of Aurora Hollow. I make it my business to see everyone has what they need."

"Leah Kent," I told her. "I appreciate that. I think I'm going to like it here."

"Course you will." She stepped over to my easel. "You an artist?"

"I dabble," I replied. "Portraits and landscapes mostly these days." I tried to ignore the tug in my heart, the frustration of broken dreams. Ambitions I'd never be able to fulfil.

I forced them aside. Regret wouldn't change a thing.

"Is that right?" She picked up my sketchpad from the table and flicked back a couple of pages. "Huh, you're pretty good." She seemed surprised.

"I'm okay," I said.

Like any creative person, I saw the flaws in my work in ways others didn't. A line here that was too straight. Shading there that needed an extra touch. Fingers that were slightly too long. "There's always room for improvement."

"Well, if you ever need a model, I'm good at sitting still." She closed the book and placed it back on the table, almost with reverence.

"I'd be honoured to draw you," I said honestly. "I could use the practice." And she had a fascinating facial structure.

"Then we can make time," she said. "Like I said,

I'm always down to help the people in town. Unlike some, I think the place could use some new blood. Otherwise a town stagnates, you know?"

"Any community does," I agreed. Even big cities stagnated without new people.

Carefully, I added, "Connor Ferguson and his friend Riley don't seem to think the way you do." I didn't know why I was bringing them up. They'd probably laugh their heads off if they knew. Thinking they got under my skin somehow. Ha, not a chance.

Louisa snorted. "Those two wouldn't know what's good for the town if it bit them on the ass. They've always had some funny ideas. Their fathers too. Jacob Ferguson and Henry Crane, the boys' fathers, were descended from the people who founded this town. Seemed to think that means they owned the place. If I'm honest, it's past time they got over themselves. They didn't give you any trouble, did they?" She narrowed her eyes, as if she was ready to storm out and give them a piece of her mind if I said they had.

"Nothing I couldn't handle," I said. "I'm used to dealing with men like them." Arrogant and full of themselves and their own importance. They were nothing new. Admittedly, I wasn't used to them coming in such attractive packaging, but that was all it was. Pretty on the outside, asshole on the inside. Original? Not at all.

"Good for you," she said approvingly. "Don't let either of them step on or over you. They do it once, they'll keep doing it."

That was exactly the impression I got from them, and I wasn't backing down. If they wanted me to leave town, then I'd stay. What could they do to me anyway?

"Think you'll be sticking around for a while?" Louisa asked. This seemed to be exactly the gossip she'd come here for. I was happy to give it in return for a pie. I could smell the apple and spices, the scent drifting up and tickling my nose. It would taste perfect with a big dollop of cream, or some ice cream.

"I thought I would," I said easily. "I'd like to see how it looks up here when it snows. From close up." I'd seen it from a distance for more years than I could remember. For just as long, I'd wanted to come here. I used to beg, even if it was only for a weekend.

My parents were... Not disinterested. Adamant. They refused to travel up into the mountains. I won't pretend to understand why. Every time I asked, they changed the subject. Eventually, I gave up asking.

I hadn't told them where I was going when I left Vancouver, just that I was getting away. I hated keeping secrets from them, but for some reason I couldn't explain, I had a feeling this would anger them.

Maybe it was nothing more than rebellion that drew me to this place. Maybe it was something more. Maybe it was a need for fresh air and altitude. I didn't know. I just needed to be up here.

"It's something else," Louisa said. "This place is beautiful in all it's seasons and moods. The blazing sun and heat, thunderstorms and pouring rain, and freezing blizzards. If you have the right view out the window, you don't need a television. You could stand there, watch the landscape change for hours and never get bored."

"That's what I'm hoping for," I said. "I want to draw and paint all of those moods and seasons. I could do a series of paintings." For the first time in I didn't know how long, I was actually excited. My hands itched to pick up a brush or pencil and get to work.

"That sounds like a fabulous idea. We have a market once a month if you want to sell them.

Every first Saturday, behind the Frosty Brew. Usually everyone moves into the pub after the market." She grinned, showing a gap between her top front teeth.

"Jacob Ferguson, he owns the pub; he loves it. Most of the money people make selling things goes to him in the end. But we do a lot of barter too. You know, a painting for a couple of dozen eggs. That kind of thing."

"I love that," I said sincerely. That was exactly the kind of thing I came here for. I didn't mind swapping my work for things like that. Useful things. Or not so useful, because life was too short not to have a few pretty or whimsical items on the shelves around the living room. The cottage had a couple of vases, and books here or there, but it was impersonal. If I was going to stay here for a while, I wanted it to feel like home.

If I could make a bit of money and not spend it all at the pub, that would be good too.

"Me too," she said. "It's a good opportunity to get to know our neighbours, and the kids always have a ball. You must try Lyle Johnson-Jones' cheesecake. He and his husband own Hollow Bites, the best restaurant in town. Not that I'm biased to one over the others." She slid me a sly smile.

"Of course not," I said with a grin. "I'm sure the town mayor has to be impartial."

"Naturally," she agreed. "But that cheesecake is pretty fucking good."

Now I laughed. "I'm hungry just thinking about it. I admit to being partial to cheese in general and cheesecake in particular."

Louisa chuckled. "You should fit in here perfectly. We tend to bond over our mutual appreciation of cheesecake." She smacked her lips loudly.

"I knew I was drawn to the place for a reason," I said.

And I was. I got into my tiny little hatchback and started to drive, not knowing where I was going until I pulled in here. Something about the place made me stop and look twice. Something comfortably familiar and magnetic at the same time. I couldn't put my finger on what. Something needed me to be here. Like a secret waiting to be unravelled. A secret that had nothing to do with cheesecake. That could be the cherry on the top.

"I should get back to it," she said. "If you need anything, town hall is right beside the café. If I'm not there, someone usually knows where to find me."

I nodded. "Thank you. And thank you for the pie. I was wondering what I'd do for dessert." Of course,

I'd have to figure out dinner first. I wasn't much of a cook, having left that to my parents, or a microwave meal. Now was as good a time as any, to learn. I certainly had the time to spare. I spied a modem in the corner of the living room, so the cottage had Wi-Fi. I made a note to look up some recipes and write down a shopping list before heading out to the grocery store.

There was that twinge in my heart again. The endless ache I tried so hard to ignore. I came here to put it behind me and that's what I'd do. I'd draw, I'd paint and I'd learn how to cook. I'd embrace this change and all the opportunities this small town held. Now was my chance to reinvent myself and start my life over. No one knew me here. No one had expectations of me. No one but myself.

This was exactly what I needed. A new beginning.

I kept telling myself that, but it didn't ease the heaviness in my chest and it didn't help the unease when I remembered the hostility in Connor Ferguson's eyes. I didn't know why it mattered, but I knew that man and his friend were going to be a whole lot of trouble.

3

LEAH

"WHAT ARE YOU DOING HERE?"

I'd set up my easel on the edge of town, in the dappled light of a couple of tall oaks. My easel angled so I could paint and observe the town. People came and went from stores with white stucco and wood, stained dark, contrasting with bright awnings and buckets of late summer flowers.

No one passed anyone else without saying hello. Many stopped for a quick conversation before bustling on. Others lingered for a few minutes, enjoying the sunshine before they went on their way. The whole atmosphere was slower and friendlier than the city.

Aurora Hollow was a true little community. Like something out of a storybook. Hopefully not like those British shows where they solved a murder every episode.

No, the scene that unfolded on my canvas was warm and friendly. The opposite of the voice that spoke behind me.

I glanced over my shoulder to see Riley Crane leaning against his pickup, legs crossed at his ankles, arms over his burly chest. He looked just this side of hostile. I did my best to ignore the fact he was also this side of delicious.

"Never seen anyone paint?" I turned back to my easel.

"I've seen plenty of people paint." His shoes crunched on the ground as he stepped around to stand beside me. "I would have thought you left town by now."

"Why would you think that?" I added some shading in front of the café, deepening the shadows that surrounded the doorway. I wanted anyone who looked at the painting to wonder what was inside. Maybe they'd come out here to find out for themselves. If not, maybe they'd imagine.

That was one of my favourite things about art. It inspired imagination. Everyone saw every piece in a different way. They all brought their life experiences to that moment, interpreting based on what they knew to be true. Which could, of course, be completely different to what the artist knew. Or intended.

"Connor wasn't very welcoming," Riley said, leaning in to take a closer look at my brush strokes. Close enough that his nose bumped against the canvas, leaving a dot of green on the tip. "Then I went and smudged your little painting."

Little painting?

I couldn't tell if he'd done it on purpose or not. It might have been an accident, and it might be an attempt to piss me off. As if somehow if he did something bad enough, I'd pack up and get out of town. I wanted to laugh. He'd have to try harder than that.

He raised his hand toward the canvas as though he could rub the mark away. Like it was nothing more than a smudge on a phone screen.

I dropped my brush and caught his wrist. "It's fine, I can fix it." I ignored the way his muscles flexed in his arm before I dropped my hand.

"Maybe you should wipe that off." I glanced up at his nose. "Just in case it's toxic."

He wiped at his nose with the sleeve of his dark grey Henley. "You wouldn't paint with toxic paint, would you, sweetheart?"

I cleaned my brush and fixed up the spot he smudged. "Of course not, but I try to keep it off my face." He didn't need to get that up close and personal with my painting.

"Oh yeah? Where do you like it?" He took a step back and looked me up and down. A small streak of paint still decorated the side of his nose.

I decided not to mention it.

"On my canvas." I dabbed at the spot until I was satisfied it was fixed. "Where else?"

Was he trying to flirt with me or get a rise out of me? Did it matter? He wasn't going to succeed with either. No more than he and Connor were going to chase me out of town.

"You know, you're pretty good," he said grudgingly. "Do you do nudes?"

"Sometimes," I said, not looking in his direction.

He gave off that 'I know I'm attractive' air already without me stroking his ego. Dark hair, squared chin with a dimple, and blue eyes; no doubt he got more than his share of attention. Did he flirt with people he took on adventure tours? That seemed likely to me. He probably flirted with anyone who stayed still for long enough. All the more reason for me to stay away from him. Between his and Connor's frigid welcome, and this disingenuous bid for my attention, Riley Crane was trouble with a capital T.

"Will you paint me?" he asked.

"Why would I do that?" I dabbed my brush in the red and touched up the H on the front of Hollow Bites. It was a little too vibrant, where the actual letter was faded. Well loved.

"Why wouldn't you?" he countered.

"I'm sure you're too busy to stand still for a few hours," I said. "Not to mention, like you said, I might not be in town for long."

"You wouldn't stick around to paint me naked?" he asked. "Plenty of women would."

"Then you won't have any trouble finding someone who will," I said. If he thought he'd impress me with the suggestion of competition, he was barking up the wrong tree. I learned the hard way not to get involved with players.

"That's true," he agreed. "They're practically lining up."

"Yeah, I know, I painted them all." I gestured towards the canvas. A whole two vague figures stood near the pub. A man and a woman, leaning with their heads close, talking about something. They weren't anyone I'd seen today, just figures I thought should be there. Something to add a hint of mystery to the painting. People could speculate who they were and what they were saying to each other. 'People' included me.

"You're missing a few," he said with a grunt.

I put down my brush and leaned back to appraise my work. "Looks perfect to me."

"How much?" he asked.

I glanced up at him in surprise.

"What?" Was this another attempt to get a response from me?

"How much for the painting?" He waved a hand at it. He'd pushed his sleeves up to his elbows, so the veins in his arms were visible, obscured here and there by tattoos.

"You want to buy my painting?" I forced myself to focus on his face, not his veins and not the way his biceps were pushing at the seams of his shirt. "What for?"

"What do you think I want it for?" He frowned. His brow slowly smoothed out and he smiled. "You think I want to put it on the front of my dartboard and take potshots?" He mimed doing just that, closing one eye as he aimed at a pretend target.

"Do you?" I asked.

"That would be a waste," he said. "I was thinking I

could hang it over my fireplace. I'll be sure to leave room for my nude."

"I'm not painting you naked," I said.

Seeing himself through my eyes would only inflate his ego further. He was a pain in the ass, but he was too attractive for his own good. I'd bet he wasn't born with a humble bone in his body either. Or his vocabulary.

"I was thinking you could do a self-portrait," he said easily. "Then anytime anyone walks into my house, they can see your pretty little pussy." His gaze dropped to the apex of my thighs as though he could see straight through my jeans.

I could almost see him mentally stripping them off me. Tearing my panties away and pressing his fingers into me.

Heat crept up my face. "I don't do self portraits," I mumbled. Especially if he was planning to turn it into something dirty. Nudes were supposed to be artistic. A celebration of the human body. Not cheap porn.

"What about I paint you then?" he said.

"Can you paint?" I arched an eyebrow at him, trying to regain my composure.

"Only houses." He grinned. "But I'm willing to give it a try if you are."

"I think I'll pass." I started to pack up my things. It was almost time for lunch and I was starting to get stiff from sitting for so long. I should know better, but when I was caught up in something, it took up all my attention. When I used to be able to…

I forced myself not to head down that line of thought.

"Suit yourself," he said with a shrug. "You don't know what you're missing."

"I have a pretty good idea," I said, managing to sound suitably unimpressed.

"I think you just implied I'm a two pump chump who doesn't know how to find a clit." His frown was back.

"I didn't imply anything, but if that's where your mind went, maybe you should get some help," I said lightly.

He didn't look like the kind of man who couldn't find a clit. He looked like one who knew how to make a girl scream two or three times in quick succession. I carefully avoided looking in the direction of his groin. At half a glance, I could already tell he was packing.

"See, that's the problem with city girls," he said slowly. "They think they know everything. I've got news for you, sweetheart, you don't know fucking *anything.*" He was looking at me the way he was in the café on my first morning in town. Like I was a waste of the clean air up here in the mountains.

"I don't think I know everything." I crossed my arms, pushing my breasts up in my tank top.

His gaze dropped down to them, widening slightly before he looked back at my face.

"You should get out of town while you can," he growled softly.

"Or what?" I asked. He was a few inches taller than me, and a lot wider, but I still wasn't intimidated. All I had to do was shout and half the town would come out to see what was going on.

He leaned in to speak in my ear. He smelled of leather and some kind of fuel. Earthy and heady. The men back home didn't smell like this. I was more accustomed to cologne and clean laundry. Pleasant, but not intoxicating like this.

When he spoke, he spoke slowly, barely breathing. "Or you'll find yourself on your knees, choking on my cock. I see the way you look at me. You think you don't want me, but you do. If you stick around town, you're going to be begging me to fuck you."

"In your dreams," I whispered. No way was I going to let him see he was getting to me. It was only because he was so close and it had been so long since

I'd been intimate with anyone. A dry spell like that would make any girl lose herself for a few moments.

He brushed a dark curl off the side of my cheek. "I think you mean in yours, sweetheart. So, how much?"

I was taken aback for a moment before I realised he was asking about the painting again. Of course he was. He really had me on the back foot. Somewhere I wasn't used to being.

"I'm not sure if it's for sale," I said. "It may need to be touched up when it's dry. When it's ready, I'll have it available at the community market."

"I'm a patient guy. When I want something, I know how to wait." His gaze dipped toward my breasts again.

"You'll be waiting for a long time for that," I told him. "Approximately...forever."

His lips curved up, but the smug expression never wavered. "We'll see." He shoved his hands into his pockets and strode away like he owned the town and everything in it.

Including me.

4

———

LEAH

"I'M NOT THE BEST COOK," I said apologetically as I handed Fiona a bowl of fusilli Alfredo and a glass of red wine.

"Anything is better than having to cook for myself." She set her glass down on the patio beside her Adirondack chair and picked up a fork. "This smells amazing."

I sat down beside her and took a gulp of wine before starting on my own food. After a couple of mouthfuls of pasta and mushrooms, I had to nod.

"Okay, it's not bad." It could do with an extra sprinkle of cheese, but other than that, I gave myself a mental pat on the back.

"Thank you for asking me over." She went to push a forkful of pasta into her mouth when it fell off the fork back into the bowl. Her eyes widened in surprise when she found empty prongs. She giggled and stabbed them into the rebellious pasta and tried again.

"It was the least I could do after you welcomed me into town," I said.

The evening air was still warm enough to be comfortable, but with a hint that cooler nights were coming soon. In front of us, the sun was setting, casting a golden glow over the ragged landscape. The smell of leaves and wildflowers was carried on the air like a subtle perfume. The kind you could never get tired of smelling. If I could bottle it, I'd make a fortune. If I wanted to share it with the world, that was. I wasn't sure if I did, to be honest.

In spite of how many tourists came here at different times of the year, right now it felt like a hidden secret up here in the mountains. A special place just for us. No wonder Fiona never left. I might not have either, in her shoes.

She made a dismissive sound in the back of her throat. "That was nothing. Anyone else would have done it if I hadn't. Besides, it's partially selfish. I've had all sorts of people staying next door. You looked quiet and sane in comparison."

"In comparison," I echoed, smiling over at her.

She laughed. "You know what I mean. It's great that so many tourists come here, but sometimes it can get…loud. Although, it's better now Sarah is older. When she was a baby and wasn't sleeping, I could use all the peace and quiet I could get. I was an exhausted mess back then. As opposed to being a hot mess now." She patted her dark blonde hair with her spare hand as if all of it was in disarray.

"You are not a mess," I assured her. "But if you were, at least you're a hot one."

"I knew I liked you." She grinned. "You have good taste. So do I, come to think of it. In friends and kids."

"It must be hard doing that on your own," I said carefully. I didn't know what her circumstances were yet. I was curious, but didn't want to be nosy.

If she was annoyed with me asking, she showed no sign. If anything, she seemed happy to talk about it. It didn't take a genius to figure out Sarah was her favourite topic of conversation. Not that it was the only thing she talked about, but she clearly adored her daughter.

"It has its moments," she agreed. "But her father was an asshole, so it could have been worse." She caught the expression on my face and smiled. "It's okay, you can ask. For the record, he was a hot asshole. Call it a moment of weakness. I don't regret it, or her."

"So he's out of the picture?" I guessed.

"All the way out," she agreed. "He gave up any right to her before she was born. He leaves us alone and I don't ask him for money. It works out for both of us. And since my parents live a block away, I'm not completely on my own. They love having her once in a while to give me a break."

"Are you their only child?" I chased a mushroom around my bowl before successfully stabbing and eating it.

"I have an older brother, but he's away in the military." She gazed wistfully out over the valley. "We only see him a couple of times a year. What about you?"

"I have an older stepbrother," I said. "My mother told me they wanted a bunch of kids, but we were all they got." And I still wasn't good enough. "You must miss your brother a lot."

"Sometimes," she agreed. "I used to want a bunch of kids, but I think Sarah might be it. Sometimes I wish… But then I count my blessings, because she's a good kid and she and I are tight. Check back when she's thirteen; that might have changed." She looked rueful.

"I'm sure you'll do fine with her, even when she's a teenager," I said. "You both seem to have your heads screwed on right."

"Can you tell my mother that?" She picked up her wine and smiled as she took a sip. "I think she still hopes I'll get married someday. Something about having someone look after me when her and dad are gone. They can be old-fashioned when they want to."

"They sound like my parents," I said. "It's like they can't handle the fact that we grew up."

Fiona groaned. "I know, right? I think mine would like to have bonsaied me and kept me a kid forever. I guess that's why they like grandkids. Someone they can fuss over when their own kids have gotten too old for it."

"Is there such a thing as being too old to be treated like you're fragile?" I said with a snort.

"Good point." She pointed her fork at me. "Probably not. Don't tell my parents. It'll encourage them. Speaking of them, you have to come over for a barbecue sometime. Half the town turns out when they throw one. I'll convince them they should have one asap. They usually don't take much convincing.

Any chance for my father to get his hands on the grill. And my mother will take any chance you can get to have a night off from cooking. I guess that runs in the family."

"Do Connor and Riley go to their barbecues?" I asked, trying not to look too much like I dreaded seeing either of them again.

"Usually," she said. "Did you have more trouble with them?" She looked like she was going to storm over to their houses and kick them in the balls on my behalf. If she was going to do that, I'd have to insist on tagging along to watch. Something like that couldn't be missed. Or recorded on my phone for shit and giggles.

"Just a conversation with Riley," I said, trying to keep my tone light, as if I didn't care. After all, I shouldn't let it bother me. I certainly shouldn't let it get me hot and bothered. "He seemed to like my painting." I waved my fork in the direction of where it still sat on the easel, a couple of metres away.

"I like it too," she said carefully. "Why do I sense there's more to this? Was he an asshole to you?"

"Not exactly," I admitted. "He flirted with me. And then he suggested it might be better for me if I leave town."

She frowned. "You're not going, are you? Because if he and Connor make any trouble for you…"

"I'm not going anywhere," I said firmly. "I like it here. Everyone else has been lovely. Whatever they have going on," I waved my own fork in the air, "that's their problem."

"Agreed," she said. "But if they give you any trouble, let me know. I have no trouble whipping their asses for you. I've done it before."

I believed her. "I can handle them," I said. I'd start by staying away from them as much as possible. Sooner or later, they would get over me being here and move on to something or someone else.

"Of course you can," she said firmly. "You know what, you should come to the pub with me after we're finished here. A couple of the girls are going to be there. They'll love you."

"Sounds like fun," I said. It wouldn't hurt to make a few more friends in town. Maybe

I'd never leave. I wondered how Riley would respond to that. He seemed certain I'd fall into bed with him at some point. He might take me staying as a challenge.

Whatever, let him. He'd figure out soon enough that he didn't own me and I owed him nothing.

"It will be," she said. "Whitney and Holly are

going to love you. And since I don't have Sarah, we can all get as drunk as we like."

"I can't even remember the last time I got drunk," I said, deadpan.

Fiona stared at me for a few moments, before my words sank in. She tipped back her head and laughed.

"I'll bet you can't. Neither can I. Apparently I had a good time. According to Whitney, I was dancing on the tables in the pub. Lucky those things are sturdy." She grooved in her chair for a few moments while taking a few more sips of wine.

I wouldn't be dancing on any tables, that was for sure, but it would be nice to let loose for a while. To forget about what brought me here to Aurora Hollow in the first place.

"Let me guess, you were wild when you were a kid," I said with a knowing smile.

"Not just then." She shook her finger at me. "I'm still wild now when I get the chance. Just a bit less young and dumb than I was back then."

"I guess we all have to grow up a little bit eventually," I said.

"Just a little." She held her hand up, her fingers slightly apart. "No more going home with people I regret."

"Did you ever... With Riley or Connor?" I grimaced. Did I want the answer to that? For some reason, it was reassuring to know neither of them fathered Sarah. I didn't know why that mattered. Possibly because I liked the kid and she deserved better than to be related to them. Yes, that was all.

She grimaced even harder. "Hell no. Those guys are like brothers to me. That would be icky and weird."

Why did I feel a wash of relief? It wasn't as though I was interested in either of them anyway. I liked the idea I wasn't the only one immune to them. Yeah, that made sense. They thought they were irresistible. Or Riley did anyway. But they weren't. Not at all. That could be their exact problem. Us women see right through them and their bullshit.

"You're not interested, are you?" Fiona asked.

"In either of them?" I pulled a face. "No way. They made it clear they both don't like me. That goes both ways." No way in the world was I going to end up on my knees choking on either of their cocks. Painting their likeness and putting them on a dartboard for target practice on the other hand? That wasn't off the table. With any luck, they'd leave me alone from now on. No doubt they had better things to do with their time than harass me. I had better things to do than be harassed.

"Right," she said slowly. But the expression on her face suggested she didn't completely believe me. That was okay, she was just another person I needed to prove wrong.

5

CONNOR

I POURED myself a bourbon before stepping out from behind the bar. I spent enough hours stuck behind it for one day. Zara and Luke could handle the crowd.

If you called a couple of dozen people a crowd. Everyone pretended they weren't bored as fuck during the lull, but Thursday night they always ended up here. Whatever, it was good for business. One that would be mine someday. No time fucking soon if I had my way.

"Hey," Riley greeted me as I stepped over to the table where he was sitting, shooting the shit with Blaise Edwards and Ryan Evans. Both guys we went to school with. Ryan was built like a tree trunk, and Blaise like a whippet. Both of them were okay, I guess, for dumbass mountain boys with no ambition.

"Hey." I toasted Riley with my drink before taking a gulp. I needed the burn as the liquor travelled down my body. It soothed and numbed, taking the edge off. "What are you assholes up to?"

"Riley here was telling us there's some new chick in town," Ryan said.

For some reason, his words irritated me, but I shrugged it off.

"What's new? There's always new people in town."

"Not a tourist," Blaise said, his eyes on me like he was watching my reaction carefully. Who knows why? He was always thinking too much.

"He's talking about the woman living in the cottage beside Fiona," Riley said. "Leah. She paints." He looked pleased with himself for some reason.

"How do you know she paints?" Blaise turned his searching look to Riley.

"She showed me." Riley sipped his beer. Now he was the one watching me for my reaction. His eyebrow twitching at the way my jaw worked back and forth.

"Is that all she showed you?" Ryan asked.

"For now." Riley sat back in his stool, cocky as fuck. "She's hot for me. She was almost ready to drop to her knees and suck my cock."

"Bullshit," I said. "If she was ready for that, you'd let her." Asshole could be persuasive.

He shrugged one shoulder. "A guy can play hard to get."

I snorted loudly. "Since when have you played hard to get?" I fixed him with a steady look to remind him he never turned me down. Of course not, Riley Crane and I had been tight since high school. We'd gone through all sorts of shit together. Shared women and each other. He was many things, but celibate wasn't one of them.

He pretended to be offended. "I hardly know the woman."

I stared at him for a moment before barking out a ha. "That's never stopped you before. How many times have you fucked a woman without so much as asking her name?"

"How many times have you?" He levelled the accusation at me without flinching.

"This isn't about me," I said. I nodded my thanks to Zara, who placed a fresh bourbon in front of me and took away the empty glass.

"She told you no, didn't she?" Ryan grinned at Riley.

Riley flipped him off. "It was a 'not yet,' not a no. Trust me, she wants me."

"Was she sober?" Blaise asked.

Riley's brows dipped. "Of course she was. Just because you have to get a woman drunk to fuck her..."

Blaise drew himself up, his face turning stony like he was ready for a fight. "I would never—"

I put a hand on his shoulder to push him back into his stool.

"Don't take the bait. Riley is messing around."

Blaise huffed out a breath, but drew himself back in and nodded. "Right."

"Speak of the devil." Riley's eyes were on the door.

At first I assumed it was him trying to stir up more shit, then curiosity got the better of me. I slowly turned to see my sister Whitney walking in with Fiona, Holly and the woman from the other morning in the café. Leah. She walked in with her chin raised, dark hair tumbling around her shoulders. She wore a skirt that fell to just above her knees, showing off legs that went for days. Under an old leather jacket, her top was cut low, framing cleavage that looked good enough to lick. Her lips were painted cherry pink, the perfect shade for decorating my cock.

"Fuck." I wasn't sure who said that until I realised

it was me. And that my dick was half-mast at the sight of her. Realising the other guys' eyes were on me, I scowled. "What's she doing with my sister?"

Right now, she seemed to be heading to the bar to get a drink, the women talking and laughing about fuck only knows what.

"Girls night out?" Riley asked. "Looks like an open invitation to me." He'd been known to crash plenty of girls' nights before. And a few bachelorette parties. The guy was shameless. I only went along with him to keep him out of trouble. It was nothing to do with the horny women who enjoyed a quick fuck in the washrooms before going back to their friends.

There was a reason I encouraged Dad to install a condom machine in there. What was the point of having a father who owned the pub if you couldn't benefit from it once in a while?

"Didn't your sister kick you in the balls the last time you interrupted one of her girls' nights out?" Ryan asked.

"Only verbally," I said.

Whitney was a whole lot of bark, without the bite. Besides, her friend Holly liked sucking my cock. Although, looking at her now beside Leah, the only thing I felt was disinterest. As if she was a pretty leaf beside a gorgeous fucking rose. If that was the case, then I was one of the thorns. Sharp and prickly.

"Shame." Riley grinned.

I punched him in the shoulder. "Fuck off." He liked my balls as much as I did. We both knew it, but we didn't talk about that in front of the other guys. As far as I was concerned, it was none of their business. If they didn't already know then they were blind to what was right in front of their eyes.

"So that's Leah?" Blaise watched her carefully as she manoeuvred around the tables, smiling at something Fiona said.

I wanted to punch him for saying her name. Riley gave him the exact same look, like he was ready to tear his balls off and make him eat them.

"Yeah, that's her," Riley said.

I'd seen lust in his eyes plenty of times. Right now, it was directed toward her. I didn't need to look to know his cock was trying to break the seams of his jeans. I was well acquainted with his dick and all its moods. Hard and ready, soft and satisfied; everything in between.

"I'm going over there." Before the others could say anything else, or even move, I was up off my stool, bourbon in hand, stalking over to the bar.

"Connor!" Whitney squealed, waving her wine glass at me. "Did you bring your scowly face over here to buy us girls a drink?" She had that expression on her face. The one that said she was going to have too much of a good time and no regrets. My sister liked to grab life by the balls and live every day as big and loud as she could. The exact opposite of me. People actually liked her.

Hell, *I* liked her. It was almost impossible not to.

"Looks like you've already got one, Whit." I threw back the rest of my bourbon and nodded for another.

"Connor's paying for our drinks for the rest of the night," Whitney announced loudly.

"I can pay for mine," Leah said. She gave me a narrow-eyed glare, like she'd sooner jump off the Aurora Falls than accept anything from me.

"I'll bet you can." I returned her look twofold. The more she gave me that haughty city girl vibe, the more I wanted her lips wrapped around my cock.

"I haven't left town." She tapped her phone on the card reader and pressed the buttons to give a generous tip.

"So I see." I leaned my elbow on the bar, watching her every move.

She smelled like strawberries. Did she taste like

them too? I wanted to place my hands on her hips, pick her up to sit her on the bar, open her legs and taste her. And keep on licking her until she screamed my name.

"I like it here," she said.

"Good for you." Could she read my thoughts? I wasn't sure if she'd like the place so well if she could. On the other hand, she might like it even better. Would she let me get her off in front of everyone here? My father would kill me but I didn't give a shit. It would be worth it.

"I thought so." She took a sip of her bourbon, her golden brown eyes turned toward me. Was she trying to get a rise out of me by drinking the same thing I was?

I waited for her to react to the heat of the liquor, but all she did was smile. I totally didn't get harder from that look. Okay, I fucking did. I wanted to taste the bourbon on her mouth. Would it taste like strawberries too?

"Why?" The question was out of my mouth before I could stop it.

"Why what?" She took another sip and raised her eyebrows at me. I noticed she didn't leave any of her lipstick on the glass. Shame, I preferred when it rubbed off.

"Why do you want to stay in Aurora Hollow?" I asked. Did I want the answer or did I just want to see her lips move?

"Because it's awesome and you're paying for the alcohol." Whitney hooked her arms through Leah and Fiona's, pulling them away toward a table. Holly glanced at me before following.

I rolled my lips and watched them walk away. Irritated until Riley stepped up beside me and put a hand on my shoulder.

"She rejected you too?" he asked.

"I thought she was panting for you." I gave him a sidelong look. I wouldn't consider that a rejection, just another volley in our little war.

"She was, she just doesn't know it yet." He patted my shoulder and turned to the bar to buy another drink.

"Yeah, I got that vibe too," I said. The one where she didn't realise she was mine to fuck. It was a good thing that she hadn't left town. I was almost certain she'd stayed to piss me off. Did she know why it was so important for her to get under my skin? If she didn't, she soon would. Before the winter rush started, she'd be coming around my cock. At the same time, she could suck Riley's. Between us, we'd fuck her into oblivion. She'd thank us for every orgasm we generously let her have.

"Nothing like a challenge," Riley said softly.

"There really isn't," I agreed. I might even buy all of their drinks tonight. But I wouldn't touch Leah when she was full of alcohol. No, I wanted her stone cold sober when she surrendered to me. Sober and begging me to fuck her.

"Fucking hell," Riley growled.

His sudden change in tone made my face swing toward him. Then toward the door where he was scowling, pure loathing flashing in his blue eyes. Of the two of us, he was usually the most chill. It took a lot for him to be rattled, much less oozing anger the way he was right now. Only one person I knew got that reaction from him.

I followed his gaze. My blood turned to white hot ice.

"What the fuck is he doing here?"

6

———

LEAH

"Uh-oh." Whitney's head turned like she was watching a hockey game, sliding from her brother to a man who stood just inside the doorway.

The six-foot-four wall of muscle watched Connor approach, dark eyes unflinching, as openly hostile as Whitney's brother.

"What do you want, Lachance?" Connor snarled.

"Who is he?" I whispered to the other women.

Holly hadn't said much, but it was her who answered now. "Dash Lachance. He and those two have had bad blood since forever." She nodded to Riley, who stood at Connor's side, no less angry and aggressive than his friend.

"That's an understatement," Fiona said. "Those

three *hate* each other. They'd throw each other off the falls given half a chance."

I caught Whitney giving her a sharp look.

One of Fiona's eyebrows twitched, but she was unrepentant.

"Why do they hate each other?" I asked.

"You'd have to ask them that," Whitney said. She gave both women a warning look. This time they pressed their lips together. Whatever was going on, they'd closed ranks against me.

"It's a free country, Ferguson." Dash shouldered past Connor and strode toward the bar.

"Not here it's not," Connor said. "You're not welcome. You forgot after last time?" His hands were curled into fists.

"Maybe he needs a reminder," Riley said.

"I'm just here for a beer." Dash leaned against the bar like he had all day.

"Get it somewhere else," Connor snarled. "Get out before we throw you out on your ass."

Dash turned slowly to face him, his lip curled. He had at least ten years and a couple of inches on Connor, and Connor was angry. Angry men tended to make mistakes.

To me, it looked like Dash was giving him and Riley enough rope to hang themselves.

"Why shouldn't he drink here?" I found myself on my feet, speaking loud enough to be heard through the whole room. Too late, I realised all eyes were on me.

Shit.

"He can pay, can't he?" I asked. If he couldn't, then he might as well leave, but I didn't think this had anything to do with him skipping out. No, whatever was going on between these three, it went deep.

"Mind your business," Connor snapped to me.

I stepped out from behind the chair and closer to him. "Is his money not good enough for you?"

"Not nearly fucking good enough," Connor agreed. "He could put a million dollars over the bar and I'd set it on fire."

I rolled my eyes at him. "That would be sensible," I said sarcastically. "And I don't believe it."

"Believe it," Riley said. "His money isn't worth shit here. And neither is he."

"He's right," Dash said. "I'm not worth getting your pretty little pussy in a twist over."

I squinted at him. I didn't know why I defended him in the first place. Clearly he neither needed nor wanted any help from me. It was possible whatever bad blood there was between them was justified. Who was I to get in the middle of that?

I just... I really hated when people ganged up against other people. Especially when it might come to blows, which it looked as though it was. I didn't want to help pick up teeth or clean up blood off the floor.

I raised my hands to either side. "No twisting here. I just figured if these guys were going to be dickheads..." I shrugged.

"They're always dickheads, sweet cheeks, but you know what?" He leaned toward me. "So am I. Ask anyone here." He jerked his head toward the rest of the room. "It's been...entertaining." He gave me a sarcastic, loud air kiss before stepping around me and back out into the night.

"And stay the fuck out," Connor shouted after him. He drew in a furious breath and loudly let it out. "That fucker seriously needs to stay out of town."

Was Dash the one they were talking about in the café the other morning? They'd walked in the door raging about someone. Connor said similar words then about him staying out of Aurora Hollow. Was it strangers in general he didn't like, or just me and Dash in particular? Presumably the latter, since his livelihood depended on strangers coming to town.

Although, he could be a good actor around them,

pretending they were welcome until they were parted from their money.

"Does every man in town have a goddamn chip on their shoulder?" I slid back into my seat. It certainly seemed like it. They got bigger with each one I met.

"Just those three," Fiona said. "They might get over it someday."

Whitney laughed. "Connor and Riley hold grudges like their lives depend on them. They're gonna keep hating him until he's dead, or they are."

"It must have been bad," I said. "Whatever caused this. Was it over a woman?" They wouldn't be the first guys to lose their shit over someone. They wouldn't be the last.

Yet, this seemed to be about something else. What could be so important it would cause so much anger and animosity between them? Dash was too much older than Connor and Riley to have gone to school with them. What else might it be then?

Honestly, I could guess until the flying pigs landed and still not be right. I might be better off not knowing if it was that bad. Staying away from all of them would be a better option. For me and them.

"Like I said, you'll have to ask them," Whitney said. Once again, she gave Fiona and Holly a warning look. After a beat or two, she said, "Let's lighten things up, shall we? Fiona said you like to paint and draw. Any chance you want to come and do a class with my kindergarten kids?"

"She teaches at the local school," Fiona supplied. "Holly too, but Holly teaches high school gym."

"I'd love to give a class," I said. "That sounds like fun." I liked kids and their enthusiasm for art. They were always so imaginative and creative, until they were told birds could only have two legs, and that pigs didn't really fly. I vividly remembered those days. I stubbornly refused to let them influence my creative eye. If I wanted pigs with wings, I'd make them, or draw them.

In fact, I had. I filled notebooks with flying pigs of all shapes and sizes, but never showed anyone. My rebellion was a quiet one. In class, I'd follow the teachers' instructions. As it happens, learning to draw and paint realistically worked out for me in the long run. Those pieces of art were easier to sell.

"Great." Whitney smiled warmly. "Let me know when and I'll pencil it in."

"I'm not saying I don't like hairdressing, but that sounds like fun," Fiona said with a sigh.

"Told you to go into teaching," Whitney said. She gave the other woman a lopsided smile that suggested this was an old conversation, only brought up now as a joke.

"Told you being with kids all day everyday would drive me insane," Fiona retorted. "Once in a while is enough for me."

"Wait until Sarah gets to high school," Holly said. "I swear, most of the class spends the entire year waiting for pond hockey season. That's all they care about. Hockey, hockey, hockey." She bobbed her head to either side with each word, while rolling her eyes toward the ceiling.

"Is there another sport?" Fiona frowned at her, but the sides of her mouth were tugging upward as she fought back a smile.

Holly plucked the paper straw out of her drink and threw it at Fiona. "Of course there is."

Fiona's hand shot up to deflect the straw. It bounced off her palm and landed back on the table, leaving a trail of droplets behind it.

"No goal." She grinned.

We all laughed.

"There is another sport, baseball," Whitney said. "And to a lesser extent, field hockey." She glanced at me and asked, "What about you? What are you into? Wait, let me guess." She put up a finger in front of her. "Cage fighting."

I laughed. "Why cage fighting?"

"Why not cage fighting?" She spread her hands up to either side. "I mean, someone has to watch it, right?" She raised her hands and dropped them.

I thought we were about to have our own version of it a few minutes ago, without the cage, but decided not to remind her of that. She seemed invested in not talking about it. Who would have won a fight between those three anyway? I had a feeling Dash could hold his own against both Riley and Connor. Was it wrong that I was slightly disappointed not to find out?

"I'm not really much of a sports person like that," I said. "I was never really allowed to watch or participate, then... I got busy." I ended the sentence on an exhale.

All three of them looked at me like they knew I was going to say something else, but none of them was going to pry. Their response was another reminder of the difference between me and them. They grew up together, I'd known them for a handful of days.

Getting to know each other well enough to open up would take time. If it ever happened.

"You'll have to come and watch pond hockey when the lake freezes," Fiona said. "Practically everyone goes out to watch. And play. Sarah is in her second year with her little team. They take it seriously." She smiled indulgently, but I suspected she was just as passionate about it as anyone else.

"I'm sure she's adorable in her skates and padding," I said. Seeing her out there on the ice must be nerve racking, but I got the feeling Fiona couldn't have held her back if she tried. Sarah would have found a way.

"She is," Fiona agreed. "Looks like I need another drink." She held up her empty glass before standing and heading over for a replacement.

"Me too." I rose and followed, my heels clicking on the floor as I walked. Everyone else in the place was in jeans, making me feel somewhat self-conscious. I liked wearing skirts, but I didn't want to look like an outsider forever. The city girl who turns her nose up at anything and everything. Especially when I didn't turn my nose up at anyone.

Correction, I raised my *chin* when I passed the table Riley and Connor were sitting at. Both of them and the guys they were sitting with, followed me with their eyes all the way to the bar.

I ignored them. Whatever their problem was, I wasn't going to make it my problem. If they wanted to have chips on their shoulders as wide as the

Rockies, so be it. They weren't alone in holding grudges. I held a few of my own. I might add them to the list. They were both attractive, but my clit wasn't in charge here. My brain was. It had to be.

The way she throbbed when I was around them, my clit would lead me to do things I'd definitely regret.

"Those are paid for," the woman behind the bar said, pushing our drinks toward us.

I turned slowly to glare at Connor, who raised his drink to me.

"I can—" I started to say.

"Just say thank you," Fiona said. "Trust me, it's not worth getting into. If he wants to pay, let him. He needs to spend his money so badly, we can enjoy it." She picked up her wine and took a big sip. "Remind me to order the expensive stuff next time."

Reluctantly I picked up my bourbon, wrapping my fingers around the glass. It wasn't his money or my enjoyment I was worried about.

It was what he wanted in return.

7

—————

LEAH

"It's a perfect day for a market." Louisa stopped at my table as I put the last of the paintings out on display.

"It really is," I agreed. I only had a handful of paintings, but no chair. Even if I thought to bring one, I didn't have a fold down one I could carry around. Tomorrow was going to suck unless everything sold quickly. Given the way pockets of people were standing around chatting, I suspected buying wasn't their priority.

"These are nice." She squinted appraisingly at my work. "I might have to buy one for the town hall. They'd look nicer there than an abstract cactus." She waved a hand at me. "Don't ask. The previous incumbent had…interesting taste."

I smiled. "Art is subjective, but I'd be honoured to have my work hanging in there. If you don't like any of these, I can paint something different. If you'd like something in particular." I preferred to be inspired, but I took commissions because I also needed the money. Rent was a lot cheaper here than at home, but I still needed to pay it and eat. Not to mention keeping my car running.

"I'd like something that represents the town and shows it in just the right light. Literally and figuratively. Let's discuss that further at a later time." She nodded, her long plait swinging to the side.

"Absolutely, you know where to find me," I said. I adjusted a couple of paintings as she moved on.

"Leah!" Whitney came hurrying over, Fiona and Sarah a few steps behind. "Are you kidding? Your paintings are gorgeous!" She gave me a hug. "I'm never going to be able to decide which one I want."

"There's a simple solution to that," Fiona said.

"Buy them all!" Sarah shouted.

"I can get behind that solution," I said with a grin. I offered the kid a fist bump. She bumped with enthusiasm while clinging to her mother's hand, dragging Fiona to the side.

"Hey, careful kiddo," she laughed. "No one wants to see me face plant on the grass."

"I refute that statement." Whitney's eyes were shining. "But wait until I have my phone out so I can video it." She gave Sarah a 'come on then' gesture with her hand.

"How about you don't?" Fiona said, pulling Sarah back toward her. She playfully scowled at Whitney.

"Spoilsport." Whitney sniffed in pretend indignation, a smile pushing at the corners of her mouth. "Seriously though, Leah, these are amazing. I wish I could paint like that."

"Me too," Sarah said. She touched one of the canvases carefully and gently with the tip of her finger. "I feel like I can smell the trees and feel the wind."

"That's what I was going for," I said softly. I liked when people got what I was trying to say through my work. For me, it wasn't just about making something pretty, although that was part of it too. I wanted people to feel like they were right there. Like they could step into the canvas and be in the exact spot I sat and painted.

"You're talented," Fiona said.

My face was still heating from the compliment when a couple of shadows stepped into the corner of my sight.

"Talented?" Connor scoffed. "Let me see, Whit."

He all but elbowed his sister out of the way to stand in front of my paintings. The way he looked at them made me want to hide under the table.

I couldn't read what he was thinking, but my mouth was suddenly dry and I swallowed hard.

"I think she's pretty good." Riley stepped over between Connor and Whitney.

"You wanted to buy one the other day," I pointed out.

Connor looked at him sharply.

Riley shrugged. "Maybe I felt sorry for you. Sitting there all by yourself for hours."

"How did you know that?" Fiona asked. "Riley Crane, are you stalking her?" Her eyes narrowed.

He snorted. "Yeah, right. I happened to see her there, that's all."

"Sure." She drew the word out. "You two are full of..." She glanced down at her daughter. "Doo-doo."

Sarah giggled. "Mummy said doo-doo."

"Doo-doo is the perfect word for both of them," Whitney said. "Did either of you want something or did you just come to be assho— asshats?" She looked at them both up and down like she didn't care much for what she saw.

"Everyone is allowed to come to the markets if they want to," Connor said defensively.

"No one is disputing that," Fiona said. "It's your critique we're questioning."

"Exactly," Whitney agreed. "Leah happens to be very talented. If you don't agree, move along." She gestured with her fingers for them to go away.

"It's okay," I said. "Their opinion doesn't bother me. Like I was just saying to Louisa, art is subjective. They don't have to like mine." I really needed to sit down. My feet and legs were already starting to ache. I went on smiling, hoping none of them could tell. I didn't want sympathy from my new friends, or to give Connor and Riley ammunition against me.

"Thanks for your permission," Connor said sarcastically. He frowned for a beat before adding, "Wait a minute, turns out we don't need it." He smirked at me.

Would the world judge me too harshly if I picked up a painting and hit him with it? Probably not, but I'd hate to damage my work. He wasn't worth it.

"You're a prick," Whitney told him. "I swear, one of us must be adopted. I think it's you, because I look like Mom."

"And I look like Dad," he retorted. "You know you love me." He stepped over to put his arms around her and kiss her cheek, but she turned her face and pushed him away.

"Ewww, no. I'm not touching you until you stop being an ass."

"I guess you won't be touching him ever again," Fiona remarked.

Connor flipped her off with both fingers. "Come on, Ri. I don't need to stand around here and be insulted."

"I'm sure there's plenty of other people around here waiting for their turn," I said dryly. "Wouldn't want them to miss out."

He'd taken a step away, but stopped and looked back at me.

I thought I'd see disgust or derision in his eyes. Instead I saw pure heat. Like all he wanted to was shut my mouth up with his cock.

He opened his mouth to say something, then shook his head and stalked away.

Riley glanced at the painting he'd wanted to buy, with a hint of regret before following Connor away.

"Ugh, I'm so sorry about those two." Whitney pressed a hand to her chest. "I swear, sometimes they should be on a leash."

"It's okay," I said.

I'm not going to lie, the idea of them restrained wasn't the worst thought I'd ever had. One of the hottest, maybe. Was I even thinking right now? Had he given me that look on purpose, trying to mess with my head? Was he aware of having done it? I hadn't looked at him the same way, had I?

I pressed a hand to my cheek, as if I could actually check.

"I really don't know what their problem is." Whitney shook her head.

"Egos the size of the entire Rockies?" Fiona suggested.

"They're big doo-doos?" Sarah said, looking gleeful.

"They're very big doo-doos," Whitney agreed. "I never thought I'd say this, but I'll be glad when it starts snowing. We hardly see them then. If they're not taking out tourists, they're skiing and snow-boarding. And whatever else those two get up to."

My mind should not have gone to where it went. I did not need to think about Connor and Riley kissing each other. Their hands wandering over each other's bodies. Touching. Tasting. Fucking. I wasn't even sure they had that kind of relationship, but the mental image was hot enough to melt panties off just about anyone.

I shoved the thought away as hard as I could, before it showed on my face.

"It's only a few short weeks," Fiona said wistfully.

"Unfortunately, it goes hand-in-hand with being cold as heck. I guess we have to take the good with the bad. Now, how much for that painting?" She pointed at the one Riley smudged with his nose. "That'll look perfect over my fireplace."

Whitney almost squealed. "It *so* will! Now I'm jealous I didn't think of that first. But this one would look amazing in my place." She lived near Fiona's parents, about five minutes away from the cottage I was renting.

"Ohhh, it really would," Fiona agreed. She caught sight of something off to the side and her expression changed. Her smile faded and her eyes became sad.

I followed her gaze to a man in his late fifties making his way through the market with the help of a walking stick. He was looking in front of him, but his eyes didn't seem to see anything. His mouth was turned down and a deep crease mark to the centre of his forehead, between his bushy eyebrows. Something about him was familiar, but I couldn't place him.

"Who's that?" I asked softly.

"Gavin Clarke," Fiona whispered as if she didn't want to intrude on him, even at a distance. "He used to own the bakery here in town."

"Used to?" I echoed.

"Yeah," Whitney said. "I don't really remember it, but to hear them talk, he used to be the life of the whole town. The one who held everyone up. Who supported everyone, y'know? When anyone needed a shoulder, or a laugh, he was there. Then his daughter died. They say he changed overnight. Became reclusive and…broken. He lost his marriage and the bakery."

"These days, we take care of him," Fiona said. "People take turns checking in on him and bringing him food. The community nurse makes sure he keeps clean and washes up after him. Mostly he walks around town as if… I don't know, like he wants to find her again." She looked close to tears.

"That's really sad," I said, my eyes following his slow progress. People nodded at him as he walked past, but he didn't seem to be aware of it. He went on shuffling until he disappeared out of sight past the stall selling fresh fruit and vegetables.

"It's nice you take care of him. A lot of people wouldn't bother." In the city, would anyone have noticed what he was going through? Would they have cared? He would have withered away, largely unnoticed. The thought was heartbreaking.

"We always bother," Whitney said. "That's what we do. We look out for each other. We support each other and encourage each other." She pushed a smile back onto her face and nodded down to the painting she'd chosen. "We make sure no one goes without."

"I don't know if I can take your money," I said uneasily. They'd both been so sweet to me, taking me under their wings. Including me on nights out and inviting me to a barbecue next weekend. They could as easily have ostracised me the way Riley and Connor did.

"Of course you can." Whitney pulled out her purse and handed over a couple of bills. After a moment, Fiona did the same, then picked up her painting and tucked it under her arm.

"Thank you," I said sincerely. For their support and because this money would go a long way. "You're so sweet."

"That's us." Whitney grinned. "Sweeter than pie." She batted her long eyelashes.

"We have good taste, that's all," Fiona said. "Which reminds me, I need to buy some chutney. I'll see you both later."

"Oh, I need chutney too." Whitney blew me in and kissed before hurrying after Fiona and Sarah.

I sagged with my palms on the table in front of me once they were gone. An hour down, three more to go. I could do this.

8

CONNOR

I DRIED the last glass and placed it back in the rack, ready for the evening rush.

"Where's your shadow?" I didn't want Whitney to think I gave a shit, but every time I saw her lately, she was with Leah fucking Kent.

Whitney wiped the last of the tables vigorously and tossed the washcloth across the bar, straight into the sink.

"She shoots. She scores!" She raised her hands victoriously and made a sound like a cheering crowd.

"She didn't answer the question." I smirked.

"She didn't think you were serious." She smirked back. "Who are you talking about anyway? Fiona, Holly or Leah?" She planted her hands on her hips and cocked her head, making her blonde ponytail fall to the side.

Hearing her say Leah's name should not have made my body react. I shouldn't even be thinking about the city girl. I should be focused on getting the Frosty Brew organised and planning for next weekend's white water rafting bookings. Thirty city slickers wanted to take on Aurora Rapids and I was here for it. Nothing got my blood going faster than sliding down the water, hoping like hell not to end up smashed against the rocks.

I shrugged and turned my back on her to rearrange the bottles of alcohol on the shelves at the back of the bar. None of which were out of place. "The city girl," I said over my shoulder.

"Does my baby brother have a crush?" Whitney teased.

A bottle of whiskey in each hand, I turned around to scowl at her. "Of course not. She just seems to turn up wherever you are these days."

I placed the bottles on the glass shelf and slid them until they were exactly the same distance apart from all the other bottles. Dad could be a real dick about details like that. As if customers cared.

"Interesting that you noticed," Whitney remarked. She slipped around the side of the bar and leaned her hip against one of the fridges. "It's okay to like people, you know."

"Why would I like anyone?" I adjusted the tequila and vodka bottles before deciding they'd live up to our father's standards. "People are pains in my ass."

"Except Riley." She tipped her head back to look at me in that big sister way she had. Like she had nothing better to do than call me out even if there was nothing to call out.

"Riley's okay." I stepped over until she was out of my personal space and checked the straw dispensers. Wouldn't want those to be empty.

Whitney snorted. "Riley Crane is practically your shadow. I'm surprised he's not here helping."

"He had things to do." He often helped out here the same way I did, cleaning up while dad was busy paying the bills. Today, he was helping his father in their garage. Fixing up some old rust bucket for one of the local guys.

"So, it's not true what they say." She slid me a sly look. "You're not literally joined at the hip."

"What if we are?" I didn't give a shit what anyone said about my relationship with Riley. The only person whose opinion mattered was his. And mine.

"You know what you need?" I turned away from

the straw dispenser to fix her with a firm look. "You need a love life so you can stay out of mine."

She barked out a ha. "With whom? I'm related to half the town, and grew up with the other half. Why would I want to date a guy I saw eating crayons in kindergarten?"

"Beggars can't be choosers," I told her.

"Who's begging?" She straightened the straw dispensers as if they weren't exactly where they were supposed to be to start with. "I'm stating a fact. What I need is some hot city boy to swoop in and sweep me off my feet. Preferably disgustingly rich."

"See, that's a problem," I said. "Your standards are too high."

She arched an eyebrow at me. "My standards are just fine, Connor Jacob Ferguson. A girl shouldn't have to settle for less than exactly the right guy for her."

"You've already ruled out the crayon eaters, what does that leave?" I grabbed a clean washcloth to wipe down the beer taps. "The glue eaters? The guys who always had their hand up first when the teacher asked a question? That one kid who ate so many carrots his skin turned orange?" Kid must have been pissing orange. I liked the vegetable as much as the next guy, but not as much as him. I preferred my skin tanned brown, with the odd freckle here or there. I didn't want to look like fruit. Or a vegetable. Whatever.

"Out, out and definitely out." She grimaced. "The fact I know exactly who you're referring to in each case is exactly why I need a city boy to rescue me. A knight in a shining Lamborghini."

Her expression turned to a dreamy one. Typical Whitney. She always had her head up in the clouds. When she went away for university, we all thought she'd only come back for holidays, if she came back at all. Taking the job at the local school shocked the hell out of the whole town. Holly too, come to that. People left Aurora Hollow without so much as a glance back in the rear view.

Very few of those who left ever bothered to come back and make the place their home again. Now both of them had, they might encourage others to do the same. With more locals, the town could grow, welcome more tourists. Put us on the map. Some of the townsfolk would say that's a bad thing, but if I could grow my business, I'd welcome it.

"I wish you luck with that," I said. "You might find one next weekend. There's a whole pile of them coming in to thrill seek."

"I'll be sure to be as hospitable as I can." She smiled.

Already the wheels in her mind were turning around and around, making plans to see and be seen. Although, the truth was she was more of a social butterfly than she was a gold digger. She loved nothing more than to talk to people she never met before. If anyone was good at making folks feel at home here, it was my sister. She should give up teaching and become the town ambassador or something. Was that even a thing? Whatever, it could be. If it was, I'd vote for her.

"Yeah, you do that," I said. "I don't need to hear about how hospitable you were to them." My sister's sex life was not something I wanted to hear about. I didn't even want to think 'Whitney' and 'sex life' in the same sentence.

"Spoilsport." She pouted playfully. "I thought you'd want a—"

I raised a finger. "Don't finish that sentence." I braced myself, ready with a disgusted look.

"Blow by blow description," she said with a grin.

I closed my eyes and shook my head. "Whit, gross. Pass me the brain bleach."

She laughed. "Don't be such a prude. It's not like I don't know what you get up to and who you get up to it with. I mean, you were the one asking about Leah." She looked pleased with herself for bringing the conversation right back around to that. Of course she was, she always found a way.

"I was curious, that's all," I argued. "I don't want to bang her."

I so wanted to bang her.

Whitney rolled her eyes. "Sure. Because I like you, some of the time, I'll tell you I haven't seen her today. She went home after the market looking tired. I guess us locals wore her out." A crease crossed her brow, just for a moment. One that for some reason made concern settle on my shoulders.

I told myself I didn't give a shit. Why would I? She clearly disliked me as much as I disliked her. The smart thing to do would be to stay the fuck away from her. But no one ever claimed I was smart. Including me.

"Okay, I think we're done here," I grabbed up the washcloths to take them out back and throw them in the washing machine. "Thanks for the help."

"Any time, bro." She grabbed up her bag and phone and headed out the door.

I watched the door for a minute or two after she left before I made up my mind. I stuck my head into Dad's office.

"I'm heading out for a bit. Everything's ready for tonight."

He glanced at me, his face an older version of mine. Grey hair at his temples, hazel eyes a bit more faded than mine. Button down shirt rolled up to his elbows and jeans that had seen better days. Hell, everything in the office had seen better days. Including the old desktop computer in front of him. How was that piece of shit still running? Slowly, if I had to guess.

I made a mental note to talk to Whitney about putting our money together to buy him a new one for Christmas. That was the only way he'd accept something like that from us. Except for me, Jacob Ferguson was the proudest man I knew.

He nodded. "Thanks, son. I appreciate the help." He always looked like asking me to come to work here full-time was on the tip of his tongue. He never did though. He knew I was committed to my business with Riley. Some day I'd take over from him, but for now I was too busy having fun and feeding the adrenaline junkies. Sitting behind a desk for hours at a time didn't appeal to me. Would it ever? That was a question for future me.

"Yeah, any time." I backed out and slipped out the back of the building.

My hands in my pockets, I strode down the main street of town, nodding to the people I passed, but not stopping for a chitchat. Every single face I went by was one I'd known since I was a kid. I could tell you what they did for a living, where they lived and who their friends were. I knew their favourite drinks and how they took them. I knew who skied, who snowboarded, and who preferred to sit in front of a fire and keep warm.

I'd been to the city plenty of times and it always felt so impersonal. No one said hello to anyone else and no one knew your business. Sometimes that was a good thing. Sometimes not. In a place like this, you got used to nosy neighbours. Most of us fit that category.

Trying to look like I wasn't up to anything at all, I strode past a couple of hotels on the edge of town. One a little fancier than the other. We got all sorts here. People wanting a five-star experience and those who wanted something a bit more budget friendly. When people arrived in town ready to spend their money, we weren't too fussy about their means.

Across a side street was the cottage where Fiona lived with her kid, Sarah. Fiona was mouthy as fuck, but Sarah was okay. Except she'd probably grow up just like her mother. Mouthy and giving the boys a hard time every chance she got. Hell, she was probably doing that already.

I stopped outside the cottage beside hers, looking for some sign to tell if Leah was home or not.

I should walk away. Chances were she wouldn't open the door to me anyway. Irritated by that thought, I marched over to the front door and hammered on it. If she was home, she better open up.

After a few moments, the shuffle of footsteps came from inside. The door opened slowly.

I stared. "You look like hell."

9

LEAH

I should have listened to my instincts and not opened the door. Having to lever myself off the couch and make my way over was difficult enough. Every step, slow and painful.

Then to see him standing there, just when I thought my day couldn't get any worse.

Fucking great.

He looked me up and down, his brows dipped low. "You look like shit."

"Thanks." I started to close the door, but his hand shot out and pushed it open.

"What happened to you?" He followed me when I took a couple of faltering steps back.

"Nothing, I'm perfectly fine." I wasn't fine. Far from it, but I didn't need him in my business.

"Bullshit." He closed the door behind him. "Your feet are swollen. Your legs too. Fuck." He rubbed a hand over the back of his head.

"Yeah, well." I lifted my hands and dropped them to my sides. "I'm fine, okay? You can go now." I turned away so he couldn't see me wince, and headed back to the couch.

"Leah," he said to my back. He followed me over, watching as I lowered myself down carefully.

If I didn't know better, I'd think he was worried. For the life of me, I couldn't think why. In spite of the look he gave me at the market that suggested he wanted me, he'd given me no reason to think he gave a shit about me one way or another.

"What do you need?" He sat down beside me, on the edge of the couch. "What is this?" He waved in the direction of my legs and feet.

"It's nothing you need to worry about," I said. "Please, just…go."

I leaned back gingerly, trying to keep the discomfort from my face but knowing I failed miserably.

"I'm not leaving you like this," he said. Much gentler than I would have expected of him, he knelt in front of me and picked up one of my feet. "Is this from standing up so long yesterday?" His hands were warm as he started to gently massage the ball of my foot and down to my toes.

I wanted to pull away, but it felt good. Too good. Instead, I sat back and let him work.

"Yes," I said finally. "I always get a flare-up after standing for too long."

He glanced up at me. "Someone would have brought a chair if you asked. Don't tell me: you didn't want to be a bother."

"Would you have asked?" I narrowed my eyes at him.

He hesitated for only a moment before admitting, "No, but I don't get swollen feet." He worked his way up to my ankle before lowering my foot and starting on the other one.

"Why are you here?" I asked.

"I didn't realise we were having an existential conversation." He carefully massaged each toe, one by one.

I snorted-laughed. "I mean here in my house," I said. "You were the one who knocked on the door, remember?"

"I was hoping to catch you in the shower," he said. "In case you were the kind of girl to answer the door naked."

"You're full of shit," I said. Was he actually worried about me?

"I figured you'd have an insult or two saved up. Wouldn't want to waste them," he said. "So, what have you got?"

"Nothing off the top of my head." I half-closed my eyes. My feet actually felt a little better, even if they were still swollen. "I'll think of something."

"Lie back," he told me.

My eyes snapped open. "I'm not going to—"

Connor smirked. "Your legs are swollen. I'm no expert, but I'm pretty sure elevating them would help."

"Right." My hands to either side of me, I swivelled around to lift my legs and place them on the length of the couch.

"Good girl," he said softly.

I didn't expect the jolt of heat at his words, or the careful way he started to massage my legs, his hands gentle but thorough. Or the knowing smile he gave me as he went on working. Prick.

"What is this?" he asked. "Your knees are swollen too."

"Early rheumatoid arthritis," I whispered, not wanting to speak the name of the monster out loud. "It comes and goes."

"They say the same about me." He smirked.

"I'm sure you're just as painful." I smirked back.

"No doubt." He rubbed my knees for a few minutes before rising to his feet and heading deeper into the cottage.

"What are you doing?" I sat up straighter.

"Running you a bath." He disappeared into the bathroom, quickly followed by the sound of water.

"Connor," I called out after him. I would have gotten up, but right now my legs didn't want to behave. They'd happily stay here on the couch and let him rub them forever. Traitors. My clit was thinking along the same lines.

I closed my eyes for a moment until he spoke.

"The bath is almost full. Do you need help getting naked?"

Did he have to make that sound so enticing?

"I can do it," I said. After a moment, and with a ton of reluctance, I added, "But I can't get into the bath."

He stopped halfway back to me, looking confused and uncertain for the first time since I'd met him. "You can't?"

"Not... Not like this." I gestured towards my still swollen legs. He was right, the water would help, but supporting myself on one leg and then the other with a bath as high as the one the cottage had? It would hurt like hell.

"I'll help you in," he said as though nothing was simpler.

"You don't have to do that," I argued weakly.

"And miss the opportunity to see you naked?" He managed a cocky grin. "Not a chance."

I rolled my eyes at him. "I'm sure you have better things to do."

"Not really." He stepped over and offered both of his hands. His expression became serious. "Look, you need help. I know you think I'm a massive douchebag."

"You said it, not me." I gripped his hands and let him ease me to my feet.

"I deserved that," he said. "But that's not how we are around here. If someone needs help, we give help."

"Even if that someone is an outsider?" I asked.

He regarded me for a moment. "Seems like you're sticking around." Without warning, he leaned down and scooped me up into his arms.

I let out a short squeal, but didn't try to stop him from carrying me into the bathroom before carefully lowering me back to my feet.

"Take your clothes off," he said.

Part of me wanted to tell him to fuck all the way off, but the steam rising from the bath, and the tower of bubbles on top of the water were enticing.

"Turn your back," I said.

He gave me a disbelieving look, then slowly turned around to face the wall.

Satisfied he wasn't looking, I stripped down to my underwear, placing my clothes beside the sink. Very much aware I was dressed in only a matching set of dark purple panties and bra, both with sheer lace. My nipples both responded to the rush of cooler air, and his presence.

"Okay, if you can help me into the water," I said with further reluctance. I liked to be independent. Flare-ups fucked with that. On top of that, I was practically allergic to asking for help. I couldn't think of many things I hated more.

He turned around slowly and ran his gaze up and down my body.

"Beg," he said.

I blinked at him. "What did you say?"

"I said if you want help into the bath, be a good girl and beg," he said.

"Please," I said, trying to ignore the increased throbbing between my thighs.

"Please what?" He cocked his head, and raised one eyebrow.

"Please, Connor," I said. "Can you please help me into the bath?"

"Good girl," he soothed. His eyes on mine, he took my arms and placed them around his neck before scooping me up and lowering me into the water.

I let out a long sigh as the warm water engulfed me, soothing my aches and warming me from the outside in.

"I shouldn't have put in so many bubbles," he said.

"It looks perfect to me." They covered me so completely, I sat up and unhooked my bra. Sliding it off my arms, I tossed it out onto the black and white tiles on the bathroom floor. Looking right at him, I pushed my panties down and leaned to grab them before tossing them aside too.

"I like making you wet," he said. He closed the lid of the toilet and sat on it to watch me.

"Only wet with bathwater," I said. We both knew that wasn't true. Between his care and praise, my body craved more.

"Why are you doing this?" I asked. "Apart from it being 'the Aurora Hollow way'." I used air quotes. "You could have asked Whitney, Fiona or Holly to help me. Or you could have walked away and forgot all about me."

"Would you have preferred that?" he asked, already knowing the answer.

"You don't even like me," I pointed out. "You've made it clear you can't stand me and are counting down the days until I leave town." I frowned. "This isn't where you hold me under the water until I stop breathing, is it?"

On a good day I wouldn't be able to fight him off. On a bad day, I stood no chance.

"I'm an asshole, not a murderer," he said with a short laugh. "My sister likes you, so I suppose you're okay. Besides, this way I guess you owe me one."

"Owe you one what?" After him paying for drinks the other night, I was starting to build up some kind of debt to him. At least, that was how it felt.

He shrugged one shoulder. "A favour? A good deed? I don't know. Something'll come up."

"I'm sure it will," I said with a glance to his groin.

"I like that's where your mind went," he said with a shit-eating grin. "I guess I should call you good girl a few more times."

"And what should I call you?" I said without thinking.

The sides of his mouth drew up in a slow smile. "How about sir?"

I let my head drop back and laughed. "Keep dreaming." His ego was big enough.

"Sounds like a challenge to me," he said in a low voice. He leaned forward, resting his elbows on his thighs. "You see, I figured out a little something."

My pulse ratcheted up until it was racing almost painfully through my body.

"What's that?" I asked.

"I figured out that you're mine, Leah Kent. You asked me why I'm here. That's your answer. You wanted to know why I'd take care of you like this, that's why. I know you're going to fight it, because that's the kind of woman you are. And I know one other thing."

I gave him a questioning look, but no words managed to work their way out of my mouth.

"I know you're going to need help getting out of that bath." He looked very pleased with himself.

Shit, he was right and I was naked under the bubbles. No wonder he looked so smug.

"I'll find a way," I said. "I feel better now after the massage and hot water." Not enough to make the flare-up die down completely, but some.

"I'm staying until I know you got out without

falling and knocking yourself out on the side of the bath," he said, unmoved. "Whitney would kill me if I even *thought* about leaving you alone."

"We wouldn't want your sister to kill you," I said with an edge of sarcasm.

"No, we wouldn't," he agreed. "Now, are you going to let me help you out?" He stretched out his arm.

10

———

LEAH

I STARED AT HIS HAND, totally not wondering how it would feel between my legs, his fingers sliding inside me.

"Turn around."

"I can't help you with my back turned," he said. He was starting to look irritated.

"Close your eyes then," I insisted. "You don't need to see you to help me."

He stared at me for a moment. Drew back his hand and pushed his sleeve up to his elbow. Before I could say anything, he plunged his hand into the bath, down between my legs and pulled out the plug.

"Now, are you going to sit there and get cold, or are you going to let me help you?" He straightened up and shook water and bubbles off his arm.

"That was a dick move." I watched the water turn in increasingly rapid circles as it disappeared down the drain.

"What can I say, I'm a dick." He shrugged and offered his hand again.

"Just remember you said it." I grabbed his hand and levered myself to my feet before carefully stepping over the side of the bath and onto the floor. I snatched a towel from the rack and wrapped it around myself before he could get too much of an eyeful.

"That wasn't so hard, was it?" He took a couple of steps back and leaned against the wall, his half-lidded eyes on me. Yeah, he'd seen plenty. And he seemed to like what he saw.

"Is that something you want to admit?" I dried my hair with another towel and wrapped it around my head.

He grinned. "I have no problem in that department, honey."

"If you say so." I stepped past him out of the bathroom. "Thanks for helping me." My joints still ached, but they'd be better tomorrow. Sleeping during a flare-up was often almost impossible. Every time I rolled over, my body screamed at me. I didn't want to rely on Tylenol, but some days I had no choice.

While I dressed quickly in a pair of sweatpants and a tank top, I heard him rustling around in the kitchen, opening cabinets and pulling things out. Walking carefully and gingerly, I stepped out to see what he was doing.

"You don't have much," he said over his shoulder.

"I've been meaning to stock up." That was today's plan before the flare-up had other ideas.

"I'll bring you some things for dinner, then I need to get back to the Frosty Brew." He closed the cabinet in front of him and stalked towards the door.

"I can manage," I said.

He stopped with his hand on the doorknob and looked back. "How?" His gaze travelled down my body to my swollen feet. "They still hurt."

I glanced down. "Yeah, but—"

He cut me off. "Then lie down. Or sit down. Stream a romcom or two, read a book. I won't be long."

I wanted to argue, but all of that sounded too good. Everything except the bit where he'd want something in return at some point.

"What's Riley going to say?" I asked.

"Why would he say anything?" Connor asked. Yet, he didn't seem surprised by the question.

"He seemed to think I was hoping to choke on his

cock," I said as I lowered myself onto the couch. "He also seemed to want me to leave town. I don't want to cause trouble between you."

Although, if there was trouble between them, they'd be the cause of it, not me. I was an innocent bystander.

"He needs to get to know you," Connor said. "He'll realise you're not leaving. Don't worry about getting *between* us. When that happens, it'll be completely consensual." He smiled slowly, very sure that would happen. Certain, like he was of everything else.

"What makes you think I'm interested in being the meat in your sandwich?" I asked.

Was I? Okay, yes I was. There'd be worse things in the world than being between two hot mountain men, even if they were assholes.

"What makes you think you have a choice?" With that, he twisted the knob and stepped out of the door, leaving it ajar behind him.

I gaped, but I knew he wasn't being literal. His hands on my feet and legs and the way he made the bath the perfect temperature told me I always had a choice. Connor Ferguson was gentler than he tried to let on. The asshole mountain man routine was a façade. A mask against…what? I didn't know, but in spite of myself, I was curious to find out.

I grabbed up the TV remote from where I left it on the coffee table and rolled through the streaming services on the big screen TV. Not looking for a romantic comedy. I finally settled on a cooking show, where the host was making some kind of elaborate dessert. The kind that made me put on weight just by watching them add ingredients to the bowl.

I half-watched it while I kept an eye on the door, and listened for his footsteps outside. Honestly, I wasn't expecting him to return at all. I might have been his good deed for the day, and now he was done. If that was the case, I'd order food in. I'd have to be careful of my dwindling finances, but a girl had to eat. Having sold all of my paintings at the market the day before helped, but it wouldn't last long. I needed to draw and paint more, be ready for the next influx of tourists. With any luck, they'd be hungry for a visual reminder of their time here. If I had to, I could do caricatures of them, but that was a last resort.

"Honey, I'm home." Connor pushed the door open and stepped inside, bags in either hand.

"You don't live here," I reminded him. "You

shouldn't have got all of that for me either." It looked like he spent a small fortune on groceries.

"I'm not taking it back." He placed the bags on the kitchen counter and started to unpack and put everything away in the fridge and cabinets. "I bought a couple of things for you to heat up, so you don't have to cook until you're ready."

"If you're not careful, you're going to ruin your reputation of being an asshole," I said.

"No, I won't, because no one would believe you if you told them." He smirked over the door of the fridge as he placed a bottle of milk inside.

"I should have videoed this," I said with mock regret. "Then I'd have proof."

"I'd make you delete it," he said.

"You think you can make me do anything?" I leaned against the back of the couch and watched him move around the small kitchen like he belonged there.

"I know I can." He closed the fridge and folded the empty grocery bags, leaving them carefully piled on each other.

"Okay." I watched the television chef scrape ice cream into neat balls and place them on the dessert plate. The whole thing looked fancy and delicious.

"Leah," Connor said.

I ignored him and instead watched the chef dig into the desert they'd just finished making.

"Leah." Connor pressed. He stepped over and knelt down between me and the TV.

"Is this where you threaten to spank me for not replying?" I asked.

What was I saying? I couldn't believe those words came out of my mouth. Now they had, I waited for his response, my breath hitching in the back of my throat.

"This is where I say I have to go," he said with regret. "The spanking will have to wait for another time." The look in his eyes suggested it was definitely a when and not an if.

I glanced down to where the front of his shirt was open, showing a sprinkling of dark hair.

"Seriously, thank you," I said softly. "Flare-up days are the worst. Usually I just... I don't know, push through. You made it easier today." Without him, I would have relied on heat packs and pain pills, doing my best to manage the inflammation while attempting not to lose my shit and cry at the frustration of my body betraying me like this. I knew some people had it a lot worse than I did, but it still sucked. It felt like a sentence I'd been given without knowing why.

He might never know how much his help actually meant to me. I might not even admit it to myself. Pride was a difficult thing to put aside, especially given everything I'd lost to my semi-broken body. The things I didn't want to think about right now.

Connor glanced away. He seemed as comfortable with receiving gratitude as I did with asking for help. Like he wished he was anywhere but there in that moment. Doing just about anything.

"Don't mention it," he mumbled. "Really don't. Like I said, no one would believe you anyway." His mouth turned down and his brow creased. His grumpy mask was pushed firmly back into place.

"Why do you want everyone to think you're an asshole?" I asked. The more I saw of him, the more I realised there was a lot more to Connor Ferguson than he let on. He was arrogant and smug on the outside. On the inside, there was someone decent. A man who cared about people other than himself.

His gaze settled on my lips, as if he was thinking of kissing me. "Because it's easier."

"Easier than what?" I asked. "Easier than people thinking you're actually a nice guy?"

"Easier than people hoping I'm a nice guy and being disappointed." He pushed himself to his feet and stalked out the door, closing it forcefully behind him. The doorframe rattled from the impact, making me wince. His footsteps slapped on the ground as he walked away.

"I'm not sure that's what they'd think," I whispered to my empty cottage. Was I reading too much into this? Just because someone was nice once didn't make them a good person. He'd probably spend the rest of forever being a dick to me, just to prove he really was one.

If that was how he wanted to play it, fine. Either way, I was going to have to find some way to repay him for this.

Whether he liked it or not.

11

____

RILEY

"Okay, out with it." I placed a beer in front of Connor, and slipped into a stool. "You've been moping around like an angry bear all night."

"No I haven't," he snapped.

"Look around," I said. "Everyone's left and it's barely nine p.m."

"It's a Sunday," he said, as if I didn't already know that. "They don't hang around late on a Sunday."

"They didn't hang around tonight because you glared at everyone like they kicked your puppy." I ran a finger down the side of my glass, swiping at the condensation that gathered there.

"I did not." But he glanced around and saw I was right. He and I were the only ones left, except for Zara, who was finishing up behind the bar. "Fine, I did. Some days a guy isn't in the mood for socialising."

If his dad was here, he'd kick his ass, but he went home early too. Connor insisted we had things under control because the night was already quiet.

"Which brings me back to—" I gestured at him to spill. "You're even grumpier than usual. What's going on?" I gave him my best 'out with it' look. How could he not tell me what was on his mind?

"I did something fucking stupid," he said after a few more moments of pointless hesitation. "I got it into my head something was up with Leah and I went over there."

I squinted at him. "Did you fuck her without me?" I wasn't bothered, because I didn't do jealousy. Not really. I'd pretend to be pissed off with him for a while, but that would pass quicker than a summer storm. I held grudges against everyone but him. I knew he wondered what he did to deserve that, but he tried not to take it for granted.

"No, I did not fuck her," he said. "I did see her naked though. She's fucking gorgeous." Slowly, in detail, he told me what he did, from rubbing the aches out of her feet, to pulling the plug on the bath. He even admitted to buying her food.

I sipped my beer and shook my head at him. "No

wonder you've been in a bad mood. To balance out doing something nice."

"It wasn't nice," he growled. "She needed help, that was it. What was I supposed to do? Walk away and leave her in pain?"

I wouldn't have walked away either, but I said, "You could have called Whitney or Fiona." I paused. "Or Holly. She would have helped Leah, then sucked you off after."

"I don't want Holly to suck me off," he snarled. "She's just a friend, okay?"

"Because you want Leah to suck you off," I said. "And me."

"If you keep saying 'suck you off,' I'm going to make you get under the table," he said. As if that was some kind of threat. I could almost see him thinking he should do that anyway, even with Zara present. No doubt she'd seen worse.

"You say that like I'd object." I grinned and took a gulp of beer.

"My dad would fucking kill me," he said regretfully.

Not that Jacob Ferguson cared what Connor did and who he did it with, but if he did it here in front of the staff, he'd be pissed. He was known to check in on things at the end of the night from time to time, without warning. It would be just my luck if he did it tonight while I was on my knees, my mouth around his son's cock.

"He'd fucking kill both of us," I said with a sigh. "I guess we better get out of here then." I glanced towards the door.

"We're not going to Leah's," Connor said before I suggested it. "She's probably asleep by now anyway."

"I guess." If I got a massage, then a hot bath, I'd be asleep. After fisting my cock. Was she lying awake right now, thinking of us? Thinking of me? Pushing her hand under the waistband of her track pants and between her legs? Circling her clit with her fingers, rubbing herself until she got off with my name on her lips?

My cock was swelling at the mental image.

"My place then," I said. "Unless you'd prefer to mope around here all night?"

"I should help Zara." Connor swallowed down the rest of his beer in a gulp and slid off his stool.

"I'll give you a hand." I finished my beer and followed him behind the bar.

I placed our glasses in the glass washer and caught the washcloth he tossed me to get to start on wiping the tables. He made it his job to tidy up the liquor bottles and take the empties out to the recycling.

Between the three of us, we got the place packed up quickly. He turned the lights down and followed us out, locking the doors behind us.

"See you tomorrow," Zara said cheerfully before heading to her small apartment above the souvenir store across the street.

"Night." We stood and watched until she disappeared into the building to be sure she got there safely. The distance was short but Connor wouldn't be doing his job if the staff weren't safe, especially a woman. No one was hurting any of his father's employees on his watch. Or mine.

Don't read anything into it, we're still assholes.

"Remember the time we went into the city to watch hockey?" I tilted my face back to look up at the expanse of sky above us. "We couldn't see any of the stars. They look so fucking big from here. Like you could reach out and grab one."

"They're not big, we're up high," Connor said gruffly. "And you can't grab them, the fuckers are made of… I dunno, whatever the sun is made of." He shrugged.

"Fuck." I gave him a look. "Be romantic, why don't you?" I dug my elbow into his side.

"Sorry if I gave you the impression I was romantic," he said sarcastically.

But he took in a breath of clean air and stared up at the stars. "I guess they're kinda cool."

On a night like this, I could make out hundreds, thousands of them winking at us. If I remembered anything about constellations from high school, I could tell you which ones I saw, but I didn't. I preferred to make up my own patterns anyway. Like that one there? It looked like a dildo.

"I'd call running a bath for someone and buying them food romantic," I said after a few moments.

"Don't," he said. "It's not. It wasn't about that. It's…what we do. That's all. I've taken food to Whitney too, when she's sick. And Fiona. And Carly." The woman who worked in the café was old enough to be our mother. "What I did was a gesture of habit, not kindness."

"Yeah, but I don't remember you stomping around with that angry bear face after helping them," I said. "And I don't remember you saying you saw them naked. Or wanting to. It's okay to admit when you're attracted to someone, you know?"

We started to walk down Main Street away from the Frosty Brew, past stores closed hours ago.

"It's just physical," he said. "I want to fuck her. That's all it is."

"I never said it was more," I said, not bothering to contain my amusement. "I want to fuck her too. Why not? We're not related to her. We didn't grow up with her. She's a new pussy to play with."

"Yeah, we didn't see her eat crayons." He told me about Whitney saying that and smirked.

I laughed. Whitney was right though. Knowing everyone in town had its downside. Too many things couldn't be forgotten or unseen by them or me. I'd done some dumb shit in my day. I didn't need to be with someone who'd remind me of those things at the worst possible moment.

One of the good things about Connor was that he'd done those things with me. Instead of laughing at me, we reminisced. Laughed at each other. Wondered how the hell we both made it to adulthood. Like the time we thought it was a good idea to ride lawn chairs down the white water. We survived, the chairs didn't. Much to the irritation of Connor's mother. Sometimes I think she would have preferred the chairs make it, not us. The chairs were a lot less trouble.

"Everyone in town feels like a sister to me," I said. "Everyone except Leah. I don't know about you, but

I don't want to fuck my sister. Yours on the other hand..."

He glared at me. "Stay away from my sister." As if he needed to warn me.

Even if I wanted to, Whitney wouldn't have gone there. For so many reasons. Including the fact she wouldn't be interested in fucking someone her brother was also fucking. That would be weird.

"I prefer her brother," I said, my voice low.

"Good answer." Connor seemed appeased by that.

"I thought so." I grinned.

My hand brushed past his. I wanted to grab it, lace my fingers in his. Even out on an almost empty road, I didn't.

That side of me, of us, it was still something I needed to come to terms with myself. Not because I was ashamed, but we never discussed what we were to each other. We'd fallen into a pattern of behaviour that was a lot of action and a few words. Panting, sweating and giving each other orgasms, but never pillow talk. Not really. Not beyond surface level conversation and banter.

I knew he was as scared as I was. What was he afraid of? The same thing he was always afraid of. That he'd put himself out there and then I'd decide it was time for me to leave Aurora Hollow.

If I was honest with myself, I always worried I'd *have* to leave. That I'd be forced to move to the city. Make a solid career that didn't rely on seasonal tourism. A job that paid a reliable, consistent wage. Why wouldn't I want that? What we did, it was the best job in the world, but it came with no guarantees. Tourists might stop coming. They could find another, favourite playground. Hell, we couldn't be sure we wouldn't break our necks next week. Or next month. Or next year.

Connor had the Frosty Brew to fall back on. What did I have? He'd have to step away from our business some day, to run the pub. He talked about expanding it. Setting up a restaurant. A hotel. He had ambitions.

One day I might not be enough for him.

"Do I want to know what you're thinking?" he asked.

No, he definitely did not. It would bring him down. I'd insist I had no intention of leaving, but it would linger in his mind the way it lingered in mine. He'd assure me taking on the pub was years away. Maybe tonight it was, but that could change when the sun rose.

"I was thinking how good your cum tastes," I lied.

He looked over at me without missing a step.

"You're full of shit, Riley Crane. You're right, but you're full of shit." Of course he wouldn't buy my bullshit. He never had. Why would he start now?

"How do you know how good your cum tastes?" I was happy to change the subject and push the dark, morbid thoughts away. They took hold too easily and never seemed to want to let go.

"Because I've tasted it on your lips," he said. "It adds a delicious, salty layer to your mouth. Not to say your mouth isn't delicious already." He slid his tongue across his own lips, smiling slowly. Savouring the memory as if the taste was right there.

"Of course it is," I said as if I was offended by the suggestion. "But you're right, tasting you in my mouth is next level." I wanted to taste him right now. Right here.

As I had that thought, we walked past Leah's cottage. The windows were in darkness, not even a faint glow coming from between the blinds. Once again, I pictured her with her hand between her legs, thinking about me while I stood just outside.

"I bet she tastes good too," I said softly, breaking through my thoughts. "Tell me again what colour her nipples were."

"The perfect shade of pink." He sighed. "And the hair on her pussy matches the hair on her head."

"I wish you could paint as good as her, so you could paint me a picture," I said. "It would keep me going until I see the real thing."

I wished he took a photo so he could show me. I could look at it myself whenever I thought of her. Whenever I imagined how soft and warm her skin would be under the calluses of my fingers. It wouldn't be too long until I touched them, parted her legs to lower my face between them. I wanted to hear her moans as she came on my tongue.

"Come on." I started walking again, a little faster now. I needed to be away from her and alone with him before I lost my load here on Main Street.

Leah fucking Kent was going to be the end of me. If I wasn't the end of her first.

12

LEAH

Walking a little easier than I had a couple of days before, I made the camping store top of my list to visit. The temperature dropped, leaving a bite to the air. The trees had already started to turn, red and gold brilliant between the evergreens.

The breeze on my face, I crossed the road that split off from Main Street and headed down to Lake Aurora. The waterskiing capital of the area in summer, according to Whitney.

I slipped through the doorway into In Tents, a bell above it tinkling to announce my presence.

"Mornin'," an older man called out from behind the display of camp ovens. "Let me know if I can help with anything."

"Thank you," I called back.

I wandered around the store, admittedly not knowing what half of it was for. Apart from a friend's birthday party as a kid, I'd never been camping. Since that was in the backyard of their home, could I even count that? I decided I could. After all, it involved toasting marshmallows and sleeping on an uncomfortable air mattress in a tent. I'd ignore the fact we were right beside the poolhouse with access to a shower and toilet.

In the back corner, I found the section with foldout camp chairs and stools. The double foldout chair with the awning and drink holder was cute, but I didn't need two of them. The stools were small and compact, but I might have trouble getting in and out of them, especially on a bad day.

Chair it was then. But what colour? Black, grey, blue or purple? I only took a moment to settle on purple. I liked a little colour in my life, where possible. Besides, I wore so much black, the contrast would be nice.

I lifted it out of the stand and grabbed the handle. I was about to head to the till when I spotted a matching thermal cup. Who could resist having coffee in a cup that went with my chair? Sometimes it really is the small things in life that make a difference. Also the mug had a picture of the northern lights on the side, dancing in brilliant colour. I hoped to see them for myself in a couple of months, when they lit up the night sky. I know, it was very touristy of me, but I couldn't resist.

I snagged up the mug too and carried them both over to the register.

"New in town?" The same man who greeted me, stepped behind the counter to ring up my purchases.

"That's right," I said, half waiting for him to make some comment about city girls.

"Welcome then." He smiled warmly. "If you ever need anything, don't be shy to ask. Name's Henry Crane." He stuck out his hand.

"You're Riley's father," I said. I could see the resemblance now. Same blue eyes and dark hair. Henry seemed friendlier than Riley and a lot less inclined to suggest I'd look better on my knees. Given the wedding ring on his left hand, that was just as well.

"Guilty." He chuckled. "I hope that young hellion isn't giving you too much trouble. Sometimes I think he has too much time on his hands." He was clearly fond of his son, while at the same time not blind to the fact he was a handful. No doubt the grey hairs around his temple were because of Riley. Although, the same could be said about the laugh lines around his eyes and mouth.

What could I say? He wasn't wrong. The girls had said as much as well. The guys were restless at this time of year.

"Nothing I can't handle," I said, hoping my smile looked sincere.

"I'm sure, I'm sure." Henry nodded. "You seem like the sort of girl to have her head on straight. Maybe you could teach him a thing or two."

I didn't doubt that either. Vice versa, more likely. Whether or not we wanted to learn from each other was another thing. He told me I'd want him, and Connor said the same thing, but fucking and having an actual relationship were two different things. Seeing a different side of Connor made me curious what else there was to him. If he was a nice guy under the asshole exterior, maybe Riley was too.

Did I want to find out? Saying I had nothing to lose was easy, but the truth was, there was always something to lose. If they were playing with me, it could be my dignity. If they weren't…

That was a thought for later.

Henry found a box for my cup and placed it inside, before putting that and the chair into a large, canvas bag before I could say anything.

"I don't mind carrying them," I said. After all, the chair came in a bag with its own handle.

"It'll make it easier." He handed the bag over the counter. "But when you're done with the bag, if you want to bring it back, that'd be appreciated. Around here, we reuse and recycle everything we can. Getting things up the mountain takes time and is expensive." He grimaced.

"I'm sure it is." Shipping was horrendous at the best of times, much less to somewhere as remote as this. Thinking back, I only remembered seeing a couple of delivery trucks in town since I arrived. Aurora Hollow wasn't on any major highway or route across the country. I only stumbled on the place after taking the turnoff on a whim. Tourists came here deliberately because it was so quiet and isolated.

I grabbed the bag's handle and lowered it to my side, careful not to let it hit my leg. Both were still tender after my flare-up.

"I'll drop the bag back later, thank you."

"Any time. Don't forget to stock up on gloves, scarves and hats for winter. You're gonna need them in a few weeks." He gave me a smile and a nod before heading back to rearranging stock on the shelves.

He was right about stocking up on warmer

clothes. I'd have to do that another time, what I brought with me wasn't going to be enough.

Careful not to knock anything over, I stepped out of the camping store, back into the morning sunshine.

The moment I did, I sensed something was off. Whatever it was, it put me on edge, on guard. At the same time, I knew it wasn't dangerous. Not exactly. Not like it might have been in the city. I was safe here, but something made my skin tingle.

I stopped and let my gaze wander up the street and back down.

Walking past the café, walking stick firmly in hand, was the man from the market. What was his name? Gavin Clarke. The man whose daughter died. He was heading away from me, his steps slow and faltering, like he wasn't sure which way to head.

In the corner of my eye, I caught more movement. Tearing my gaze from Gavin, I saw the guy from the other night at the Frosty Brew, the one Connor and Riley said should leave. Dash. His dark eyes were on Gavin, watching him, his mouth pressed in a flat, tight line.

He would have been right at home in the shadows in the middle of the night. His black jeans were fitted like they were painted on. His black T-shirt was moulded around his broad chest and huge biceps. His boots, although scuffed, were also black. His hair was only a shade lighter than his clothes. Same with the stubble on his chin.

He must have realised I was staring, because he turned his face and his lip curled.

"What do you want, city girl?"

You to tell me to get on my knees.

Okay, where did that thought come from? Sure, he was hot as hell, but he was wound tighter than a coiled spring, ready to explode and take out half the block.

I shrugged. "Just enjoying the sunshine. Anything wrong with that?"

He mimicked my shrug. "It's a free country, so they say."

"You don't believe it is?" We weren't talking about the country and we both knew it. We were talking about the other guys and their insistence that he leave town. As if he had no right to step foot in Aurora Hollow.

As far as I knew, neither of them, nor their parents, owned the town. Why then, were they so adamant he didn't belong here?

"I wouldn't know." His gaze dropped to my chest, ghosted down to my feet and then back up again. His tongue slid across his lips like he knew exactly what to do with it. "Some people seem to get away with more shit than others."

"You mean Connor and Riley," I stated. "They—"

"I don't want to talk about those fuckheads," he snapped. "Why are you talking to me? Shouldn't you be getting a pedicure or something?" He sneered like I was some precious princess who shouldn't be out on the street by herself. Like maybe I'd break if I stepped on a crack in the sidewalk.

"I've never had a pedicure in my life," I said evenly. My mother would have suggested that kind of self-care was an expensive indulgence. I made a note to book one. To rebel against her, not him.

"First time for everything," he said.

"Are you offering, Dash?" I asked, not caring if I was poking a hornets' nest. I was going to give as good as I got.

His face reddened. "Don't fucking call me that," he snarled. "My name is Josiah. Josiah Lachance."

His anger was enough to make me take half a step back. If he was a coiled spring before, now he was a grenade, ready to blow a hole in the sidewalk.

"Sorry, Connor and Riley called you—"

"I know what they fucking call me," he said. "Because they both have their heads up their asses so high they can't see the sunrise." He sucked in a harsh breath through his mouth and forced it back out again. His expression wasn't pure fury. There was anger, and a lot of it, but something else too. Hurt. Whatever happened between the three of them was still a raw, open wound.

"Why do they call you that?" I asked softly. Whitney wouldn't tell me and I was in too much pain to think to ask Connor. Would Josiah tell me the truth?

I knew the look of someone who needed another person to talk to. I saw it in the mirror often enough. The need to confide deepest, darkest secrets to a friend who wouldn't judge. Friends like that were few and far between in my experience, but what was the harm in reaching out to him? I've been told plenty of times I'm a good listener.

"Josiah." Henry stepped out of the camping store before Josiah could say a word. He wasn't aggressive like his son, but he clearly wasn't happy to see the younger man outside his business.

"I was just moving along." Josiah gave me a long look, his expression unreadable, before turning on his booted heel and stalking away.

"You'd be better off staying away from him, girl," Henry said softly. "Josiah Lachance is trouble." He hesitated for a moment before shaking his head. "That is to say, trouble finds him."

I knew the feeling. Trouble seemed to be a fan of mine as well. I didn't get the impression Josiah was trouble on purpose. He seemed troubled instead. Outcast from the community that prided itself on being so close-knit. That made me more curious about him, not less.

"I should get going so I can get this bag back to you," I said.

"Just think about what I said," Henry said before disappearing back into his store.

That was an easy promise to make. I wasn't sure I'd think about much else.

13

LEAH

I BARELY GOT HOME and closed the door behind me when someone knocked. I turned around and opened it again.

Connor and Riley stood on the other side, both puffing as though they'd run here.

"Is something wrong?" I asked. I couldn't think of any other reason why they'd be out of breath.

"You were talking to Lachance." Connor stepped past me, into the cottage. Riley gave me a glance before following him in.

"Josiah. Yes I was, so what?" I put the bag containing the chair and the cup, on the dining table and stood with my hands crossed under my breasts.

"Why?" Riley demanded.

"Why, what? Why was I having a conversation on the main street of town with someone?" I lifted my chin and stared him down. "Why do you care? How do you even know?"

"It doesn't matter how we know," Connor said.

"Of course it does." I turned my gaze to him. "Are you stalking me? Is someone stalking me on your behalf?" Whichever one it was, I didn't appreciate it.

"I saw you," Connor said. "I was coming out of the Frosty Brew as Riley's dad chased him away."

"No chasing took place," I said evenly. "Riley's father barely said a word to him."

"Enough to make him leave." Riley seemed pleased at that.

"I haven't had enough caffeine for this conversation." Giving them both the side eye, I stepped over to the kitchen to turn on the coffee maker. "What is your problem with Josiah anyway? You both seem to have it in for him."

"It's a long story," Connor said.

I leaned my back against the counter and spread my hands. "Seems like we have time right now. Why don't you enlighten me?"

"You should stay away from him," Riley said, his voice low.

I rounded on him. "Why? You can't say that and not explain it." If they wouldn't explain, I might seek him out and spend time with him to spite them.

They exchanged looks.

"If you don't tell me, I'm going to assume you don't like him because his cock is bigger than both of yours put together," I said.

Hell, that might be accurate for all I knew, but I didn't think so. Judging by the bulges I'd seen in the front of their pants, they could hold their own. I tried not to think too hard about holding them for myself.

I totally wasn't curious about seeing them naked. Okay, yes I was, I was only human. But now wasn't the time.

Connor barked a laugh. "He wishes."

"Maybe we should tell her." Riley scrubbed his face with his hand. "If we don't, someone else will."

I didn't bother to tell him I'd asked and no one else would explain. They might decide to never tell me.

"Yes, you should tell me." I gave them an 'out with it' gesture with my fingers.

"You do it." Connor stalked away, rubbing his temples with his fingers.

Riley scowled after him, but let out a breath of acceptance.

"You saw Gavin Clarke at the market the other day," he started slowly. "The guy with the walking stick and the broken eyes."

That was more poetic than I expected from him, but I nodded. The description was an accurate one.

"I saw him. He was on the street today. Josiah was watching him walk away. Did something happen between them?"

"I guess you could say that." Riley glanced over his shoulder to Connor before looking back at me. "Josiah was supposed to be watching Gavin's daughter, Coral."

"The daughter who died." Something scratched at the back of my mind. I must have seen something about it on the Internet. Judging by what Whitney said, I was too young to remember the incident myself, if it was on the news. Tragic things like that had a way of lingering in people's memories and being talked about long after they happened.

"Yeah," Riley said. "I don't remember, but we used to have play dates and shit. Me, Connor, Coral, our sisters and friends. Dash— Josiah was her neighbour. He watched out for her when her dad was working.

He was supposed to keep an eye on her. They used to live by the creek. Above the falls."

He paused, his expression solemn.

"When he wasn't looking, she fell in."

My heart bottomed out.

"She drowned?" I whispered. I could only begin to imagine how everyone must have felt. Her father must have been beside himself. What about her mother?

Riley shrugged one shoulder. "The river took her and she was never found."

"But *Josiah*," Connor spat his name like it was an insult, "refused to admit what happened. He said someone took her. Said he ran after her. *Dashed*, that's why we call him Dash. Cops never found any sign that anyone was there. He made it all up so he wouldn't look bad for what happened to her. But it's his fault she died. That's why we don't want him around here. She should have grown up with the rest of us."

"That's really sad," I said softly.

"Yeah, tell that to her dad," Riley said bitterly. "He trusted Josiah. When Coral died, he fell apart. Her mother left. He broke into a million pieces. No one around here can forget what happened. We take care of him as much as we can, but you can't mend the kind of brokenness that happened to him."

His lips twisted to the side, his emotions barely contained. Anger, pity, and the sadness that lingered after something horribly tragic happened. The whole town must have been in mourning for a long time. Years. Terrible things didn't happen in small towns without touching every single person who lived there. Everyone's heart breaks.

"I understand, but it was a long time ago," I said carefully. "What happened to her was a tragic accident. Unless you're suggesting Josiah pushed her in."

Was that what they were trying to explain? If that was the case, he belonged in prison, not walking around Aurora Hollow like a bruised soul.

"No," Riley admitted. "But he might as well have."

"He still lives there?" I guessed. "Above the falls?"

It was Connor who said, "He's the caretaker for Aurora Lodge. It's a ski resort at the top of the mountain. Popular with the hipster crowd." He didn't seem to have a particularly high opinion of the place. No doubt he and Riley had plenty of customers who stayed there though. I didn't suppose he had any problem taking their money, despite their choice of accommodation.

"What about the rest of the year?" I asked. "When it's not snowing?"

Connor shrugged. "He's up there alone. That's his fucking problem."

"How old was he?" I asked. "When she died?"

"Thirteen or fourteen," Riley said. "We were about four."

Around the same age I would have been back then. Fiona too. She didn't seem to have the same hatred of Josiah these two did, but she didn't seem interested in welcoming him to town either. The whole town had closed ranks against him.

In some ways, he was more of an outsider than I was.

"That's a long time to hold a grudge against a teenage boy," I said. "Especially for an accident." No wonder Josiah was defensive. He probably spent the better part of the year alone on the top of the mountain, being hated for something that wasn't his fault. He was still a kid himself at the time.

"It wouldn't be so bad if he admitted he looked away, or was taking a piss," Connor said. "He's stuck to the story about someone abducting her all this time. He won't take any responsibility for what happened because he's chickenshit." He all but spat out the last three words. His hazel eyes burned with raw hate.

Hate he was probably taught by his father, because he had to have been too young to make the connection himself. Hate that must have been taught to Riley by Henry, in spite of how mild he appeared. Unless Henry had mellowed over the years. It certainly hadn't mellowed the way they felt about Josiah.

"Is there any chance he's telling the truth?" I couldn't help asking.

They must have considered that possibility, right? I understood holding on to a grudge like it was a comfortable blanket, but it wasn't healthy for anyone involved. If they weren't careful, it could eat them alive from the inside out. Without doubt, it was doing the same to Josiah.

Silence fell, except for the sound of coffee dripping into the pot. The smell was starting to waft through the room. Any other time it would have been welcome, but today it turned my stomach. The whole story was both sad and sickening. What must that poor girl have gone through?

"The police said no one was there," Riley said finally. "The whole town searched for her, but nothing was ever found. No sign of any strangers or a car either. Nothing to say anything happened except her falling into the water."

"She wouldn't have survived going over the falls," Connor said. "She was long gone before anyone knew anything happened. That's why we blame him. All he had to do was admit what happened and we would have… I don't know, started to forgive him."

It didn't seem like full forgiveness was ever on the cards, but maybe they could have dialled it down to mild hostility.

Honestly, I wasn't sure what to think. Josiah didn't seem like the sort of person who would be anything other than bluntly honest. On the other hand, if he panicked, he might have said almost anything. He must be stubborn as hell to stick to that story for what must have been at least twenty years.

Either way, I felt sorry for him for being ostracised by the whole town, even if it was because of a lie. What difference would the truth have made? What difference would it make now? It wouldn't bring Coral Clarke back. It wouldn't put the pieces of her father's heart back together.

"Don't feel sorry for him," Connor said. "He's had plenty of opportunities to fix this."

"Has he?" I asked. "Or do you chase him out of

town the first moment you see him? Would you even listen to him if he told you he wanted to explain?"

They both grunt-laughed.

"We don't want to hear anything he has to say," Connor said. "Chances are, he'd try to spin some other story. More bullshit. Some reason why they didn't find any sign of a kidnapper."

"Aliens," Riley said ominously. "Or a giant Kraken, rising up out of the river to snatch her."

"Or maybe she was eaten by a moose," Connor said dryly. "Or a beaver."

"Or disappeared into a magic book." Riley seemed to be enjoying this a bit too much.

"Have you tried giving him a chance?" I asked, trying to get the conversation back on topic.

"What for?" Connor shrugged one shoulder. "The damage is done. Nothing he says is going to change anything. Besides, he's an asshole. He belongs up there on the mountain, not down here in the hollow."

"And that's why you should stay away from him." Riley stepped closer to me. "If he tries to come near you, I'm personally going to see he ends the way Coral Clarke did."

"Only if you get to him first," Connor said darkly.

"We can do it together," Riley told him. "It'll be more satisfying that way."

"You did not just threaten to murder someone," I said.

If I thought they were serious, I'd be more worried. But these two were more bark than they were bite. I suspected the same could be said of Josiah Lachance.

"You don't get to decide who I spend time with and who I don't."

"Don't we?" Riley placed his hands on the counter, to either side of me.

14

LEAH

I TILTED MY HEAD BACK, my gaze settling on his. Heat radiated off him. Half a step forward and we'd be pressed against each other, chest to chest.

"No, you can't," I said without flinching. Desperately trying not to let on that he was getting to me. He smelled of pine and leather, earthy and heady at the same time. And something else. Soap? It seemed like an innocent smell compared to the rest of him. The contrast had my mind in a spin. Who was this guy really? Who were either of them?

They prided themselves on being assholes. That was a mask. A layer I wanted to peel back to see what was underneath. Not just their clothes, but them.

"You hear that, Con?" Riley said over his shoulder. "She thinks we can't tell her who she can spend time with."

"I heard, Ri," Connor replied.

Riley leaned in closer, still not touching me. His mouth was a centimetre or two from my throat. His breath was light and warm on my skin.

The pulse between my legs raced. I pressed my thighs together and kept holding his gaze. He was the predator and I was the prey. I shouldn't be the one to blink first.

I blinked.

One minute he was right there, then he was stepping away, grabbing my hand to pull me with him.

"Come with us." He smiled, all the way to his eyes, like a boy who wanted to have some fun.

"Where are we going?" He wasn't tugging me in the direction of my bedroom. Instead, he opened the front door and led me outside.

"Same question." Connor followed us out and closed the door behind him.

"Do you trust me?" Riley asked.

While Connor responded that he did, I gave Riley a 'what do you think' look. He hadn't given me any reason to yet.

"Come with me anyway." He laced his fingers in mine and positioned me between him and Connor.

We walked a block before taking a side street and stopping at a two-storey, stone and timber house.

I thought he meant for me to go inside. Instead, he led us around the back, where two quad bikes were parked side-by-side.

"Ever been on one?" Riley asked.

"As a matter of fact," I said slowly, "no. You expect me to drive one of those?"

Riley laughed. "No, I expect you to sit on the back while I drive." His smile faded slightly. "If you can stay on comfortably." He looked down at my legs and feet.

My face heated. "You told him?" I squinted at Connor.

Connor was unapologetic. Of course he was. "I don't keep any secrets from Ri."

I doubted that. Everyone had secrets. I knew I did. This one wasn't his to tell. I was torn between walking away, and climbing on a quad bike and aiming it at Connor.

Since I wasn't given to violence, I chose the first option, turning away from them both before Riley grabbed my wrist.

"Don't be mad at Connor. He wears an asshole mask well, but it's just a mask. He told me because he gives a shit."

"So he goes around telling everyone your deepest, darkest secrets because he cares about you?" I retorted.

Riley smirked. "I have no deep, dark secrets."

I smirked right back. "Bullshit. Everyone has secrets. Everyone has things they don't want the rest of the world to find out. Why would you be any different, Riley Crane?"

"Fine, I have secrets." He shrugged. "That doesn't change anything. Connor told me and now I know. Can you get up on the back of my quad bike or do I need to pick you up and put you there?"

"Who says I'm getting up there?" I yanked my wrist free from his grip. "Maybe I had plans for the rest of the day."

"Ditch them," Connor said. "We're going quad biking."

"And if I don't want to?" I countered. What were they going to do, kidnap me? Tie me to the back of the quad and force me to enjoy myself? If they tried, I'd scream the town down. No doubt someone would come running.

"You smell that, Ri?" Connor sniffed the air. "Smells like bullshit to me. Come on, honey, you know you want to ride with us almost as much as you want to ride us."

I opened my mouth to retort, but instead stood with my lips slightly apart. Did he have to be right? On both counts?

I should walk away and not look back over my shoulder, but my feet wouldn't obey. My clit wouldn't let them. Traitors.

"She's not denying it," Riley pointed out.

"No, she's not," Connor agreed. "You want to ride with me instead, honey?" He raised his hand slowly like I was some kind of wild animal, and stroked down my cheek with his knuckle.

"I called it first," Riley said. "She's coming with me." He made no effort to hide the fact the wording was deliberate.

"I'll ride with you," I said softly. "On one condition."

"Name it," Riley said, not taking even half a moment to hesitate.

"Take me slowly," I said. "I haven't been on one of these before and I don't want to fall off."

"Sweetheart," Riley said, "I'll take you as slowly as you want. Just tell me when you want me to go harder." His gaze dropped to my lips as my tongue slid across them.

"I'll let you know." I let him help me up onto the

back of his quad before he slid into place in front of me.

"Put your arms around me," he said over his shoulder. "Hold on real tight."

Scowling, Connor climbed onto the other quad bike and started the engine, pulling out around the house and leaving us to follow.

I wrapped my arms around Riley's firm body. His muscles bunched under my arms as he got settled, sitting forward to give me more space to be comfortable.

He revved the engine before starting after Connor, driving carefully off the block and onto the road.

After a kilometre or two, we pulled onto a dirt track that led deeper into the forest and higher up the mountain. The roar of the engine, the wind whipping my hair and the bike between my legs drew a smile from me, then a laugh.

"Having fun, sweetheart?" Riley called back over his shoulder. "Ready to go faster?"

"Just a little bit," I called back.

He pushed the quad bike a little faster, trying to catch up to the speed Connor set. He disappeared out of sight around a bend for a few moments before we swung around, dust flying out behind us.

The trees went past in a blur of green and brown, with the occasional burst of red and gold. Birds startled, flying out of the bushes as we roared past.

Riley let out a whoop of excitement and accelerated a little harder, until we were almost on Connor's heels.

Connor glanced back over his shoulder, grinned and drew away.

"He thinks he can beat us!" Riley shouted. "Are we going to prove him wrong?"

Did I want to go any faster than we already were? Apparently I had a reckless streak I didn't know about before, because yes, I did. If we were in a race, I wanted to win.

"We can catch him," I called out.

"Hell, yeah, we can." Just like that, the quad went even faster. Fast enough to take away each breath as I exhaled. The trees were nothing but a wash of green, the ground nothing but dust. My heart raced like crazy, but I couldn't stop grinning.

Someone let out a shout of excitement. It took a moment to realise it was me. I felt like I was flying. Adrenaline pumped through my veins, racing through my blood faster than we were going. If that was even possible.

The track widened and Riley steered us over

until we were side by side with Connor and his vehicle.

"Assholes!" Connor shouted.

Riley laughed, the wind whipping the sound back to me. "First one to the lookout gets to taste Leah first."

I was ready to come undone on the back of this bike as it was. His words left me panting, wanting more. Needing more.

Connor shot us both a look before leaning over the front of his bike and putting his foot down harder. He pulled away from us, leaving dust in his wake.

Riley's body shook with laughter, but he gave chase until we reached an open area in the trees. Finally, both guys slowed their bikes and drew them to a stop.

"Wow." I sat and stared at the view laid out in front of us. The mountain dropped off, revealing land that went on for days. Somewhere down there were houses and towns. People going about their daily lives.

All I saw was an endless green and cloudless sky.

"Do you trust me now?" Riley slid off the quad bike and offered me his hand to help me off.

"Because you brought me somewhere pretty?" I

asked. "The jury is still out." I did accept his hand and walked with him over to the edge of the lookout.

"You're a hard woman, sweetheart." He didn't stop smiling. "If I could, I'd build a house right here. With huge windows that look out over that view. And a massive fireplace with a big rug in front of it for fucking."

"It would be a beautiful place to live," I said. "It'd be a shame to ruin it with a house though." Not to mention that no vehicle bigger than a quad would manage the track up. It would be an isolated place to live.

"I'd make one that fits into the landscape," Riley said. "Lots of timber and glass." He sighed softly.

"Where's the creek from here?" I asked. Was this near the lodge Josiah worked at?

"On the other side of the mountain," Connor said. His expression suggested he wouldn't consider taking me anywhere near it. Which of course made me want to go even more. "Now, there's the matter of my prize."

"Riley made that offer, not me," I pointed out, although my body buzzed. If I didn't get relief soon, I was going to end up with a blue clit.

"Riley has a way of knowing what people want before they do," Connor said. He stalked toward me, placed his large hands to either side of my face and slammed his mouth down onto mine.

My first instinct should have been to pull away, but instead I melted into him. Let him press his body to mine, his tongue sliding between my lips and stroking. I couldn't stop the moan that came from the back of my throat. The growing need between my thighs.

He walked me backwards until my legs hit one of the quad bikes. He gripped my hips and lifted me onto the seat before breaking his mouth away from mine. He stepped back to look at me sitting there, before he curled his fingers into the waistband of my leggings and pulled them down to my knees.

"Black," Riley said, admiring my lacy panties. "How wet are they?"

I swallowed hard.

"Be a good girl and answer him," Connor said. "Put your hand down there and tell us how wet you are."

I lowered my hand down to my stomach before inching it under the waistband of my panties and down between my thighs. Between my lips.

"So wet," I whispered.

"Show me," Connor said.

I pulled my hand back out of my panties and

pulled them aside, putting my pussy on full display for them both.

"Fuck," Riley whispered. "So wet."

"Take them off," Connor said, his eyes dark.

I hesitated for a moment before pushing my panties down and taking them and my leggings all the way off.

"Good girl," Connor whispered. "Open your legs wide and give me a good look."

I glanced at Riley before doing what he said, spreading my thighs wide for them.

"Good girl," Connor said again. He placed his hands on my thighs before lowering his face to my pussy and inhaling. "You smell so good." He swiped across me with his tongue. "You taste like fucking heaven."

He took a moment before diving back in, licking me and suckling on my clit.

"That's so fucking hot," Riley whispered. He lowered his face to kiss my lips softly while tugging down the front of my T-shirt and bra. Slowly, he kissed his way down my cheek and throat, down to my chest. He teased one of my nipples with the tip of his tongue before drawing it between his lips and sucking.

"You like that don't you? Having both of us touch

you."

"So much," I whispered. I'd never been with two men before. This was incredible. Out here under the open sky. Exposed, but I didn't care. I was lost in the moment.

Connor slid a finger inside me, then another, stroking me while licking and biting my clit. He curled his hand around and fucked me with it, up there on the quad bike. Not caring if I left my release on the seat. Maybe wanting me to.

"Such a good girl." Riley moved to the other nipple. "So fucking ours. Come for us."

Connor looked up at me and worked me harder and faster. Forcing me right to the edge and over like I was falling off the side of the mountain itself.

I threw my head back and screamed so loud it echoed back to me. And back. And back. My whole body was consumed with pleasure, pulled under as I was shattered into a million pieces and brought back again.

My orgasm was so intense it took me a solid couple of minutes to catch my breath again and come back down to earth.

"Good girl," Connor said. He drew his face away from my pussy and slid his fingers free. "You come so perfectly." He angled his body toward Riley and kissed his mouth, letting the other man taste me on his lips.

Watching them kiss was unbelievably hot. Even after one incredible, intense orgasm, I was aroused as hell.

Riley groaned. "Fucking delicious. Next time she comes, it will be on my mouth."

15

CONNOR

"WE SHOULD HEAD BACK," I said, hating everything about the idea.

The taste of Leah and Riley lingered on my lips. The sound of her moans as she came. His mouth sucking her nipple. They echoed through my brain over and over on a continuous loop.

I should have recorded them so I could listen to them again. Better yet, we could recreate it as soon as possible. I wanted to know how many times we could make her come before she was completely boneless. And I desperately wanted to slide inside her and come, fill her with my release. I wanted to watch Riley do the same. Pumping into her before he orgasmed inside her body.

My dick hard, I pulled Leah to me and crushed

my mouth against hers before saying, "You're riding with me on the way down."

I expected her to argue, as usual, but she didn't. I couldn't discount the possibility she thought we'd leave her up here if she decided to be difficult. We wouldn't, but we'd absolutely pretend to. On the other hand, maybe we should. I wasn't doing a good job living up to my asshole reputation. I'd have to work on that, but not today.

"Eat my dust." Riley kissed her quickly, then raced over to his quad, vaulted onto it and roared away. Not the way we'd come.

"Where is he going?" Leah squinted after him. Her body stiffened like she wasn't sure if she wanted to get back on and go the way he'd disappeared. Like it was safer to stand still and watch the dust settle.

It was, but we weren't here to be safe. We were here to show her one of the most incredible places in the world. Places few people knew about. We were here to show a wilder side of life she'd never seen before. And we were here for her to learn her body belonged to us. We'd be the ones to make her come. It wouldn't be long before she understood that. Before she'd be begging both of us to fuck her.

I grinned. "The way down. It's even more fun than the way up." I all but pushed her back onto the bike, climbed up in front of her, and gave chase. Leaving the stunning view behind and heading into the trees.

The track we rode down was barely that. It was wide enough to fit the bikes, but we frequently had to duck under the branches and swerve around fallen logs. While the track up was relatively smooth, this was rough as fuck, making for a bumpy ride that had me grinning the whole time.

Leah clung to me like her life depended on it. At this speed, maybe it did.

"This is crazy!" she shouted, but she laughed while she said it.

Yeah, Miss Straight Laced city girl was as much an adrenaline junkie as Riley and me. They usually were. Lipstick and stilettos on the outside, wild on the inside. Begging for that part of them to be unlocked. I was happy to be the key. Hell, I was happy to tear off the padlock and throw it away. Life was too fucking short to live in fear, suppressing any part of ourselves. Any day I didn't take a risk was a wasted day.

"You ain't seen nothing yet," I called out over my shoulder.

"What are you—" She squealed as we drove right through a stream that crossed the track. It exploded in a burst of water that drenched our legs before the rush of air started to dry them again.

"That was cold!" she shouted.

My blood was so hot, I barely felt the drop in temperature. I wouldn't have cared anyway. I liked the cold, almost as much as I liked the heat. If it was extreme, I was here for it.

I laughed. "Wait until it's snowing up here." The ice made it slippery as hell and dangerous, but that was part of the fun. If we weren't taking risks, were we really living?

I'd already come to terms with the fact I'd probably die doing something stupid, why bother fighting it?

"You're insane," she said.

I couldn't see her, but I was sure she was shaking her head at me.

"Haven't you heard? All the best people are," I called back.

She laughed. "If you say so."

She wasn't convinced I was one of the best people, or even close to it. I shouldn't care if she never believed it, but I did. The moment I saw her, I wanted to sink my dick into her pussy. I wanted to fuck her, and for her to then fuck off back to the city.

Now… I was starting to like the woman. I liked the way she stood up to me. I liked the way her eyes darkened when I called her good girl. I didn't want to admit it, but I was starting to feel like she belonged in Aurora Hollow. Not just to me and Riley, but as a part of the town. It almost felt like she'd always been there.

I had to remind myself she hadn't, and at some point she'd want to pack up and go back to the city. I'd let my cock get attached to her, but not my heart. When she left, I'd find someone else to fuck. Someone else to share with Riley. Some other willing, wet pussy. Or a series of weekenders. Whatever it took to forget her.

No way was I going to admit that thought hurt. Not a fucking chance. She was gorgeous, but I couldn't let her get under my skin.

Wouldn't admit she already had.

"Hang on tight," I told her. Riley just ahead of us, I swerved through a series of narrow bends and hairpin turns, barely keeping the wheels on the ground.

As far as I knew, he and I were the only ones to use this track, if you could call it that. Every few weeks, we'd go up to the lookout and come back down this way. We'd like to explore all over the mountain, but the quad bikes would damage too much of the pristine nature.

Even assholes like us had our limits.

Leah squeaked and squealed every few swerves, clinging to me even harder. As if somehow I might let her get thrown off. I wouldn't tell her, but we were riding a little slower than usual. Taking the curves with a little more care.

We were going to wreck her, not with reckless speed.

Finally, the smaller track led out to the bigger one, and then the paved road. This part was always an anticlimax. Coming down from the high like an addict. Adrenaline running with nowhere to go. If it wasn't for the promise of the next adventure, I'd lose my mind. Days like this made life worth living. One day, I'd have the funds to buy multiple quad bikes and take tourists through the forest on them. And over the frozen lake. Motorbikes too. Anything that went fast.

The engine thrumming, we followed Riley past his house and around the back to park beside him. He was grinning like the idiot he was.

"I won this time." He was practically crowing like the neighbour's rooster.

Stupid fucking thing crowed at three o'clock in

the afternoon like it didn't know what time it was. He had one redeeming quality; he liked to chase Riley every time he saw him. I'd be okay with it if he didn't end up roasted too soon. The animal was good for a laugh.

"Won what?" I killed the engine and jumped off. "I couldn't get past you if I wanted to." Not without damaging the habitat the animals relied on. I was competitive, but that was a line I wouldn't cross, even to win a race with him. On the wider track, all bets were off. No way in hell was I letting him beat me there.

He didn't stop grinning. "I don't care, I still won."

I glanced over to Leah and shrugged. "Some people are too impressed with themselves."

She gave me a meaningful look and smiled. "I've noticed."

Riley laughed. "Burn. She's got you there, Con."

"I think she was talking about both of us," I said. She wasn't wrong though. He and I were way too impressed with ourselves most of the time. Fair enough, we were pretty fucking impressive if you asked me. Of course we were, we made her soaking wet without even touching her.

"There you are." Whitney appeared from around the side of the house. "I've been trying to get a hold of you. I figured you'd be with Riley." She raised her eyebrows at seeing Leah in our company, but didn't say anything before turning back to me.

She glared at me like I'd done something wrong by existing. "Have you got your phone turned off?"

I patted my pocket. "I must have left it at home. What's up?"

"It's Dad. He's in the hospital. He had a heart attack."

16

LEAH

"THANKS FOR STICKING AROUND." Whitney looked over at me and offered a smile.

"I know I haven't been in town long—" I started.

"It feels like you have." She leaned over in the worn, plastic waiting room chair and hugged me. "You're practically part of the family now." She sat up and gave me a meaningful look before sliding her gaze towards Connor.

He was pacing through the corridor outside their father's hospital room. Deepening the already worn path in the faded blue linoleum.

"There's nothing going on," I said.

Okay, not exactly nothing. He *had* eaten me out on the back of his quad bike. But, in spite of his claims I belonged to him, we were barely friends, much less anything more.

Sure, I'd been quick enough to come here and sit in the waiting room that smelled like hospital grade disinfectant and starched sheets to be with them while they waited. I told myself I was here for Whitney, not Connor. I didn't think I convinced myself.

"Did he and Riley take you up to the lookout?" she asked a little too loudly.

Connor stopped mid-pace to glare at us both. "Whit..."

She waved him off with a flap of her hand. "We both know you don't take just anyone up there." She looked over to him. "Have you been up there with anyone but Riley? Ever?"

"This isn't the time," he snapped.

"He hasn't," Whitney told me. "I only know about the place because Riley told me one time. They won't even take me up there."

She let out an exaggerated sigh, but this was a distraction from worrying about her father. The doctor hadn't said much since we arrived, and their mother hadn't left Jacob's side. Nurses bustled around the tiny hospital, looking worried, but never stopping long enough to give any information. As far as I could tell, Jacob was still alive. That had to be a good sign, right?

"You won't get on the back of a quad," Connor said to her.

"Not with the way you drive," she agreed. "I should object to you putting my friend in danger like that." She narrowed her eyes at him in playful warning.

"Your *friend*," Connor drawled the word, "enjoyed every minute of it." His gaze settled on me, his tongue slipping over his lips. Could he still taste me there? Was he waiting outside a hospital room for his father while my release was still on his face?

My face heated. "It was fun," I said half to myself.

"It was more than fun." Riley stepped into the waiting area, carrying a tray of coffees in one hand and bags of chips in the other. "I heard you scream-ing. While we were flying around the bends."

The bends, right. I gave him a smile of thanks as he handed me a coffee and a bag of chips.

"You know what would be fun to ride up there?" Whitney asked.

We all turned to her, likely thinking the same thing. Hopefully she was thinking something different entirely.

"What's that?" I asked carefully.

She squinted at me. "A horse. What did you think I meant?" She stared for a moment longer before grimacing and waving a hand in front of her face. "Oh. Oh gross. I did not need that thought in my brain."

My face got hotter. "You might have been thinking of a motorbike. Or a bicycle. Maybe one of those motorised scooters." All of those sounded like fun, but not as much fun as her brother and Riley riding me. Or me riding them. Or them, riding each other.

Fuck, could Whitney read my mind right now? I hoped like hell I wasn't too obvious. Or if I was, she'd pretend I wasn't.

"A motorbike would be much better," she said quickly. "If it's not ridden by a maniac like my brother. I swear, he has a…" She must have remembered where she was and why, because she clamped her lips shut and glanced towards the door to Jacob's room.

"I don't have a death wish," Connor said, his tone low but dark. "The opposite. I want to live my life." Coffee in hand, he stalked away to flop down beside Riley, at the other end of the waiting room.

"If you're wondering if he's always been an

asshole, the answer is yes." Whitney followed him with her eyes before turning back to me. "I'm pretty sure he was born with two middle fingers raised, right at the doctor."

He flipped her off with his one spare hand.

"That sounds like him," I agreed. "Except maybe one for the doctor and one for the rest of the world."

Whitney laughed. "Yeah, that sounds about right. Riley probably came out ass first so he could moon them."

"Projecting much?" Riley grinned. "If you want to see my ass, you only have to ask."

"Hard pass." Whitney held a hand up in front of her face, palm out. "That'd be like seeing my brother's ass. I have some fun kinks, but that's not one of them."

"TMI, Whit." Connor grimaced.

"Don't be such a prude," she told him.

"Don't be a pain in my ass or I'll tell you exactly what we were doing up at the lookout with your friend," Connor said. He toasted me with his coffee before taking a sip. He made a face like he was ready to spit it out. "Ugh, what is this, fresh mud?"

"It is pretty bad," Riley agreed. "That's hospital coffee for you."

"I'm sure it's not that bad." Whitney tentatively

took a sip. She looked a lot like her brother when she grimaced at the taste. "I stand corrected. And spare me from the details, please. I'll approve if I have to but I don't need facts."

"Don't need your approval, Whit," Connor said. "Who I fuck is my business."

"If you don't stop, I'm going to stick my fingers in my ears and start singing," she warned.

"Anything but that," Riley groaned. "I just had my eardrums repaired from the last time."

"Fuck off," she said. "I'm not that bad."

They both looked like they were going to argue when the doctor appeared from Jacob's room. All three of them shot to their feet. I was a moment behind, feeling like I was intruding on something I shouldn't be present for. I thought about stepping away, but Whitney grabbed my hand and held it, hers trembling.

"How is he?" Connor asked.

"He's going to be just fine," the doctor said. "The heart attack was mild and he got here in time. He's going to need to rest for the next while, but I expect him to make a full recovery."

"Thank goodness," Whitney whispered. "We'll make sure he rests, won't we?"

"Absofuckinglutely," Connor agreed. The relief on his face was tinged with something else. A hint of frustration? I couldn't get a read on it before it was gone, firmly pushed away with a firm nod.

"Thank you, Doctor Blair," Whitney said with a lot more genuine enthusiasm. "Can we see him?"

"For a little while," the doctor said. "No letting him overdo it or I'll have to throw all of you out." He nodded before disappearing down the short corridor into a room at the end.

"I'll wait out here." I gave Whitney's hand a squeeze before letting it go and sinking back into one of the chairs.

"Me too." Riley pressed a quick kiss to Connor's mouth before flopping down beside me.

Arms around each other, Connor and Whitney stepped into Jacob's room, closing the door behind them.

"They must be super relieved," I said.

"I would be," Riley said. "I mean, if it was my dad in there. Or my mum. How about you?"

I shifted uncomfortably, not just because of how hard the chair was under my rear.

"I dunno. I guess. My mother and I aren't close, but I don't want anything to happen to her."

"What about your father?" Riley asked.

"He left when I was little." I sipped the terrible coffee, which was quickly getting cold. "My stepfather and I aren't that close either." He always made it clear I wasn't biologically his.

"Any siblings?" Riley peeled off the lid of his coffee before downing the last of it.

"One stepbrother, Brooks. He's a couple of years older than me."

"Are you close?" Riley asked, eyebrows dipping as he smiled.

I made a face. "No. And especially no, not like that. My stepbrother is, I don't know, the golden child of the family."

My stepfather made sure he had everything, whereas I was never extended that same courtesy. Brooks had birthday parties and extravagant presents. I got practical gifts, like shoes. He was given a car. I had to buy my own. I was basically ignored when my stepfather's family spent Christmas with us. Reminded I wasn't biologically related to any of them except my mother. Although, she was just as cold.

"Why do I want to punch him in the face?" Riley mused.

"I don't know. It's not his fault how they treated us," I said. "I don't know if he had it much better, to be honest. My parents had high expectations for him. If he didn't meet them, they'd always grill him about why. Why was his report card straight As instead of A-plusses" I didn't know why I was telling him all of this. It was nice to have someone to confide in, I supposed. I would have told Whitney or Fiona, but the opportunity hadn't arisen. So, here I was, telling Riley instead. Or at least, telling him first.

"Did you get all A-plusses?" Riley asked. "Let me guess, you did and they didn't notice?" He seemed offended on my behalf.

"I didn't, but they wouldn't have noticed," I said. "I did okay. I was always better at art than anything academic."

"Painting and drawing," he said.

"Yes… And… Sculpture." Just saying the word made my heart ache. "Creating art out of things nobody wanted, that was always my thing. Making something pretty out of trash."

"That explains your attraction to me and Connor," Riley said jokingly.

"You're not trash," I argued.

"Plenty of people would disagree with that, but

thanks." He gave me a smile I hadn't seen from him before. A real, genuine smile.

"Now I'm the one who wants to punch someone," I said. "I'm sorry people make you feel that way."

"I'm sorry your parents made you feel that way." He reached for my hand, wrapping his fingers around mine. "No one should do that to anyone, especially someone as sweet as you. Tell me about your sculptures. Why haven't I seen you making any? Have you been hiding them in a secret room in your house?"

"I haven't been making them," I said. "I—"

Connor and Whitney stepped out of Jacob's room, both looking a lot more relieved than when they went in.

"Bastard is tough as shit," Connor said. "We might have to tie him down to keep him from working too hard."

"We'll help out," Riley said. "Whatever you need."

"Yeah, I can too," I said. If I was going to stick around town and become part of it, then I wanted to help out the townspeople the way they helped each other. I wanted to be a part of that. The warm community that looked after its own.

"Thank you," Whitney said to us both. "Don't

think we won't take you both up on that. Because we absolutely will."

"Shit yeah, we will," Connor said. "Let's get something better than that crap coffee."

"Yes please." Whitney hooked her arm through mine, pulled me to my feet and we headed out of the hospital, into the evening air.

17

LEAH

"SHOULD YOU BE STANDING SO MUCH?" Connor gave me a look up and down.

"I'm fine." I gathered up a stack of empty glasses to carry back behind the bar. I was going to hurt tomorrow, but I'd help out where they needed it. Right now, that was keeping the Frosty Brew going. Connor disappeared into the office to do the paperwork his father usually did, leaving me and Fiona to clean up out here. He only just reappeared, his hair tousled like he'd run his hand through it several times.

"We're almost done." I loaded the glasses into the glass washer and closed the door.

"Leah," he said warningly.

I turned around, my hands on my hips. "I said I'm

fine. Don't tell me you didn't need the help." He and Fiona would have been here all night without the extra pair of hands. Or they would have had to call in Zara on her night off.

"Not if it means..." He shut his mouth with a click of his teeth as Fiona stepped around behind the bar.

"You two are getting intense," she teased. "Should I leave?"

Connor's side eye suggested she should, but I lowered my hands to my sides, trying to appear less confrontational.

"I think we're both done here," I said. Fortunately the place was quiet enough tonight to close early, but the weekend was imminent. I was going to have to pace myself, or sit out. Honestly, I didn't care for either option.

"Yeah, thanks," Connor said with a grunt. "I appreciate the help." He took a step to the side to let Riley pass, carrying a keg on his shoulder. He disappeared into the cool room, followed by the clang as he lowered the keg to the concrete floor.

"That's the last one," Riley said, stepping back out and rubbing his shoulder. "I signed for the delivery."

"Great." Connor slapped his shoulder. "I'll put it

into the system before I forget. You know what Dad's like with shit like that."

"Yeah, he'd lose his mind if you don't put it in thirty seconds after the truck pulls in." Riley grinned.

"Fifteen seconds." Connor sighed and disappeared back into the office.

"He acts like a fucking grizzly, but he really is grateful," Riley said. "This is more than his father's business. It's important to the whole town. Wait until summer when we get live bands here in the beer garden. The whole town comes. It's like one big, dysfunctional, more or less happy family."

"It really is," Fiona agreed. "Those are the best nights around here." She put a hand up over her mouth to cover a yawn. "I should get going. It's almost Sarah's bedtime and I have to run a couple of things over to Gavin Clarke first."

"Can I come?" I asked.

I ignored the widening of Riley's grin. I hadn't forgotten his promise that the next time I came, it would be on his mouth. My trusty vibrator might prove him wrong, but we'd see.

In the meantime, I was curious about Gavin. Should I be? It felt a little morbid, but I couldn't help myself. After the guys told me about his daughter, my heart hurt for him. If I could help look out for the man, that could be another way for me to settle here in town.

"Of course," Fiona said lightly. "Later, Ri."

"Later, Fi." He gave her a brief nod. "Later, sweetheart." He looked like he wanted to kiss me, but he tucked his hands into his pockets and leaned back against the bar to watch us leave.

"He's got it bad," Fiona said as we stepped out into the still of night.

I glanced back to see him still watching, his gaze on my ass.

"I wouldn't go that far." He wanted to fuck me, but chances were he'd forget me the second we were done. I'd be another notch in his belt. Did I want that? Ugh, I didn't care for that line of thought. I didn't want to be thrown away like a disposable coffee cup the minute it was empty. I already lived that life. I deserved better.

I pushed those thoughts away and focused on the moment. "What are we taking to Gavin?"

"A few things for breakfasts and lunches," Fiona said. She stopped to pick up a couple of bags that sat by the back door of the pub, out of the way. "Mostly bread, peanut butter, things like that." She peered into the bags, the sides of her mouth turned down.

"Does he eat them?" I asked gently, guessing the reason for her expression.

"Some of it," she said. "We throw out a lot. Louisa and Carly from the Snowdrop Café check on him when they can, and make sandwiches and things. Sometimes I think…"

"Connor and Riley told me what happened with his daughter," I whispered. If that was why she was holding back from finishing that sentence, she should know I understood. Or at least, I had the situation explained to me.

"Right." Fiona looked up. "Sometimes I think he wishes he was the one who fell into the creek. I've seen him over the lake, staring into the water like maybe he'll… I don't know. Jump in. If it happened to Sarah…" She sniffed.

"It must be hard on him," I said.

I'd never loved anyone so much I wanted to follow them under the water. I knew a couple I might *hold* under there, but I kept that distasteful thought to myself. I'd never act on it anyway. I could barely slice meat without feeling bad about the animal it came from.

"Yeah." Fiona pushed the door open with her back and stepped out, leaving me to hurry behind her.

My legs felt a little stiff and achey. I didn't need

to look to know they were beginning to swell. I'd try to have a bath when I got back home. Maybe I could prevent the worst of a flare-up.

"So, you went up to the lookout with those two," Fiona said when we were about half a block away from the pub.

"Let me guess, you've never been there either?" I asked.

She glanced over and smiled. "Oh, I have, but not with either of them. I was seeing a guy for a while. Things didn't work out."

"I'm sorry," I said. "I'm sure you deserve better."

She laughed. "I really do. He was sweet, but he always had one foot out of Aurora Hollow, you know? I wouldn't leave and he wouldn't stay."

"Definitely his loss then," I said. "Where did he go?"

"Last I heard, he was playing baseball in Toronto. Professionally. I mean, I guess I can't blame a guy for leaving to do something like that. There aren't many professional baseball teams in town. Specifically… none."

I laughed. "Yeah, okay, I get that. Do you think he'll ever come back?"

"Reese?" She looked thoughtful. "Maybe. I mean, he comes back for holidays and during the off-season. Sometimes we hook up, sometimes we don't. But I don't know if he'd want to stick around permanently. Why would he when he has fans chasing him. What's the baseball equivalent of a puck bunny? Ball bunny? Bat bunny? Jersey chaser?"

"I have no idea," I admitted. "If he picks them over you, then he's crazy."

"I agree completely," she said. "I told him I wouldn't wait for him, and I won't. Even if I didn't deserve better, Sarah does. I don't want someone in her life who's ready to walk out the door at any moment. I want her to have stability, to be able to trust the people around her."

"You're a good mom," I said. "She's lucky to have you."

"I'm lucky to have her," Fiona said. "It was a high risk pregnancy. The doctor suggested I not go through with it, but I couldn't bring myself to end it. Although, there were times when I had morning sickness so bad I thought it would end both of us." She scrunched up her face.

"That sounds terrible," I said sympathetically. I'd never given much thought to having children. Getting around was difficult enough, and if I passed my arthritis onto them…

"It was. I became very intimately attached to the

bathroom floor, in front of the toilet," she said with a laugh. "But Sarah is completely worth it. I wouldn't have changed those days for anything."

"Can I ask you something?" I asked carefully.

"That depends what it is," she said. "You can ask, but I don't guarantee to answer." She smiled, showing she was at least half joking.

That was fair.

"Sarah's father. You said he's not around?"

"That's right," she said lightly. "It's not Reese, if you're wondering. He would have stuck around for her. And I would have spent my life feeling guilty about tying him down."

I told her what I told Riley about my father taking off when I was little. "I know how it feels to have an absent father. My mother was physically present, but she was otherwise absent. At least Sarah has you."

"That's terrible," Fiona said. "I can't imagine having a kid and not giving them everything they need as best you can. I know I can't do everything for her, but I try. You know?"

"I do know, because I've seen you together," I said. "She adores you. I can't help wishing... I had what you give her." A mother that cared whether she succeeded or not. That supported her and nurtured her. The kind of parent I wished for every child. Parents who wanted their offspring. That didn't seem like a whole lot to ask to me.

"I wish you did too," Fiona said softly. "I wish you grew up here in Aurora Hollow. I bet we would have been like sisters. Doing everything together and all that shit. Whitney and Holly are great, but they're older than me. When they started high school, I barely saw them. We drifted apart for a long time. We kinda didn't hang out again until a couple of years ago. But you and I, we could have given Connor and Riley a bunch of shit. And the other guys in town too." She made it sound amazing.

"That would have been wonderful," I said wistfully. Even if my family was distant, I would have been surrounded by found family. There was no reason I couldn't have that now. It already felt like I did. I could certainly have worse sisters than Fiona, Whitney and Holly.

"Well, you're here now," Fiona said. "We can make the most out of that."

"I hope to," I said. I'd never been anywhere that felt like home like this town did. More than anything, I wanted to belong. To be a part of this place and the people in it. A valuable member of the community, not just someone who lived here. I wanted it so much my heart ached.

She was silent for a few minutes as we made our way down the street. We crossed an empty side street and stopped in front of a cottage with a facade made entirely of river stones and timber. Judging by the wear on the heavy wooden door, it must have been standing for at least a hundred years. In the centre, an iron door knocker in the shape of a horse shoe was shiny, like hundreds of hands had gripped it to announce the visitor's presence.

The mat in front of the door showed signs of once having words or patterns on the surface. What-ever it was, I couldn't make it out now. It could have been anything from the word 'welcome,' to a picture of a moose or maybe a kangaroo, its tail out behind it.

"This is where Gavin Clarke lives." Fiona nodded towards the door before she pushed it open and stepped inside. "Gavin?"

I hesitated for a moment before following her in.

18

LEAH

THE PLACE WAS DIMLY LIT, but cosy. Low ceilings welcomed me inside, like a warm hug.

I followed Fiona into the small, open plan living and kitchen area.

Dark blue walls contrasted with white crown moulding and wainscoting. A brick fireplace off to one side was cold and empty.

"Hey, Gavin." Fiona placed the bags on the kitchen counter.

He sat on an armchair near the window, staring at a small television. I recognised the show, featuring a family who renovated a resort in the Bahamas. Somewhere I'd love to go someday.

At first, I didn't think he knew we were there, but

slowly he turned his face. His brows dipped when he looked at me.

"This is Leah." Fiona flapped a hand in my direction before starting to pull out groceries from the bag. "Have you eaten today?"

"Leah." Gavin seemed confused, like his mind wasn't putting all the pieces together.

"That's right," I said softly. "Leah Kent. I'm new in town."

"Leah Kent," he echoed.

"She's my friend," Fiona said. "Now, have you eaten? You know what, let me make you something anyway. It doesn't look like anyone's made anything here today." She bustled around, pulling out a microwave meal and putting it in to heat up.

"Can I do anything?" I asked, directing the question to both of them.

"Can you take these?" Fiona dug through the fridge, pulling out items that needed to be tossed away. She handed me half a loaf of bread, a couple of half-rotten apples and a sock. "I don't know either," she said before I could ask. "Its pair might be around somewhere."

"Right." I threw the food away in the trash and the sock in the laundry hamper by the bedroom door. I caught a glimpse of a big four-poster bed that didn't look recently slept in. Unless someone came by during the day to make it for him. Since the hamper was empty, I assumed he or someone else washed his clothes.

The microwave pinged happily. Fiona opened it and eased the meal out. Gingerly, her brow creased in concentration, she pulled back the wrap and let it sit too cool for a couple of minutes.

"How have you been, Gavin?" She leaned against the kitchen counter, her hands to either side of her.

"Same old," he said in a rough, gravelly voice that was strangely soothing. The kind of voice that could put someone into a comfortable, restful sleep.

The tune to an old lullaby came to mind. I couldn't remember the words, only a vague, soothing sound. I must have heard it on some TV show or movie, because I didn't think my mother ever sang me a lullaby. My stepfather definitely didn't. Gavin's voice was the same kind of soothing.

"Louisa came by with pie," he added. "Maybe that was yesterday." His brow creased again.

Fiona glanced at me, then back at him. "It could have been." Clearly she thought it was much longer than that. "Was it good pie?"

"Her pies are always good," he said. "The best.

Almost as good as…" He blinked a couple of times, as if trying to remember.

"They are so good," Fiona said quickly. She grabbed a fork and stirred the meal, it looked like spaghetti Bolognese, before carrying it over and handing it to him. "Make sure you eat it all."

"Bossy," he teased. He gave her a sideways look before tucking into the food.

"I'm not bossy, I just care," Fiona said tartly. "We can't have you fading away, can we now?"

He grunted in response, but went on eating as though he hadn't seen food in days. I suspected he hadn't. At least, not today.

When I was engrossed in a piece of art, I sometimes forgot to eat, so I could relate to being that hungry. Losing his daughter must really have shattered him. He seemed totally aware at moments and completely lost in others. Thankfully he had the town looking out for him.

After a couple of minutes, he finished everything and looked mournful.

"Still hungry?" Fiona guessed. "Lucky I brought you a surprise." She took the empty tray and fork, and dug into one of the bags to pull out a plastic container. She peeled off the lid to reveal several cupcakes.

"Your favourite colour." She held the box out to him so he could take one.

"Purple was Coral's favourite colour," he said. He bit into the cupcake, leaving a smear of purple icing on his nose.

He reminded me of Riley with paint from my painting on his face.

"Purple is a great colour," I said. I picked up a cupcake when Fiona offered me the box. She took one herself before tossing the box back into the bag.

"Purple is the best colour," Fiona agreed. "It's like blue and pink had a lovechild."

I laughed before biting into mine. "This is so good," I moaned.

"Of course they are, Carly made them," Fiona said. "Everyone knows she's the best baker in town."

"Carly is the best," Gavin agreed. "I asked her to my prom, but she said no. She wanted to go with Henry Crane." He grunted in the back of his throat, like she should have had better taste.

"Riley's dad?" I asked. Of course, many of the families in town lived here for a couple of generations. It made sense they all grew up together, like my new friends all had.

"Yep," Gavin agreed. "But Henry only had eyes for Briony. He waited years for her to break up with

Jacob, then he pounced." He mimed doing that with one hand before wiping the icing off his nose.

"It all sounds really incestuous, doesn't it?" Fiona giggled. "My parents met when they were five. They've never dated anyone else. So they say, at least."

"That must have been nice though," I said. "Always knowing who you're going to end up with."

Fiona finished her cupcake and washed her hands. "I suppose so, but I've always been a big fan of 'try before you buy'. I don't want to get stuck with someone who can't…" She glanced at Gavin and her cheeks turned pink.

"Get you off, " he finished for her. "I'm not all there sometimes, but I wasn't born yesterday. I know what orgasms are."

"Of course you do," she said with an awkward laugh.

He hummed his agreement. "Don't marry anyone who can't give you lots of them." He tossed the rest of the cupcake into his mouth and chewed slowly.

"That sounds like good advice," I said.

He looked confused. "What does?" In a matter of moments, he disappeared back into himself.

Fiona sighed softly. "Us going and letting you get

some rest. I'll make sure someone comes by in the morning to be sure you have breakfast."

"Suit yourself." His shoulders dropped and he curled in on himself, his eyes back on the TV screen.

I watched him for a moment, my heart hurting for him. What would his life have been like if his daughter hadn't died? He could be laughing with her, maybe a couple of grandchildren. Not here by himself, trapped in his own brain. I wished I could help more, but all I could do was feel incredibly sad. And remind myself to live my best life as much and as often as I could. I had no choice but to slow down on flare-up days, but the rest of the time? I should be out there living better.

Although, I was living better here than I was back in the city, so that was a start.

Fiona watched him for a minute or two before grabbing up the bags and starting towards the door.

"Good night, Gavin."

He didn't answer. The only sign he heard was a twitch in his cheek. Otherwise, he didn't move.

"Should we...?" I whispered.

"There's nothing we can do," she whispered back. "Trust me, we've tried. Once he's had enough, he's had enough."

I hated to leave him there like that, but I stepped towards the door.

"Good night, Gavin," I said softly.

I didn't know why I expected a different response to the one he gave Fiona, but it seemed rude to walk away without saying anything.

"Good night" he said without glancing at me.

Fiona looked surprised as she gestured out of the door in front of her. "I think he likes you."

"I'm probably a novelty," I said. "New face in town and all." Like I was with Connor and Riley.

"I guess so," she agreed. "I never expected him to say the word orgasms." She smiled before pulling the door closed behind her.

"It really was good advice." I walked beside her as we headed back to our cottages.

"Is that why you went up to the lookout with Connor and Riley?" she teased.

"You really want the answer to that?" I turned to raise my eyebrows at her.

"Now you mention it, not really," she said with a laugh. "That would be like listening to you talk about fucking my brother."

"I won't answer the question then," I said. I wouldn't want to hear if she got involved with my stepbrother. Although, I suspected they'd loathe each other. She was a small town sweetheart and he was a city asshole, through and through. She deserved a lot better than Brooks Kent.

"Thanks for coming with me tonight," she said. "It was nice to see Gavin a bit more lively than usual. Sometimes he just watches the TV and doesn't seem to notice I'm there. I could do a dance routine in front of him and he wouldn't blink."

"You dance?" I asked.

"Badly," she said with a laugh. "That could be why he wouldn't watch. I'm pretty bad."

"I'm sure you're not that bad," I said. I would be. Right now in particular. My legs and feet were starting to ache. The sooner I got off them and into a bath, the better.

"You haven't seen me," she said. "Wait until I get a few tequilas in me and then you can enjoy the show. I'm the definition of 'dance like no one is watching.' Of course, I never say anything like this in front of Sarah. I don't want her to grow up thinking it's okay to put herself down."

"I like that," I said. "We're really good at being mean to ourselves too much of the time."

"We really are." She nodded vigourously. "And we don't need to be, especially with guys like Riley and Connor around. I think they get off on being mean to us on our behalf." She said it lightly, like she didn't really believe it.

For all their barbs toward each other, it was more teasing than it was nasty. She made the comparison to siblings; that sounded accurate to me. They bickered like brothers and sisters, but at the end of the day they all had each other's backs. If anything happened to Fiona, I didn't doubt guys would come running. Ready to take a swing at anyone who'd try to hurt her.

"I'm glad I found this place," I said softly, as we crossed a street and stopped in front of my cottage.

"I'm glad you found it too." She threw her arms around me and squeezed me tight. "I hope you never leave."

"I might not." I squeezed her back. "Why would I want to?

"I can't think of a single reason." She laughed. "I guess you better stick around." She lowered her arms and waved at me while walking backwards a few steps to her place.

I watched her until she turned around, then headed inside for a long soak.

RILEY

"ARE you sure this is a good idea?" I asked.

"It's a great idea." Connor tried the door of Leah's place before pulling out a key and unlocking it.

A couple of summers ago, he and I painted the insides of several of the rental properties on the street. To make it easier, the owners made several copies of the keys. Evidently some of them never made their way back to them.

The sound of splashing water convinced me that maybe this was, in fact, an excellent idea.

Connor stepped inside, leaving me to close the door behind us.

"Is someone there?" Leah called out from the bathroom. She sounded nervous. Like she thought people broke into the place to do inappropriate things to her.

We didn't break in, but if we hadn't had a key, we would have. As for the rest…

"It's just your friendly neighbourhood assholes," Connor called back. "Are you naked?"

"Please be naked," I said with a grin.

"What are you doing here?" Her voice was higher now. "How did you get in?"

Connor stepped over to the door, dangling the key from his fingers.

I was right behind him. To my disappointment, her body was mostly obscured by bubbles.

"Why do you have a key?" She narrowed her eyes at us.

"So I can let myself in," he said easily. "Why else? How are you feeling tonight?"

I dropped my gaze to where her feet peeked out of the water. Just the tips of her toes, nails painted deep red.

"Connor was worried about you," I said. "Because you were standing for hours." I leaned against the door frame and crossed my arms over my chest.

"I wasn't worried," he argued. "I was curious." But his hazel eyes held an edge of concern.

"He was worried." I nodded. "I think his exact words were, 'if she's overdone it, I'm going to tie her to her bed.'"

"The last part is right," he said.

Asshole wouldn't admit it, but I was telling the truth. I saw the way he looked at her when she left the Frosty Brew. She pushed herself too hard.

What I wanted to know was why. She barely knew his father. Or him for that matter. She could have walked away and left us to sort things out. Plenty of people would have. But not Leah fucking Kent. No, she had to stick around and help, even if it meant messing herself up. She was too fucking noble for her own good.

"Did you bring the rope or handcuffs?" Connor asked me.

I patted my pockets. "I seem to have misplaced them. There must be something around here long enough to go around her wrists."

"Why are you really here?" Leah asked. Her cheeks were flushed and her eyes were dark, like the idea of being bound while we worshipped her body was appealing.

"Checking on what's ours," he said. "In case you had someone else here."

"As you can see, I'm alone." She gestured around the bathroom.

"Shame." He took a couple of steps toward her. "I was looking forward to kicking some ass."

"I was looking forward to *kissing* some ass," I said.

He gave me a sharp look.

"I mean it literally, not like I'm sucking up," I said. "Would you like it better if I said I wanted to bite some ass?"

He shrugged. "All of those are good."

As long as it was his ass, or Leah's, I was biting or kissing, he'd allow it. Or licking, for that matter.

"Now you've seen I'm fine and no one else is here, you can go," Leah said. "It's late."

"It's not that late," Connor said.

We weren't leaving until we were ready. She must have known that.

"Do you need help getting out of the bath?"

"It's my turn." I stepped deeper into the room and glanced over at him, challenging him. Like I'd fight him for the right to help her out of the bath.

But I hadn't forgotten he also liked to watch.

He pulled a towel from the rack on the wall and offered it to me. "Be my guest." Stepping back, he leaned against the door frame, his gaze on both of us.

There, that flicker in his eyes. He knew. He remembered. And I was going to give myself a show.

I offered my hand to Leah, who clasped it and let me pull her to her feet. Showing off her whole, gloriously wet body.

My cock was instantly hard.

She stepped carefully over the side of the bath onto the bath mat. I wrapped the towel around her. She started to take it from me, but I wouldn't let her. Instead, I dried her slowly, rubbing the towel from her shoulders, down to her biceps. In small circles, I rubbed it across her skin, wiping all the moisture from her, and leaving her pink.

"I can do that," she told me.

"Be a good girl and let him finish," Connor said.

Her eyes went darker and she stood still, her lips parted slightly.

I worked my way down lower, over her back and down to the curve of her ass. I dried each cheek like it was a work of art. One soft, round apple at a time. Carefully, I crouched to dry one leg, then the other.

"Turn around," Connor ordered.

Her eyes on him, she turned around slowly.

"Good girl," he said softly.

She swallowed hard.

I started to dry her from the ankles up, slowly

inching my way up her thighs. I pried them apart and dried in between them. Inhaling her warm, heady scent, but only gently patting her pussy. I wanted her aching for my touch. Hoping for more. Begging.

Her gaze dropped to watch me work my way up her belly and carefully over first one breast, then the other. Avoiding her stiffened nipples for now.

Finally, I patted her face dry and wrapped the towel around her hair.

"Such a good fucking girl," Connor said. "Did you like that?"

"Yes," she whispered.

"Good," he said. "Now you can be a very good girl and let Riley make you come with his tongue."

"Yes please." I hung the towel back up on the rack, making sure the ends were evenly lined up with each other, and turned back to her. My hands on her warm, bare hips, I lifted her onto the counter top beside the sink.

"Show me her pussy," Connor said.

Without a glance back at him, I gripped her thighs and parted them, putting her beautiful pussy on display for both of us.

"So pretty," he said. "How wet is she, Ri?"

I slid the tip of one finger down the middle of her

slit, making her quiver. "So fucking wet," I said reverently.

"Of course she is," he said. "Show me how you make her come."

I couched and lowered my face between her legs, swiping my tongue over her pussy. She tasted like the sweetest nectar the gods ever made. Sweeter. Headier. Addictive as fuck.

"Leah, play with those beautiful nipples of yours," Connor said.

She didn't seem to know where to look next, at me or at him, so she switched back and forth, while raising her hands to her breasts and rolling her nipples between her thumbs and forefingers.

"Just like that." In the periphery of my vision, Connor leaned his head back so he could watch both of us. His cock must have ached like a bitch. Mine did.

My erection was trying to escape from my jeans. If I was any harder, I'd burst the seams.

Connor barely seemed to notice. His attention was on the way I sucked Leah's clit and the way her hips rolled to meet me.

"Put a finger inside her," Connor said. "Now two."

Leah moaned and whispered my name.

That must have been too much for him. He

hastily undid his jeans and pulled out his cock. His hand wrapped around it, he fisted himself slowly while I licked and sucked, bringing her closer and closer to the edge.

"How close are you?" Connor asked.

"So close," she said breathlessly. "So, ahhh." She started to throw her head back.

"Eyes on me," he ordered.

I looked over to him, then back up to her face.

She dropped her gaze so I saw and felt the exact moment she came apart from my mouth. Her lips dropped open and she moaned, her whole body stiffened except her hips, which were still meeting my licks, moving automatically as if they had a mind of their own.

"So fucking hot." Connor's words came out on a ragged breath. He was close to coming himself. He pumped a couple more times while stepping over closer to us.

"How close are you?" she asked, still trying to catch her breath.

"So fucking close," he said. "I'm going to—" He came hard, squirting a string of cum, coating the side of my face and her thigh in his pearly release. He went on pumping himself, milking every drop until his orgasm faded away.

I sat back on my heels and wiped a hand over my cheek, grinning as it came away with cum. "I love it when you do that." I stuffed my finger into my mouth and licked it clean, then turned to click Leah clean.

She writhed, her hands to either side of her on the countertop. "That tickles."

I didn't stop until all the cum was gone. Then I sat back and smiled like the Cheshire cat. Or the cat that got the cream. "You were right Connor, this was a good idea."

"I'm always fucking right." He tucked his cock back into his jeans and did them back up. "Leah, do you need anything? You've got enough pain pills?"

She seemed surprised at the question, as if she expected us to stay all night and fuck her until she was raw.

We would, but not tonight. Not while she was swollen and uncomfortable because of her need to help us, and this town. When we did fuck her, she'd be completely comfortable until we were done. Then she wouldn't be able to walk for a week.

"I have what I need." She let me help her down from the counter top, but winced as she stood upright.

"Good. Pyjamas?" Connor took a step towards the door.

"In the drawer beside my bed," she said.

He nodded for me to help her into her bedroom while he rummaged around for her pyjamas and helped to get her comfortable.

"Sweet dreams," I said, leaning over her while she lay with her hair fanned out across her pillow. I kissed her forehead and stepped back for Connor to do the same.

"Thank you," she said. "For the help and the orgasm."

"Thank you for helping at the pub," I said lightly. I never felt the urge to lie down beside a woman, gather up and sleep next to her. I wouldn't tonight, but I badly wanted to.

"Any time," she said sleepily. "You can leave the key on the table before you go."

Connor chuckled. "Not a fucking chance, honey. While you live here, I'm keeping a copy."

Of course he would. Knowing he could come and go whenever he wanted to wasn't a thing he was going to give up. Not tonight. Probably not ever.

"Maybe I'll move then." She rolled onto her side and raised her eyebrows at him.

"Then I'll get a key to that place too," he said.

If she thought for a moment he wouldn't, she better think again. She was ours. We weren't giving her up that easily.

"He really will," I said. "Connor is persistent."

"Exactly," he said. "I always get what I want." He grabbed my sleeve and tugged me out the door.

20

LEAH

"I'M SO glad you're here, they've been wild this morning." Whitney's messy bun was even messier than usual. Her green-grey eyes showed how frazzled she was, but she was smiling, regardless.

"Oh, good." I grimaced playfully. "What could be better than a room full of wild five- and six-year-olds?"

Whitney laughed and patted my shoulder. "You'll do fine. They'll sit still and listen to you."

I gave her a dubious look, but stepped into her classroom.

The kids were all seated at tables, giggling and poking each other until they realised a new person had stepped into the room.

"This is Miss Kent," Whitney said, gesturing

towards me like I was the prize on a television game show. "She's going to give you an art class today."

That got a squeal in response and a bunch of kids bouncing up and down in their seats.

"Can we do finger painting?" one of them called out. A boy with straight, black hair and dark eyes.

"Not today, Kennett," Whitney said.

The class collectively groaned.

"I thought we could do some drawing," I said. "Miss Ferguson said you have pastel crayons."

"That's right, we do," Whitney said. "We only use them for *very* special occasions." She looked at the kids and nodded as she spoke.

"Is this a special occasion?" a girl with short, blonde hair asked. Her huge blue eyes and solemn expression made her look as though she was six, going on forty.

"I think so, Dakota," Whitney said. "Can you get the crayons out for the class please?"

"Yes, Miss Ferguson." Dakota pushed her chair back and walked over to a set of drawers on the side of the room. From there she pulled out four or five packets of crayons and started to place them in front of pairs of the kids.

"They don't seem so wild to me," I said softly to Whitney, giving her a sideways glance.

She snorted. "For you, they aren't. You should have seen them two or three minutes ago. They would have been throwing the crayons around the room."

"If we throw these crayons, we don't get to use them again," Kennett said, obviously hearing the conversation.

"Absolutely correct," Whitney told him. "We take good care of our special art supplies." To me she added, "Funding for them is limited. I wish we didn't have to police them, but if we're going to have anything to use for art, I have to."

"That sounds familiar," I said. My school was the same way. Most schools seemed to be. The arts weren't as valued as they deserved. Shame, because everyone was happy to consume art in the form of books, movies and music. How would we have those things if we didn't nurture talent in kids?

"What are we going to draw?" Dakota returned to her chair and sat with her hands clasped in front of her.

"I thought you could draw each other," I said. I counted quickly to make sure we had an even number before nodding. "You can draw your partner and then your partner can draw you."

"Who are you going to draw?" Dakota asked.

"She's sharp as a tack," Whitney whispered.

I could see that. "I thought I'd draw Miss Ferguson."

For some reason, the kids thought that was hilariously funny. They all burst into laughter, even Dakota.

"Can you make her look funny?" one of the boys asked. With bright blue-green eyes and a turned up nose, I bet he got away with all sorts of things he shouldn't. Riley and Connor probably looked the same at his age, but with fewer freckles.

"You think I don't look funny already, Lincoln?" Whitney teased.

"Yeah, you do." Lincoln grinned in delight. The rest of the class cracked up laughing again.

I couldn't help smiling. I didn't think I could do this day in and day out, but they were adorable for a little while.

"Let's get you all some paper." Whitney bustled around giving each of the kids a couple of pieces of paper and handing some to me. She waved to a chair to the side of the room. "Sit, sit. Where do you need me?"

"On the toilet!" Lincoln shouted.

Once again, the class erupted in laughter.

"How about you put a chair in front of your desk

and sit there?" I suggested. That way, she could keep an eye on the class while I kept an eye on her.

I lowered myself into my seat, trying not to let on that the flare-up from the night of helping at the pub hadn't completely died down. The bath and the orgasm made it better than it might have been, but the chair was low.

Still, I couldn't stop thinking about the way Connor came on me and Riley. The surge of hot cum on my cool skin. The way Riley licked it off.

I shouldn't be thinking any of this in a room full of kids, and especially not in front of Connor's sister. Not that she could read my mind, but if my face heated too much, she'd definitely notice and wonder why. She wouldn't ask questions now, but knowing her, she'd ask later. She didn't want details, but she'd want to know how involved I was with both of them. Since I didn't even know, it was best not to go there for now.

I got out my own pastel crayons from my bag and waited for Whitney to get settled before I started to draw her.

I worked quickly, outlining the shape of her face and shoulders in black crayon, before adding in detail. Every so often, I glanced at the kids. They were mostly quiet, focusing on their paper, and their partner. The occasional giggle would break out, but never lasted long.

Whitney warned me in advance they might have short attention spans, so I finished up the rough sketch of her before putting down the crayon and standing to walk around the room and look at the kid's work.

Dakota was drawing Lincoln with great care.

"Make sure you do my eyes the right colour," he said. "My mother says if you're going to do art, you have to do it right and make things look how they really are. She said people don't really have three eyes."

"Art is creative," I said as diplomatically as I could. "Things don't always have to be perfect. Lots of it isn't. If your creativity tells you three eyes is a good idea, I say go for it." I didn't want to contradict his parent, but there was no right or wrong way to be creative. If there was, no one would have ever heard of Picasso.

"Can I draw you with three eyes?" he asked eagerly.

"Of course you can," I said.

While Dakota finished off the picture of him, he grabbed up a bright green crayon and started to draw something that didn't resemble me as far as I could tell, but he seemed to be enjoying the process a lot more.

"You're good with them," Whitney said from beside my shoulder.

"I don't like to see people suppress creativity," I said. "He might be an artist too some day."

"He just might," she agreed. "Or an art teacher."

"Yeah," Lincoln said. "I can be an art teacher that plays pro hockey. And builds houses with my dad."

That was certainly ambitious. I hoped whatever he did, he'd be happy.

"My mum says I'm going to be a doctor," Kennett declared.

"I'm going to be a lesbian like my mothers," Dakota said softly.

"Her mums are the best," Whitney declared. "They're the best plumbers in town. If you ever need one, just call on Gina and Serena. They'll sort you out right quick, right, Dakota?"

Dakota nodded, still solemn but now with a hint of pride on her face. "I'm going to work with them."

"That's awesome," I said. "The world definitely needs more girls in trades."

Dakota blushed faintly before looking down at her drawing and fixing up lines here and there.

"They remind me so much of myself at that age,"

Whitney said. "I used to sit in this exact classroom. My brother's class was next door. You can imagine how many times I heard the teacher yelling at him and Riley." She made a face and rolled her eyes toward the ceiling.

"I bet you all were adorable back then," I said.

"Of course we were; we're still adorable," she replied, pretending to be offended.

"Absolutely! Of course you are." I wasn't sure that was the word I'd use to describe either of those guys. Attractive, arrogant and hot; those fit better.

"Finished!" Lincoln declared. He held up his picture, three eyes and all.

I made out a face with a ton of spiky hair and big ears. "Do I have two mouths?"

He giggled and nodded. "One to eat and one to talk."

"That would be useful." I glanced sidelong at Whitney, who was trying not to laugh. I could see what she was thinking. Two mouths would be useful for sucking two cocks at once. Except now I was thinking about sucking Connor and Riley's.

"Very useful," she agreed. She wasn't being very helpful at helping me to keep a straight face. Her expression made me want to laugh, but I didn't want Lincoln to think I was laughing at him. That wasn't how talent was nurtured. Or enthusiasm, for that matter.

"You could laugh and eat a burger at the same time," Kennett said.

"I'm starting to be envious of a drawing of myself." I was relieved to have a reason to laugh, this time at myself.

"Do you want to keep it?" Lincoln, suddenly shy, offered me the sheet of paper.

"I'd love to," I said. "But you need to sign it first. Then, someday, when you're famous, I can show everyone my Lincoln original artwork."

He grabbed up a bright yellow crayon and wrote his name in big, awkward letters before offering me the paper again.

"I'll cherish it forever," I said. "I'll put it on my fridge when I get home."

A thing my mother never did. If she kept any of my childhood artwork, she stashed it away where I couldn't see it. My stepfather had a couple of pieces my stepbrother did framed and hanging in his office, but nothing of mine. I'd cherish this picture all the more because of that.

Lincoln grinned. "Thank you, Miss Kent."

"All right, class," Whitney said.

Before she could say another word, the bell rang

and the kids bolted from their seats, grabbed up their bags and ran for the door.

"Well then." She laughed at how fast the room emptied. "Thank you for doing this today. They had a lot of fun. You're welcome back any time."

"Do you want to see my drawing?" Now I was suddenly shy. People had varied responses to seeing themselves on paper. Sometimes good, sometimes not so good.

"Of course I do." She followed me over to the table and gasped. "Oh my God, Leah, that's incredible! You made me look so pretty."

"You are pretty. I picked up the piece of paper and handed it to her. "You can keep it if you like."

"I like, I like," she said with a smile. "I like it so much." She managed to tear her eyes away from the drawing long enough to give me a hug. "You're so talented."

"I'm okay," I said modestly.

Yes, I could draw and paint, but it wasn't where my whole heart was. Although, my heart hadn't been whole for a long time. Not since my body started to be so broken.

21

CONNOR

"I'M glad you're doing better, Dad, but I've got this." What was with the prickle of annoyance at seeing him sitting behind his desk in his office? I'd been stir crazy for the last three days, waiting for the week-end, and for him to take back his job. Now he was here, I was, what? Possessive? Like somehow he was stepping into my territory, and not the other way around?

He glanced up at me and waved me away. "I'm fine. You know me, I can't lie around doing nothing."

He was right. He was as restless as I was. If things turned out differently, he'd be the one running the adventure tours. Bossing me around and making me step aside when he felt like it.

Respectfully, fuck that.

"Did you order more beer?" He frowned at the screen in front of him. "I'm not seeing anything here."

"I placed the order two days ago," I said. "It should be delivered this afternoon." Just in time for the weekend. Just as he asked me to do via text message the day after his heart attack. Of course he'd still question whether or not I did what he asked.

His frown deepened. "I can't see it… Oh, there it is. Right in front of my eyes."

Certain he wasn't looking, I rolled mine. Of course it fucking was. Right where I said it would be.

"Did you order enough?" He clicked on the link and peered at the screen.

"I ordered what you told me to order," I said. "Then a little more, because I didn't think it was enough."

He swung his face away from the screen to scowl at me. "You didn't think?"

I forced myself to hold my ground and not take a step back. "It's going to be a big weekend. Riley and I are—"

He cut me off. "Did you think to check with me?" His tone was cooler than the cool room where the kegs were stored.

"You were resting," I said, trying to match his

tone. Either he trusted me to run the place in his absence, or he didn't. Middle ground was something we rarely found between us.

"I was approachable by text, as you know. Even if you had to wait a few hours for a response." His chair creaked beneath him as he sat back.

"I made the call," I said. "I did what needed to be done. Like I said, this is going to be a big weekend. If we run out, who are they going to blame?"

"You," he said flatly. "Because you were running the Frosty Brew in my absence."

"Exactly," I said, just as blunt. "And I'd shoulder that blame. I made a decision that meant I wouldn't have to do that. We won't run out." I closed my mouth before I added 'you're fucking welcome.' He probably saw it on my face.

He and I were uncomfortably alike at times. I looked like him and I had his temper. And his inability to back down from a fight. Us Ferguson men were as stubborn as they came.

He nodded once, sharply. As close as he'd ever get to agreeing with me. Fuck forbid he'd admit I was right. Asshole.

"It better be a big weekend." He turned back to his computer.

My heart dipped. I'd never admit he was right

either. In this case, there was a possibility he was. But only a possibility. A busload of tourists was due within the next couple of hours, but they'd pulled out this late in the past. Sometimes the road up here got impassable. Fallen tree. Ice. Or the bus broke down. Any number of unforeseen things could fuck with the whole weekend. None of that would be my fault, but I'd get the blame, regardless.

"It will be," I said. If I had to drive everyone up here on the back of a quad bike, one by one, that's what I'd do. If only to prove to him I wasn't the dumbass he seemed to think I was. If I didn't look like him, I really would wonder if I was adopted. He seemed to care a whole lot more about Whitney than me. Fair enough, I cared more about her than I did about him too, but she was my sister. A parent shouldn't choose one kid over the other. Because she went away to university and I didn't, who gave a shit? Him, obviously. Yet, he still insisted I'd take over the pub someday.

What the fuck was with that? Either he trusted me or he didn't.

"Who's that girl who was helping?" He didn't look up at me while he spoke.

I should have known he'd hear about Leah lending a hand in his absence. He probably had a camera behind the bar, watching our every move. I should have had Riley eat her out there, so he could watch. Maybe I still would.

I shrugged. "She's a friend of Whitney's." Since Whitney could do no wrong in his eyes, he'd have a higher opinion of Leah as her friend than mine.

"Oh yeah?" Now he glanced over like he didn't believe me. "She new in town?"

"Does it matter?" I asked. "She was here when she was needed. Even took food to Gavin with Fiona." My dad and Gavin Clarke went way back, like everyone else in this place.

Dad grunted. "I like to know who's coming and going in my pub."

"I would have texted you to let you know, but we were busy," I said.

That was bullshit, I wasn't going to text him to ask his permission for Leah to help. I didn't need his approval to spend time with her. Since he only gave his approval grudgingly, I'd learned to more or less live without it. That didn't stop him from withholding it as often as possible.

"Don't knock her up," he said.

I smirked. He'd gotten my mother pregnant when they were both seventeen. They married when they were eighteen, right before she lost that baby.

They'd been making each other miserable ever since.

I'd never bring up the subject with him, but I suspected he cheated, at least a couple of times. With tourists, of course, because gossip spreads faster than wildfire in a town like this. For all I knew, he had another couple of kids out there he didn't know about. Whatever, he wouldn't give a shit about them any more than he did about me. Unless they were highly paid lawyers or doctors or some shit. Then they'd be his new favourite child.

"I have no intention of knocking her up," I said. Not for a while anyway. We had plenty of time for that. Or for adopting. Pregnancy would be hell for her arthritis. I wouldn't put her through that. I wanted all of her, her body, mind and heart; not for her to suffer. She belonged on the back of my quad bike, or riding my cock, not lying in bed in pain.

Besides, I wouldn't want any kid to inherit my asshole gene.

"Good. Tell Riley not to knock her up either." He gave me the briefest glance.

"I'll pass on your pearl of wisdom to Riley," I said. "I'm sure he'll be happy to take your advice."

"Don't get pissy with me, son," he snapped. "I

don't think Riley wants to be tied down with a baby and a woman either."

I'd hadn't talked about any of this with Riley, but chances were, Dad was right again. We were living our best lives, building our business. All that other stuff could come later. Once we and Leah were ready.

"Did you need anything else?" I asked. "I think I heard the delivery truck." I didn't, but it wouldn't be too long before it arrived anyway. Someone should be at the loading dock to receive it.

"No, get out of here," he said gruffly. "Get the delivery in and call it a night."

"Shouldn't you be finishing up and resting?" I asked.

"If you wanted to be my doctor, you should have gone to university," he said. "Since you didn't, go and meet the delivery driver."

Of course he couldn't resist the jab. He never could.

I responded with a curt nod and took a step toward the door. I stopped and placed my hand on the door frame.

"You might not believe it, but I'm glad you're okay."

He looked over at me, surprised, then gave me a

nod of his own. "I'm glad I am too, son. Thanks for holding down the fort while I took a little holiday."

"It wasn't a holiday," I said softly. "You had a fucking heart attack."

"You don't need to remind me," he snapped. "Don't give me another one."

I raised my hands to either side and stepped back, out of the doorway. "Wouldn't dream of it."

The thrum of an engine and the squeal of brakes announced the arrival of the delivery truck, just in time. Saved by the beer.

I could use a drink right about now too. The weekend couldn't come soon enough. I needed a hit of adrenaline even more than a drink. And in there, somewhere, I was going to fit at least one orgasm in.

I hurried away from the office without looking back, and without trying to dwell on how I wished our relationship was different. As if there was something I could say or do that would make him really see me. Something that didn't require compromising myself. Or leaving town to go to university.

I'd thought about that for a while, years ago, but it was never going to be for me. Maybe a little part of me was worried if I left, I'd never want to return. Would that have been a bad thing?

I would have missed out on a lot, including

spending time with Riley. Tearing around the forest on our quad bikes. Swimming in the lake in summer and skating on it in winter. Navigating the white water rapids below the falls. All the things that made me feel alive. Would I have found that anywhere else?

I supposed it didn't matter now. Nothing and no one would make me leave Aurora Hollow permanently. Not even my father's approval. Knowing him, it wouldn't be enough anyway. He'd find a way to disapprove of me. A reason to scowl.

"That's his problem," I muttered to myself.

"Pardon me?" Zara said as I walked past the bar to make my way to the loading area.

"Nothing," I said. Nothing important anyway.

She shrugged and went back to polishing glasses. "It's good to see your dad back on board."

I stopped before the corridor that led to the back door of the pub. "Was I that bad to work for?"

She grinned. "Nah, you're okay. I just notice you're happier when you're not working here."

"That obvious?" I grimaced.

"I don't know how to put this, but...yes," she said. "Everyone has seen it."

"Everyone in this place is nosy," I said.

"We want what's best for you," she said. "You can

be a prick at times, but you're our prick." She always did have a way with words. And complementing while insulting me at the same time, she must have learned that from my sister.

"Thanks. I think." I pretended to think that through then shrugged.

She just laughed. "You're welcome. Shouldn't you be meeting that delivery?" She jerked her head in that direction.

"Yeah." I patted my palm against the door frame a couple of times before turning and hurrying away.

2 2

———

LEAH

Main street was packed. People stepped down from buses parked on the side of the road beside the Frosty Brew. More cars than I'd seen in town before were parked in front of and behind them, as well as on the other side of the street.

And down the side streets as well, I noted as I walked past.

People strolled from store to store in twos and threes. Many carried bags with logos from various stores on them. Especially In Tents, and the little shop beside it that sold fudge and jars of maple syrup.

Most of the tourists were around my age, but some were younger and some older. All here, I assumed, for adventure tours. Some of them must be international if they were buying syrup to take home with them. Okay, now I had a craving for too much of it on a piece of bacon.

All I really needed was some milk. I was used to bigger crowds than this, but for some reason, that day it threatened to overwhelm me. I'd have to get used to them when the winter tourist season rolled around.

Still, I hurried into the grocery store, relieved to find it almost empty. A couple of people browsed the fruit and vegetable section, while Carly from the Snowdrop Café carried a small basket around the aisles.

She greeted me with a smile. "Hey there. You seem to be settling in well."

"I am," I said, matching her smile. "How could I not? Everyone's been so welcoming."

"We can be an ornery bunch at times," she laughed. "Once in a while we decide to be nice to someone."

"I can't imagine you being anything but nice," I said sincerely. She'd been kind to me ever since we met. Whenever I saw her around town, she took time to stop and talk to me. And anyone else whose path she crossed. As far as I could tell, she never had a bad word for anyone.

"I have my moments," she said. "I heard you helped out when Jacob Ferguson was recuperating." She gave me a nod of approval. Like I could have sat at home and pretended everything was fine, but I hadn't. I pitched in where it was needed.

"Lots of people helped out," I said modestly. It seemed like half the town had given an hour here or there. Did they really expect that, because I was new in town, I wouldn't do the same? Okay, city folk didn't help out as much as they did here, but I was more than happy to prove them wrong.

"Well, that's true," she conceded. Something behind me caught her attention. Her smile faltered slightly.

I turned as Josiah stepped into the grocery store, his whole body stiff like he knew he'd be watched. He grabbed up a basket from beside the door and stalked through the store like a lion seeking its prey. Ready to tear it to shreds, down to the bones.

"Is this where you warn me to stay away from him?" I asked. It seemed to be the way of things around here. Every time he appeared, someone wanted to throw him out on his ass.

"I think you're old enough to choose for yourself," Carly replied. Her blue eyes were still warm, but now they held something else. Concern. Sadness.

She was the first person since I arrived in town who wasn't immediately hostile to Josiah. If anything, she seemed sympathetic. Like she felt sorry for him because the whole town ostracised him. Was she the only one?

"I'm glad someone thinks so," I said wryly. Everyone else seemed to think it was okay to tell me who I could and couldn't spend time with. Especially where it involved Josiah Lachance.

She caught the tone in my voice and looked back at me and laughed. "Why doesn't that surprise me? I've heard about some of the company you've been keeping. No, no, I'm not judging," she said quickly. "Those boys are like their fathers, and their fathers are men who like to be in control. Mountain men." She rolled her eyes toward the ceiling, but didn't stop smiling. "They work hard, and they play harder. They take care of their own, but heaven help anyone who tries to mess with them."

"That sounds like them," I agreed. Connor in particular liked being in control, and I couldn't say I hated it. The way he told me and Riley what to do, it was hot as hell.

Which reminded me...

"Is there someone in town who can change locks?" I asked.

"Henry Crane is our local locksmith, amongst other things," Carly said. "Riley too, sometimes. Both of them do a lot of handy jobs here and there. Fixing windows, framing walls, stuff like that."

Of course they did. If I was going to change the locks, I might as well have an extra key made for Connor. He'd have Riley do it anyway. If I found a way to lock them out, I suspected they wouldn't hesitate to break a window.

I wasn't sure if that was also hot or disturbing as fuck. Maybe a bit of both.

"I should get going," Carly said. "I have to get to work for the lunch rush." She adjusted her grip on the basket before carrying it off to the counter to pay for her groceries.

I glanced around carefully, looking for the aisle Josiah was in. I found him loading packets of meat into his basket. Trying to look like I wasn't approaching him, I moved around the store, looking at the items on the shelves, stopping here or there to add things to my basket.

"Are you going to keep pretending you're not watching me?" Josiah asked without glancing my way.

"What makes you think I'm watching you?" I picked up a packet of chicken breast, pretending to inspect it carefully before placing it with my other items. I had a couple of ideas of ways I could use it for dinner. Hopefully none that involved burning it to a crisp.

"Someone's always watching me," he said. "They have no fucking idea how to be subtle."

"Including me?" I turned to face him.

He smelled like leather and wood smoke with a hint of spice. Cinnamon? I hadn't noticed a scar down one of his cheeks before, but a line of pale stubble amongst the dark hinted at a long one. What was it from? I couldn't tell, but the ragged nature of the line suggested the injury wasn't a tidy one. Probably not a knife to the face then.

He sighed. "Did you want something, city girl?" His dark eyed gaze slid to my face, then slowly down my body, taking in my cute dress and boots. Making me feel like I was naked in the middle of the store.

"I know what happened with Coral Clarke," I said softly.

"You have no fucking idea," he growled.

"I know it wasn't your fault," I insisted.

"It might as well have been," he said. "Don't feel sorry for me. I fucked up and she paid the price."

The bitterness and self-loathing in his voice was nothing short of heartbreaking. He seemed to hate himself as much as most of the town did. Of course, if you spent twenty years being told you screwed up, eventually you're going to believe it yourself.

"It was just an accident," I said. "You shouldn't be beating yourself up about it."

"Shouldn't I?" He took a couple of steps closer to me. Close enough to feel the heat of his body. To see the seams of his black T-shirt starting to fray with the effort of holding his biceps in. The smell of spices was stronger now, like early fall mixed with leather.

I held my ground. "What if you let it go? What if you forgave yourself for what happened? Wouldn't that be better than living with the shadows of an accident?"

He locked his gaze on mine, like he was trying to figure me out. Trying to understand why I was saying the things I was. Why didn't I hate him like everyone else did?

Finally, he leaned back, away from me. "It doesn't matter if I do. People around here, they never forget. They don't forgive. They don't get past anything. They decide what they know is what they know and nothing will change their mind."

"You make them all sound horrible," I said.

Even his laugh was bitter. "Because they are.

They like to think they look out for each other, but how long do you think it would be before they turn on each other after something else bad happens?"

"I don't think you're giving them enough credit," I admitted.

Sure, they gave each other shit, but they had each other's backs. They'd take care of each other if they needed to, like we had with Connor's dad. No one even thought about walking away and letting the pub fall apart.

"If you're still around in twenty years, you'll feel different," he said. "Riley, Connor, men like them." He curled his lip. "They only want one thing from you. They want you to fall for them. When you care about them so much it hurts, they'll get bored and turn their backs. Right now? You're a novelty to them. Someone new to fuck with. A warm pussy to stick their cocks in. If you know what's good for you, you'll go back to the city before that happens."

"Are you 'men like them?'" I asked.

Falling for either of them hadn't crossed my mind. Honestly, I hadn't given much thought to what Connor meant when he said I belonged to him. I hadn't taken it all that seriously. We were playing around, that was all. Wasn't it?

"Sweet cheeks, all men are," Josiah said, looking

almost amused. "Especially around here. Winter is coming and no one wants their dick cold."

"Seems like keeping it in your pants might be safer," I said. "Wouldn't want them to freeze and fall off."

He laughed, but the sound wasn't full of humour. It wasn't contagious. I didn't want to laugh with him, I wanted to feel bad for him.

He believed what he was saying, but I wasn't sure I bought it. Okay, plenty of men were fuck boys, but Josiah? He seemed almost as broken as Gavin Clarke. Instead of taking care of him, the town turned their collective back. That would screw with anyone's head.

I should know. It's how my mother and step-father treated me. Like I was barely there. Like they wouldn't care if I disappeared overnight. Had they even noticed I wasn't in the city anymore? They hadn't called to check on me. Chances were, they didn't even know it yet. I should feel sad about that, angry, but instead I was resigned.

In a way, Josiah and I were a lot alike. Two people who needed others to give a shit about us. Who were bitter around the edges because we didn't get what we badly needed.

Instead, we got derisive looks and whispers behind our backs.

"Don't," Josiah said softly.

My eyebrows dipped. "Don't what?"

"Don't go feeling sorry for me," he said. "I don't need it or want it. Not from you. Not from anybody. Especially not anyone who lives in this stupid, fucking town." He raised his voice loud enough to be heard through the whole store.

The couple of other people stopped to look around and stare. Neither of them appeared to be locals.

"Josiah—" I started.

I didn't miss the way his eyes darkened when I said his name, but he whipped away. Turning his back on me to take his groceries to the counter so he could pay and stalk out of the store.

23

LEAH

For some reason I couldn't explain, I paid for my own groceries and hurried out behind him. Fingers tight around the handles of my bags, I stopped on the footpath and scanned the street.

There he was. A hint of black wove through the strolling visitors to town. His back straight, looking ahead of him.

Careful not to hit anyone with my bags, I wove through the same gaps, following him past the Snowdrop Café and the Frosty Brew to the edge of town.

He stopped beside a black pickup truck, unlocked it and placed his groceries inside. As he closed the door, he glanced at the side mirror. His back stiffened. He must have seen me reflected in the glass.

"What the fuck do you want?" He turned around, his eyes blazing. "Why are you following me?"

"What makes you think I'm following you?" I asked. I had no answer for him. I didn't know either.

"Has it occurred to you I might be heading this way?" I wasn't the only one walking in this direction. He couldn't think everyone was following him, could he?

"You live in the other direction." He closed his mouth, his teeth clenched.

I arched my eyebrows at him. "How did you know that?" He clearly spoke without thinking, and then regretted admitting he knew anything about me. Especially where I lived.

"I saw you there one time." His mouth barely moved as he spoke. His gaze didn't quite meet mine. He was lying, but I had no idea why.

"Did you?" I cocked my head at him. "Or maybe *you're* following *me*."

Wouldn't I have noticed him outside the front of the cottage? He was difficult to miss, especially in a town this small. As far as I could tell, he was the only one who dressed entirely in black. I wasn't surprised to see his truck was black. Everything inside it was probably black as well. Did he live in a black house too? With black walls and black satin sheets on the bed?

I shouldn't be thinking about his bed. I certainly shouldn't be thinking about him lying on it, looking up at me, his eyes telling me to come closer. To lower myself onto him and ride him until we both screamed.

I forced the thought away. It didn't leave, but it reluctantly retreated into a back corner of my mind until later. At some point, it was going to be back in full force. Maybe when I had my vibrator in hand.

"Why the fuck would I do that?" he snapped. He let out a long sigh through his nose. "Sweet cheeks, you have a high opinion of yourself." One he apparently didn't share.

I straightened my head and glared. "The hell I do. I think you might be projecting, Josiah Lachance. I mean, look at you." I jerked my head forward. "You've nailed the whole brooding bad boy thing. Do you own anything that isn't black?"

"Nope," he said tightly. "Everything is black, like my soul."

I snorted a laugh. "That's fucking dramatic. You want to know what I think?"

"No. I don't give a shit." Keys in his hand, he started to turn away.

I decided to tell him anyway.

"I think you enjoy this. You like people looking at you like you're something they just scraped off the bottom of their shoe. You like them blaming you for what happened to Coral Clarke, because then you're justified in blaming yourself. If they look at you like you're trash, then you don't have to make the effort to be nice to anyone. You can go on brooding."

"You don't know shit," he said over his shoulder.

"Don't I?" I stepped closer. "Believe it or not, I'm not perfect." I ignored his smirk.

"I know how it feels to have people treat me like crap. After a while, you start to believe the things they say. Eventually, you stop fighting it, because it's easier to let them walk all over you. But you know what? It's a fucking miserable way to live. If that's what you want for the rest of your life, then…" I let out a frustrated breath. "I guess I can't do anything to help you."

"Fuck," he whispered. He turned around slowly, his gaze finding my face.

"You know what, you're right. You're not perfect and there's nothing you can do for me. Do both of us a favour and leave me the fuck alone. Whatever Girl

Scout shit you're trying to do here, I'm not interested. Go and soothe your ego with some other sucker."

He walked around to the other side of his pickup, unlocked the door and slid inside. Starting the engine, he revved it a little too hard before peeling away from the gutter and heading off down the road a bit too fast. A couple of pedestrians had to jump out of his way to avoid being struck. One of them flipped him off, but I doubted he noticed, or gave a shit. He was too angry for anything other than getting the hell out of town and away from me.

That shouldn't have stung as much as it did.

I startled as a hand covered my shoulder, the sudden pressure warm and firm.

Letting out a squeak, I spun around. The bags swung in my hand, hitting me in the thigh. I barely noticed. My heart raced from the surprise.

Riley stood behind me, his expression irritated, but not repentant at just having scared the shit out of me. Did he even realise he'd done it? His attention seemed to be on Josiah's truck, and the man driving it.

"He shouldn't talk to you like that." He glared down the street as if he could blast lasers out of his eyes and hit Josiah and his truck with them.

"I kinda asked for it," I admitted. I sighed softly. "I said a bunch of stuff I shouldn't have said."

Was I wrong though? He was brooding and letting the town treat him badly. On the other hand, he didn't need me to be as awful. Something about him made me furious, but I didn't know if it was at him or for him. All I knew was that I'd taken aim and let fly. Giving him everything that was on my mind.

"He has that effect on most of us," Riley said. "Maybe Coral ran away from him." He smirked.

"Riley Crane!" I frowned at him. "That's a terrible thing to say. Whatever really happened, a little girl died." I had a dark sense of humour myself, but not about something like that.

"Because of him," Riley said, unrepentant. "I'm never going to stop reminding him of that." He wasn't even slightly sorry.

Of course, he spent almost a lifetime treating the other man like this, and seeing other people do the same. Chances were, he never gave it a second thought. As habits went, it wasn't a good one.

"Why?" I had to ask. "Why do you have to keep reminding him of something so horrible? Do you think he doesn't know? Because what I see when I look at him…" I gestured down the street, in the direction he'd gone. "I see a guy who's beaten himself up for twenty years. I don't think he needs, or deserves, everyone else piling on him."

My breath was coming faster now, my irritation threatening to boil over. I already told Josiah what I thought, I was fully prepared to do the same with Riley. If he thought I wouldn't, he'd have to take a long, hard think again.

He closed the distance between us and raised his hand. I thought he was going to run his knuckles down my cheek, but instead he grabbed a fistful of my hair. He wrapped it around his fingers, tight enough that I couldn't pull away if I wanted to.

In spite of myself, my panties were ruined in moments.

Riley leaned in and spoke in my ear. "Don't defend Josiah. Don't follow him. Don't talk to him. Don't let him talk to you. What he touches, he breaks. I'm not letting him break you."

"He won't break me," I whispered back. "But you and Connor might."

He let go of my hair and stepped back, looking confused and angry. "Is that what you think?" He looked as shocked as I was when he came up behind me and put his hand on my shoulder. Like he couldn't wrap his head around what I said. Thinking maybe he'd misheard, but letting the words sink in gradually.

"Honestly, I don't know what to think," I said. "You and him are so possessive, but I hardly know either of you. I don't know why you've decided you want me."

I remembered what Josiah said about them wanting me to fall for them before they turned their backs on me. Was he right? They might not even go that far. They might want to fuck me and then walk away. They wouldn't be the first.

"Because you fit," Riley said. "With us. With Aurora Hollow."

"What if I want to fit with Josiah Lachance?" I lifted my chin, challenging him to think before he responded. "What if I wanted to fit with someone else?"

What were they going to do about it? Scowl at anyone I chose until he ran into the forest? What would that actually achieve? Apart from pissing me off. And potentially feeding bears.

"Do you?" His brow was scrunched. If I wasn't annoyed with him right now, I'd find it adorable. Why did men have to be so infuriating?

"I don't know," I said. "What I do know is I get a choice. The possessive mountain man thing is ridiculously hot, but I make my own decisions."

He blinked at me a couple of times, then smiled. "I've never been called ridiculously hot before."

I rolled my eyes. "Of course that's what you took away from that."

"I heard the possessive mountain man thing too," he said. Did he actually puff his chest out? "That's also accurate. We are who we are and we aren't going to change."

I resisted rolling my eyes at him. "I didn't say I wanted you to change," I said. "You don't get to control my life. Do you understand that?"

His smile didn't change. Didn't falter. "You say that now."

"I'll always say that," I insisted. Was he trying to imply that I'd surrender total control to him and Connor at some point? In the bedroom, maybe. Outside of that? Not a chance. The sooner they figured that out, the better.

"Okay," he said, clearly not believing or backing down a centimetre. "Anyway, I came to find you to see if you want to come with us. We're about to take the first group out on the white water."

"I thought you were booked out?" I said.

He shrugged one shoulder. "We are, but we have

room for one more. And a picnic lunch after. You said you hardly knew us. This is a chance to get to know us and see what we do."

I always wanted to go white water rafting, and this seemed like the perfect place to do it. If I was honest with myself, I'd like to watch them both in their element. Like I had when we went up to the lookout. When the adrenaline ran through me like a drug. Once that rush faded, I felt flat, like I needed another hit. Why not take that hit today?

"Sure, why not?" I said as if I wasn't as excited as I actually was. "As long as you don't push me overboard."

"No, but you're going to get wet," he promised.

I bet I was.

24

RILEY

I grinned as squeals and shouts echoed off the ravine walls. The raft hit a rapid and spun. The tourists on board cried out again. I righted the raft and faced us down the next section.

Most of my attention was on the river, but every so often I glanced over to Leah. Every time, she was smiling at least as big as me. Clinging to the raft, but enjoying every moment.

Connor, steering the raft in front of us, shouted out something to Charlie, who was controlling the raft with him. She worked for us for almost as long as we'd been doing this. The brunette was at least as out of her mind as we were. She'd come to Aurora Hollow from England for a holiday and never left.

She was also a constant reminder of what we had

to lose if we ever shut the business. It wasn't just us, we had staff to consider.

Right now, none of that mattered. The only things that did were enjoying the rush, and keeping the raft right-way up.

"Hold on tight, folks," I called out. "Here's where it gets hairy."

I caught a glance from Leah and grinned. Her face and hair shone from water dripping down her, but she didn't seem to notice or care how wet she was on the outside. I'd bet an entire year of earnings, her pussy was just as wet.

She smiled back, then she was squealing along with everyone else as we hit a wild section of river. The raft was thrown hard left, then hard right, dipping and swishing, threatening to tip but righting itself at the last moment.

A laugh burst out of me, pure enjoyment, pure rush. This was what life was for. These moments. These risks. If I could have held onto this sensation forever, I would. The only thing better was mid-orgasm. Those seconds when the world disappeared and the only thing left was the rush of blood through my veins.

"This is insane!" Leah shouted, but she was laughing at the same time.

"That's why I like it so much!" I shouted back.

She tipped her head back and laughed, exposing the column of her throat above her lifejacket.

I wanted to lick the river water from her neck. To taste the salty sweat on her skin. To taste all of her. To watch and listen to her come.

The raft hit another rapid and spun again, before sliding down, finally into calmer water.

Right here, a burst of irritation spiked in my chest. Disappointment that the rapids were behind us. All we had to do now was steer down the river for another kilometre or so before we were finished. I would have liked nothing more than to drag the raft back up and do it all over again. And again.

We would, but not until tomorrow. Right now, that seemed like an eternity away.

"That was fun." Leah stretched her long legs out in front of her, her hands resting to either side of her, on the edge of the raft. The sun caught her dark hair, bringing out hints of auburn and mahogany as it quickly dried.

"I knew you'd think so." The paddle trailed in the water beside us, keeping us on course in the centre of the river.

"Is that so?" She raised her eyebrows at me.

"Absolutely," I agreed.

I'd yet to take anyone out here and then have them say they didn't love every minute of it before booking to come back again. Everyone here, except for her, was a returning customer. A handful came for the summer activities and then returned in winter to get their adrenaline rush on the snow. Those were the customers who kept us in business.

"Has anyone told you you're cocky, Riley Crane?" she asked.

That drew a snort-laugh from Seth Winterstein, who sat on the opposite side of the raft. Another of our staff who'd been with us for a long time. A blow in from Ontario, he'd come to take tours with us and also never left.

Leah laughed. "I'm guessing that's a yes."

"Seth, you're fired," I told him jokingly.

Seth laughed and turned to make conversation with the woman who sat beside him.

"He never takes me seriously," I grunted.

"Poor baby." Leah leaned over to pat my knee.

I took one hand off the paddle to cover hers, her skin soft and smooth under my calloused fingers.

Fingers I would happily have slid inside her and made her come. Even in front of all these people. I'd never thought about having an audience before, but the idea made my cock twitch.

"Maybe you should come and work for me instead of him," I said without thinking.

Her smile faded and she pulled her hand back, flattening it out beside her.

"I just meant…" I started.

"I know what you meant," she said. "I wish I could."

She turned away to face ahead, toward the river as it became more and more glassy. From here, a section drained into the lake, while the rest disappeared down the mountain, into the ocean.

Every so often, I thought about Coral Clarke, and where she must have ended up. When we first started working out here on the rapids, I kept looking for her. As if somehow we'd find her after all this time, when no one else had.

Yeah, I know it was dumb, but what happened to her could have happened to any of us. It still could. I could fall off this raft right now and disappear. Except I wouldn't, because Connor would jump in after me. Plus, I was wearing a lifejacket like everyone else.

I pushed those morbid thoughts away and steered the raft over to the side of the river, where we let everyone off and pulled the craft up and out.

While everyone mingled and talked about how

much fun they had, we dragged the rafts up onto the back of a truck, ready to be driven back to the top of the river.

"You need a hand?" Leah asked. She'd undone her lifejacket and left it hanging open over her blue tank top.

I wanted to make a joke about her hand on my cock, but I caught the look on her face. The set of her jaw and the stubborn determination in her dark eyes. Her body wouldn't stand the rigours of this job, but she wanted to prove she could at least do this. I could tell her no, but she'd help anyway.

Fuck, the woman was stubborn.

"Sure. Grab on to the rope. On the count of three, we tug it up." I grabbed on myself and nodded to her. "One. Two. Three." As one, me, her and Seth pulled the raft up on top of the others, before Seth started to tie all of them down.

"Nice work," I told her.

"Thanks." Seth grinned.

I would have flipped him off if we didn't have tourists present. I could be unprofessional in private, not in public. It'd be my luck if someone took a photo and put it up online. Reputations took years to build, but they could be destroyed in seconds. I wasn't going to do that to myself or to

Connor. That would be a one-way ticket off the mountain for me.

I settled for smirking at him instead, before turning back to Leah. "We need to gather up the life-jackets and set up the picnic."

Charlie already started to pull foldout chairs out of the back of the truck and set them up around the clearing.

"I'll gather the lifejackets," Leah said. She shrugged out of hers and walked around, taking them from people's hands before tossing the pile into the back of the truck.

"It feels like she was always here." Connor pulled out a cooler and carried it over to start handing out sandwiches and cups.

"Yeah, it does." I grabbed a couple of thermoses and took them around to give everyone coffee or tea. It wasn't as good as they'd get from the Snowdrop Café, but no one seemed to mind.

"Coffee?" I asked Leah as she held up her cup.

"Please," she said.

I poured the steaming liquid into her cup and then leaned to whisper in her ear. "I like it when you beg."

"If you think that was begging..." she whispered back.

"It was good for a start." I lightly grazed my lips over her soft, smooth cheek before stepping over to fill up everyone else's cup.

Once everyone had everything they needed, I was allowed to plop myself down on a camp stool, enjoy a cheese sandwich and watch the river meander past.

For the most part, we were the only ones who came here. A hidden piece of paradise in the forest, at the end of a dirt road. A time to stop and breathe after rushing down the rapids. The opportunity for everyone to chat and get to know each other, sharing their experiences of the moment they thought the raft would tip and throw them into the water. It happened often enough, but not today.

"It's beautiful here." Leah carefully lowered herself into the chair beside me.

"Almost as beautiful as you," I said. I enjoyed the way the colour crept up her face.

She looked into her coffee, but didn't speak for a minute or two. Finally she said, "I see why you like doing this. So many places up there—" She nodded back upriver.

"No one would ever see them unless they were on the water. Or in the water. It's like…we get to see secret places no one knows about."

"I like seeing secret places." My gaze dropped to her lap.

She reached out with her foot and nudged my knee. "I'm being serious here."

"So am I." I grinned. "What's not serious about that?"

"I don't know, it's just..." She shrugged. "There are other people here."

I stared at her for a moment, then slowly looked around as if I was surprised. "There are?"

She snorted and poked my knee with her toe again. "Yes, there are."

I leaned over and whispered. "If there wasn't, I'd be on my knees, eating you out right now. Maybe I should anyway."

"I don't think that's what they signed up for." She took a swallow of her coffee.

"Sometimes we like to add bonus experiences," I said. "But you're right. I don't want them to see. If they did, I might have to toss them all into the river." I didn't want to share her beautiful pussy with all of these people.

"You wouldn't do that." She frowned at me over the top of her cup.

"No," I agreed. "It would be bad for business."

She lowered her cup. "Then there's the little

matter of being arrested and thrown in prison for the rest of your life."

"That would also be bad for business." I tossed the last corner of the sandwich into my mouth and chewed.

"Oh, I don't know. Seth seems competent." She was struggling to keep a straight face. "I'm sure he could replace you."

"Not a fucking chance," I said.

"What are you two talking about?" Connor offered us a box of cupcakes.

I snagged a chocolate one and nodded my thanks. "Leah was just saying how indispensable I am." I bit into the cupcake.

Connor grunted. "Sure she was."

I almost choked on my mouthful of cake, trying to swallow too fast. "Don't you start." I coughed a couple of times.

Connor, being the asshole he was, chuckled and moved on, handing out cupcakes to everyone who wanted one.

"You both suck," I muttered, but there was no heat in it.

"You wish," Leah said tartly.

I swung my gaze over to her. "You *will*. Come on,

it's time to get everyone out of here." I rose and brushed crumbs off my shorts, leaving her to follow.

25

LEAH

I sat between Connor and Riley as we bumped our way back toward the road. We were the last to leave, after the other vehicles carried the tourists to their cars and waiting buses.

"They'll take them up the mountain for zip lining." Connor's long fingers were wrapped around the steering wheel. "Then they'll end up at the Frosty Brew or wherever."

"Have you ever gone zip lining?" Riley curled his hand around mine.

"No," I admitted. "My mother would have lost her mind if I did." Anything that resembled risk was a no-go, as far as she was concerned. Maybe she didn't want the hassle if I broke a limb. Or my neck.

"We won't tell." Connor glanced over at me

quickly before turning his attention back to the dirt track.

"What's she going to do anyway?" Riley asked. "Leah is an adult. She's too old to be grounded."

"But not too old to be spanked," Connor said. "By Riley and me."

My face heated. "What else do you do up here? On the adventure tours, I mean." I ignored Riley's grin.

"Bungee jumping," Connor said. "I want to get one of those chairs that swing out over nothing. There's a ravine further up the mountain that would be good for that."

"Is that where Josiah lives?" I asked.

Both of them stiffened.

"Close to there," Riley said, clearly not wanting to elaborate. "Your mom kept you on a tight leash?"

I slid my gaze over to him.

"You said she'd lose her shit if you did anything fun like zip lining," he said for clarification.

"It wasn't so much that she kept me on a tight leash," I said slowly. "She would have thought something like that was a waste of time and money."

"Sounds like she needs to get out and live a little," Connor said. "You should tell her to come up here. We'll comp her a couple of tours to lighten her up."

"She wouldn't go," I said. "Her idea of nature is placing an orchid in the kitchen window."

"She sounds like a shit load of fun," Connor said sarcastically.

I didn't know how to answer that. "She did the best she could." Did she? Just because I felt like I could write a hundred pages of things she could have done better, didn't mean they weren't reasons for it. I wasn't perfect either, after all.

"And your stepfather?" Riley asked. "It sounds like he didn't try very much either. And the stepbrother I want to punch in the face."

"Stepbrother?" Connor looked as though he might stop the vehicle so he could see my response to that question.

"Yes," I said quickly. I told him what I told Riley. That Brooks was the golden child of the family and we weren't close.

"You never fucked each other?" Connor sounded like he also wanted to punch him in the face.

"No, why? Do you want to watch?" I asked.

What was it with these guys and Brooks? They didn't even know the guy. Chances were, they'd never meet him. And yet, they had some idea in their heads about him and me. Was it some kind of fantasy they wanted to live out? Some kind of stepbrother kink?

Brooks was attractive enough, but he was certain he was better than me. That somehow having a university degree in business made him superior. Even though he seemed miserable and regretful every time anyone brought it up. The one time I asked him about it, he shot me down and walked away. I never asked again.

Now Connor did slow the vehicle to a stop, letting the others disappear out of sight. He turned to me, hazel eyes flashing.

"If you ever fuck anyone but me or Riley, you better fucking do it where we can watch. We're not letting anyone touch you without our knowledge or permission."

"I don't need your permission," I said tartly.

"The fuck you don't," he snarled.

He closed his eyes and let out a long breath, while rubbing the heel of his hand up and down his stubbled cheek. "If we didn't have to get up to the zip line, I'd spank your ass, then fuck you raw."

His words lit a fire that roared through my entire body. If my panties weren't already wet from the rafting, they certainly were now. I got the distinct impression Connor was the kind of man who knew how to throw a girl around and make them scream. Riley too. Between both of them, raw would be the right word. I'd be sore as fuck afterward.

More so than usual.

Riley groaned. "They'll notice if we don't show, won't they?"

"Yeah, they will," Connor said grudgingly. He shook his head and dropped his hands back to the steering wheel. "When we're done for the day." He put his foot down, making the truck jump and almost slide on the gravel.

"Don't kill us," Riley said jokingly.

"Not today," Connor agreed. "I don't plan on dying until my cock feels the inside of Leah's pussy. And her mouth."

"If you keep talking like that, I'm going to come in my shorts," Riley complained.

Connor snorted. "Not my fault if you don't have any control."

"I have plenty of control," Riley argued. "Usually. Both of you together make my cock harder than a fucking rock. A guy can only have so much control in a situation like that. Don't tell me yours isn't ready to explode."

Connor didn't answer, but judging by the bulge in his pants, Riley was right.

The fire in my body became an inferno. Being pressed between two guys who were aroused for me was both hot and overwhelming.

I was used to artistic types. Quiet, thoughtful, always with an idea for a new piece rattling around in their heads. But these two, they were hard, rugged. Pure sex and muscle. Arrogance, attitude and possessiveness.

I'd never met anyone like them.

"We'll be driving for at least ten minutes," Connor said. "Leah, help him with his self-control." After a moment he added, "Help him to lose it."

I looked from him to Riley. Down to Riley's groin.

"I might," I said, drawing out the second word. "But I think he should beg."

Riley's jaw tightened like he didn't want to beg me for anything. Like he wanted me to be the one doing the begging. Which is exactly why I wanted him to. They thought they could control me. I wasn't giving them all of it. If they wanted me, they'd have to do the work.

"Do it," Connor insisted.

Riley swallowed. "Please, Leah. Help me out before my dick explodes. Please." His eyes crossed, clearly uncomfortable.

I snorted a laugh and placed my hand over the front of his shorts. He was right, he was hard as hell under my palm. Harder still the longer I kept my hand there. I rubbed the heel of my hand across his length a few times before tugging down the front of his shorts and boxers. His erection sprang free, into my hand. Thick and hot and ready.

"Fuck." Riley shifted a little, his eyes half-closed. What control he had was slipping fast.

I wrapped my hand around his base and adjusted my seatbelt so I could lower my face and lick pre-cum from his tip.

He groaned. "Yeah, more of that. Please."

Since he was begging so nicely, I parted my lips and took more of him into my mouth. Just a little at first, sucking lightly and teasing with my tongue.

He wrapped his fist around my hair, holding me while thrusting up oh so slowly, his other hand on the handle beside him.

The truck bumped a couple of times before Connor turned the steering wheel. The road under us became smooth.

I glanced up, assuring myself if there was any other traffic, they wouldn't see me. Wouldn't know what I was doing.

I took Riley in deeper, all the way to the back of my throat.

"That's it, gag on his cock," Connor said. "Good girl."

Those two words got me going every time. I had no idea I liked them until I heard them from him. I didn't know whether it was from not being praised enough as a kid, or if I just liked it. It didn't matter, either way it did it for me.

I sucked harder, faster, deeper. The side of my hand brushing against his balls.

"Fuck," Riley whispered. "I'm going to come. Please… Please, swallow."

I looked up at him, to see his blue eyed gaze locked right on me. I smiled with my eyes and went on sucking until he groaned and lost himself between my lips. Grunting and grinding, and shooting warm, salty cum into my mouth.

Since he begged so well, I waited until he caught his breath before sliding my mouth off him and carefully swallowing every drop. I licked my lips, making sure I got every little bit of his release.

"Good girl," Riley said, still a little breathless. "Connor, she gives incredible blowjobs."

"She can give me one later," Connor said. "Put your pants back on, we're here."

I sat back up, peering out the window to see if anyone was watching, before I fixed my hair. There wasn't much I could do about my red lips. If I was lucky, the colour would fade before anyone thought to wonder about them.

"Are you ready to go zip lining?" Riley tucked his cock back into his pants and straightened his shirt.

I couldn't see where it started from here, but I got the impression we were high up. Uncomfortably so.

"I'm scared of heights," I said tentatively.

"Good reason to do it," Connor said. "I used to hate heights, but I kept on doing it and now I don't think twice." He pushed out of the truck.

"Do you trust us?" Riley asked.

I rewarded him with a side eye. "Should I?"

He laughed. "In lots of things, probably not, but you're safe with us up here. We don't want to get sued."

"I don't think my family would bother." I followed him out of the truck.

"That makes me want to attach them to a zip line without the safety harness."

He took my hand and led me through the trees, following another track to where a couple of hand-fuls of people waited. "I'll double check yours personally. If anything happens to you, I give you my permission to haunt my ass."

"I don't need your permission to haunt your ass," I told him. "I'd do it anyway."

"That's because you like my ass so much." He tugged me along until we caught up with Connor.

"Maybe," I said. "And maybe I wouldn't want you to forget that one strap you didn't tighten properly."

He stopped me for long enough to lean down and whisper in my ear. "Sweetheart, I always do straps up properly. When I bind you, you won't be going anywhere until I let you."

His words sent a warm shiver all the way through me. If I wasn't careful, I'd be the one begging to be touched. Who was I kidding? I was already as wet as the river, and my nipples were harder than diamonds. I wanted, needed more. I could wait. I'd use some of that self-control Connor talked about.

He straightened up and led me over to a wide platform where the first of their clients was getting fitted into a harness.

26

LEAH

"Okay, your turn." Riley beckoned me over. "Connor will be waiting for you at the other end." He was still smiling, even after dealing with a long line of people. Others would have hated it, but he was in his element.

Connor and Charlie left before the first person disappeared down the zip line. Riley explained they had to be there to help them out of the harness and give the signal for the next person to go.

I had to give it to them, they had a well oiled machine here. Everyone knew exactly where they needed to be and when. Seth and Riley were perfect at settling the nerves of anyone anxious about stepping off the platform and zipping down the mountain.

For guys in their mid-twenties, they certainly knew a lot of dad jokes. They trotted all of them out, soothing nerves and making us all laugh and groan. Who knew there were so many cow puns? Or goat puns. Especially mountain goat puns. Leave it to mountain men to know those.

When he wasn't being an asshole, Riley could be quite sweet. Not that I'd tell him that.

"Are you sure this is a good idea?" I peeked over the edge of the platform.

From here, I made out the river winding through the trees. A hint of sunlight sparkling off the water every so often, between the branches. I couldn't tell if that was the same section we'd rafted down, but I guessed it was close.

When the breeze blew, it carried to the sound of the nearby falls. The white water started right below them. As far as I knew, the men had no adventure tours involving going over the falls in a barrel. Or without one. That might be too dangerous, even for them. If that was possible. They didn't seem to have a filter where risk was concerned. If risk existed, they'd take it.

Somewhere up here, Josiah lived. Where, I still hadn't gotten out of anyone. That didn't stop me from being curious. Nothing would. I liked answers to my questions. When it came to him, I had plenty of them.

That wasn't a conversation I was going to have standing on a platform on the side of a mountain.

"It's an excellent idea." Riley held the harness up. "Step through here and there. I'll…strap you in."

His deliberate choice of words had my mouth going dry, but it took my mind off how high up we were. For a minute or two anyway.

"Have you done this before?" I teased, stepping where he told me to and standing still to let him adjust and keep everything into place.

"It was my first day, but you're my thirtieth person, so I think I've got this by now." He grinned and adjusted the harness around my hips a little more than could possibly have been necessary. I think he enjoyed having his hands there, his thumbs pressed against my belly.

"He's the work experience guy," Seth teased. "I'm not sure if we should keep him on after this. What do you think?" He gave me a wink.

"I'll let you know if I get to the other end alive," I said dryly.

Seth laughed. "Fair call."

"You're a dick," Riley told him. "Come on, sweetheart. All you need to do is step off the platform and fly."

I looked down again. "I don't know. This is…"

Fear and cold sweat replaced my arousal. Did I *really* want to do this? To step off that platform and hope like hell the zip line held my weight all the way down? A laundry list of what ifs scrolled through my mind. All of them relying on the fact he knew what he was doing, and everything was set up correctly.

Hadn't I seen thirty people go down before me? Hadn't the zip line held? The only screams I heard were screams of enjoyment, right? Yes, but I was low-key terrified anyway.

Riley waited until Seth moved away, leaving the two of us alone on the platform. Everyone else had already gone before me, so we didn't have an audience. No one to see him tangle his fingers in my hair and pull my face closer to his.

"Would I bring you all the way here if I didn't know you could do this?" His voice was low, bordering on harsh. His breath was laced with coffee and the soda he'd taken sips of over the last hour or two. Keeping hydrated, but not enough to have to run off and relieve his bladder.

"You might," I said without flinching. I was more

scared of heights than I was of him. "You might get off on seeing me back down from my fears."

He huffed a laugh, his exhale warm on my jaw. "I get off on seeing people *face* their fears, sweetheart. It's one of the best parts of this job. The more scared you are, the more I want you to turn around and step off this fucking platform. I want you to enjoy every damn minute of it. I want you to want to come right back and do it again. That's what gets me off."

"And if I don't step off?" I was surprised my voice didn't waver. "Are you going to push me?"

His grip loosened and he drew his face back so our gazes could meet. Hazel eyes intense, he said, "I'd never push you off. Seth, yes. Connor, probably. But you, never. You have to want to step off. You have to need this. You have to make that choice for yourself."

I didn't think we were talking about zip lining anymore.

"Otherwise," he continued, "we can take this off you and go to town and get drunk."

I twisted my face around to take a long look at the taut line that disappeared between the trees. It was nice and tight; stable. Carefully connected at both ends. Likely subject to regular inspection and maintenance. Nothing bad was going to happen to me if I took this leap of faith.

That still left me with a question.

"Has anyone ever gotten here and changed their minds?"

Riley smoothed my hair down, back into place. "Absolutely. Some of them regret it and come back for a second try. Others spend the night at the Frosty Brew telling everyone they wished they'd done it."

"There must be some who are okay with changing their minds," I reasoned.

"I guess, but their regret comes later. When they get their credit card bill." He grinned.

I laughed. "Yeah, I can see that."

I wouldn't want to spend money on an adventure tour and not do everything I paid for. Especially if I let fear get in the way. I wouldn't judge anyone else for changing their minds, but I'd judge myself. I'd spend the rest of my life wondering what would have happened if I'd trusted that I could do this.

Hadn't I already proven I could stay on a raft on the rapids? Didn't I already know I enjoyed riding on a quad bike? This was another calculated risk. One that, when I thought about it, was a lot safer than the other two.

"So, I just step off and fly, hmmm?"

"Yep." He took my hands and placed them on the harness, in front of me. "Hang on here and enjoy the ride." He kissed my cheek before stepping back to give me room.

"That's what he said," I said as I stepped off the platform into nothingness.

Riley's laugh followed me as I started to zip down the line, dangling like a fish on a hook.

I let out a squeal, which turned into a whoop as I gained speed, flying down the side of the mountain. Past the trees. Over the river. Through the wind.

The pace was alarming but exhilarating at the same time. I tipped my head back and shouted out my excitement, probably scaring the animals in the forest, in the process. I couldn't stop myself from vocalising the adrenaline which surged through every centimetre of me. I didn't want to. I couldn't remember a time when I felt more alive.

The quad bikes were fun. So was the white water rafting, but this was something else. This was pure freedom. Something I craved for so long and never knew how to find.

Right when I thought the speed was too much, I started to slow. The angle of the zip line flattened out, drawing me closer to the lower platform and Connor's waiting arms.

He looked smug, like he was absolutely certain I wouldn't back down from this challenge.

He caught me when I was close enough and pulled me to him, bringing my ride to an end. Wrapping an arm around me and letting me feel the heat of his body.

"Hey, there." He held me until I got my footing. "For a while, I thought you weren't coming." He clearly didn't think that at all, but he couldn't help shit-disturbing.

"I almost wasn't," I said. "Then I thought, why not take a chance? That was incredible."

"It always is." He started to undo my harness and help me out of it. "It's even more fun in the rain. You should try it in the middle of a thunderstorm."

"Isn't that dangerous?" One hand on his shoulder, I stepped out of the harness.

He smiled. "Very. That's why we don't run tours during storms. Doesn't stop me and Riley though."

"You two are out of your minds," I told him.

He chuckled. "Nah, we like to live a little harder than most. Keeps things interesting."

"It's all fun and games until you get struck by lightning," I said.

He started folding the harness. "Gotta die of something."

I straightened my clothes. "Yes, but you don't need to tempt fate that badly, do you?"

"Always." He placed the harness into a box and clicked it shut. "I think of it as making fate my bitch on a daily basis. Someday, I'll be hers."

"That's a dark way to think about it," I said.

"I'm a realist. Charlie, let's get this box into the truck." He grabbed one handle and waited for her to take the one on the other side before they carried it off the platform and over to one of the trucks parked a few metres away. On the other side of that, the weekend adventurers were climbing onto the two buses and heading down to town. Laughing, talking and sounding as exhilarated as I felt.

"I can see why you like this job." I followed Connor over to the truck. "Fresh air, sunshine and excitement."

"Yeah, that's my tagline," he said sarcastically. "Fits my personality, don't you think?" He offered a sideways smile.

"I was going to suggest Sunshine was your middle name," I teased. "Connor Sunshine Ferguson."

He barked a laugh. "That would be the fucking day."

"It's perfect," I insisted. "Sunshine."

He scowled at me. "If you think that's a nickname you can use..."

I grinned.

He ran a hand over the back of his neck and shook his head. "Fuck me."

Charlie was laughing as she headed over to the other truck and climbed in.

"Your ass is going to be pink by the time I'm finished punishing you for that," Connor growled.

My arousal was back, this time with interest. I slid into the passenger seat of his truck and clicked my seatbelt.

"You talk the talk, Sunshine."

"Honey, I can spank the spank too. And I don't mean spank bank." He climbed into the driver's seat and started the engine before following Charlie back toward Aurora Hollow.

27

LEAH

"Sounds like you got the royal treatment." Fiona tapped her fingers on the arm of her chair along to the drum beat from the small band in the corner of the beer garden. "White water rafting and zip lining. Are you going to bungee jump next?" Head bobbing, she slid me a look, one eyebrow raised.

"You should," Holly said. "It's amazing." Her eyes were wide like she happily ate adrenaline for breakfast.

"You're all out of your minds." Whitney's eyes were on the lead guitarist as she spoke. "I'm going to keep my feet on solid ground."

"He's solid something all right," Fiona said slyly.

Whitney turned her face slowly to stare at her as

if she hadn't realised how blatantly she'd been staring. "What?"

Fiona laughed. "Kayden Mitchell. You've been ogling at him all night."

"I have not been ogling," Whitney protested. "I've been...admiring his finger work."

I almost choked on my bourbon and cola.

"Of course you have," Fiona laughed.

"He has some impressive finger work," Holly teased. "Maybe you should try it out when he's finished this set." She wiggled her fingers back and forth in front of her.

"You guys." Whitney shook her head. "He's at least fifteen years older than me. His youngest brother is around our age."

"So?" Fiona asked. "Age is only a number. Especially with the lights off."

"Fucking him with the lights off would be a crime," Holly said on a sigh.

"You know, you're right," Fiona told her. "Whitney should definitely fuck him with the lights on, and tell us all about it afterward." Her expression suggested the matter was settled, but her eyes shone with amusement. Clearly expecting Whitney to argue.

"When have I ever kissed and told?" Whitney's lips twisted as she frowned at them both.

"When was the most recent occasion?" Fiona's expression was all innocence. "Let me see, a few weeks ago when—" She ducked to the side as Whitney scooped up an ice cube from her drink and tossed it at her. "Hey! I'm just saying, that's all."

"Remind me not to tell you anything ever again," Whitney said as Fiona and Holly burst out laughing. She rolled her eyes and looked over at me. "Can you believe these two?"

I raised my hands to either side. "I don't know what to say, he looks pretty fuckable to me. I say you should go for it." Besides, he'd been sneaking glances at her while he played and sang. She wouldn't have to try too hard to persuade him to spend more time with her.

"He has a kid," Whitney whispered loudly. She was at least three drinks in at this point.

"So do I," Fiona pointed out. "You don't see me being unnecessarily celibate, do you?"

"Not unnecessarily, no." Whitney fought back a smile at scoring a point off Fiona.

Fiona flipped her off with both hands. "This place needs some new blood. Preferably young, hot and single."

"Amen to that." Holly dropped her gaze and grimaced. "Maybe we need to start some sort of advertising campaign." She held up a hand in front of her. "Come for the views, stay for the women."

"I could get behind that," Whitney said while nodding slowly. "Maybe we could talk to Louisa about starting something. The town could use a boost. Or two, or three. Maybe a dozen."

I considered reminding them Josiah Lachance was young, hot and single, as far as I knew, but I pressed my lips together instead. Was it because of their animosity toward him, or something else? The idea of him with any of my friends made me strangely uncomfortable. Like he was a puzzle I wanted to solve myself. If he'd ever give me the chance.

"Leah, do you know any city men who might like a tree change?" Fiona asked. "Preferably several of them."

"How many do you need?" Holly laughed.

Fiona sniffed as if she might actually be offended. "I have three holes and two hands, don't I? Why limit myself?"

"You go girl," Whitney said approvingly. "Don't forget one of those holes can take two cocks at once."

Almost in unison, we all sighed.

After a minute or two of reflective silence while we enjoyed the band, I got the courage to say, "Have any of you ever..."

I swallowed, not sure if the question was over-stepping. They seemed comfortable talking about sex, but I was still a newcomer. They might not want to discuss intimate details around me. I never would have asked anyone else a question like that though. I had friends back in the city, but not close ones and not ones who thought fucking was a conversation to have around the table.

Fortunately, none of them seemed to mind me asking. They took it in stride like they did with most things.

"I wish," Fiona said. "No one I've been with has been that creative, or wanted to bring in a third."

"Me either," Whitney said. "A girl can dream."

"She sure can," Holly agreed. "Although, Kayden looks pretty accommodating." She nudged Whitney with her elbow. "Maybe he'd invite the drummer along."

Now Whitney looked at the guitarist specula-tively. "He does look accommodating, doesn't he? But he's still a lot older than me."

"We'll be old and grey and still single and sitting around this table," Fiona complained. "Our pussies will close over from lack of use. That's what happens, right?"

"I don't want to find out," Whitney said. "That would suck. Also, not gonna happen. Not while vibrators are a thing."

"You know, you're right," Fiona said after a beat or two. "We'll be old and grey, sitting around this table and talking about the latest in vibrator fashion. We might all have robotic men by then."

"You think robotic men could do DVP?" Holly squinted at her.

"I'm sending them back if they don't." Fiona nodded firmly.

Holly looked surprised, then laughed. "Good idea. Can it be the future now?"

"Hey." Whitney frowned. "There's still plenty of time to find a couple of guys who will double stuff you. Don't give up yet."

"Wise words from Whitney Ferguson," Fiona said. "Leah, have Riley and Connor double stuffed you yet?"

Whitney stuck her fingers in her ears. "I need another drink." Holding her hands in place, she stood and hurried towards the bar.

My face heating, I watched her walk away. "Why would they… I mean…"

I hadn't expected such a direct question, although that was her style. Neither she nor Whitney held back from saying what was on their minds. Holly was only slightly more reserved.

Fiona swung her face slowly to look toward Holly. "I think that's a 'not yet.'"

"Ugh, I'm jealous," Holly said. "Not of Riley and Connor. I'm jealous of Leah, because that might be in her future." Like the other two, she grew up with both guys. She seemed to think of them the way Fiona and Whitney did, like brothers.

"You *will* give us details won't you?" Fiona leaned forward, her elbows on the table.

"There's nothing to say," I said. I wasn't going to tell them I gave Riley a blowjob while Connor was driving. I certainly wasn't going to tell them if things went further. Not in detail anyway. They didn't need to know everything about me.

They both looked at me like they didn't quite believe me, but knew that was all they'd get.

"If there isn't now, there will be soon," Fiona said. "Those guys aren't going to take anyone out on a busy weekend unless they want to impress them. The question is, did it work?"

"Am I impressed?" I asked. "I'm impressed with

white water rafting and zip lining. I might do them again."

"So you admit to doing them?" Holly teased.

I snorted. "The activities, not the men."

Would I suck Riley off again? Hell yes I would. I might be doing it now if they weren't both helping behind the bar.

They'd insisted Jacob rest, even though they had a long, exhausting day and had another one ahead of them. The moment Connor suggested it, Riley jumped in too.

Whitney and I would also have helped, but Fiona dragged us out to the beer garden for a girl's night, and the men insisted we go. That is, they insisted I go and sent Whitney to make sure I stayed off my legs. I won't lie, I was grateful not to be standing up for hours again tonight. I hated the feeling of help-lessness, but I'd pushed myself enough for one day.

At some point, I had to accept I had limits.

They both gave me a knowing look and turned back to listen to the band as they played a popular song.

"Have you finished talking about my brother?" Whitney placed a tray of drinks in the centre of the table and started to put them in front of us.

"You didn't miss much." Holly pulled her drink

closer to herself. "Mostly Leah wouldn't tell us anything fun."

"Good." Whitney pulled her chair in and settled back down. "Some things are better left unsaid. And un-thought about."

"I agree." I picked up my drink, toasted her in thanks and took a sip.

"You two are no fun," Fiona complained.

"We're lots of fun," Whitney said. "Do you want to hear about your brother's sex life?"

"Why would I want to hear about that when I can hear about yours?" Fiona teased.

"You're such a fucking brat," Whitney said but she was laughing. "Maybe I should seduce your brother so you know how it feels."

"If your taste is that bad, go for it." Fiona grimaced. "Don't come crying to me when he can't make you orgasm."

"He can," Holly said softly.

Fiona's mouth dropped open. She pressed it closed again and raised her hands to either side of her face. "You know what, Whitney's right. We don't need to talk about any of this."

"What was that?" Whitney turned her ear toward Fiona. "Say that again. Actually, wait a minute so I can record it on my phone." She picked up hers from the pile we'd made to the side of the table and turned it on.

"I'm not saying that again," Holly said. "You heard me the first time. I won't mention Fiona's your brother again if you don't mention mine."

Whitney grinned. "Deal. Let's never talk about them again. Leah, did you say something about having a stepbrother or two?"

They all looked at me with interest.

"Can I add him to the list of guys we don't talk about?" I asked.

I wanted to put Brooks behind me as much as possible. That was my old life, in the city. My past. Right now, I wanted to live in the present and let the future take care of itself.

"Can we say no?" Holly looked sideways at the other two women.

Fiona adjusted her ponytail. "I don't think we can. Not tonight anyway." She gave me a sly smile to suggest the topic would come up again at some point.

Of course it would, until I managed to convince them my stepbrother wasn't particularly interesting. I couldn't imagine Brooks being interested in them anyway. He'd think they were country girls, beneath him to even talk to.

The truth was, they were too good for him. They were better people than he'd ever be. Shame he'd never admit that. Not out loud anyway. Who knows what went on inside that head of his? He was a closed book if I ever met one. Speaking with disgusted looks instead of words. Looks that suggested he wished our parents never met.

Honestly, me too.

28

CONNOR

"THAT WAS BRUTAL." I threw the washcloth in the sink and went to lock the door behind the last of the patrons. We'd called last drinks an hour ago, but it took that long to get them to leave. The till was overflowing, but I was wiped out.

"Time for a couple hours of sleep before we do it all again," Riley said.

"Fuck." I groaned and ran a hand over the back of my neck. "Yeah."

"You okay?" He looked worried. Like maybe if he poked me with his finger I'd break. He should know better.

"Course I am." I pushed myself off the side of the bar. "Let's get out of here."

"Okay," he said slowly.

"What?" I pushed out the back door and took in a breath of fresh air. Pine and rapidly approaching fall was better than stale beer and sweat. What wasn't?

"I dunno." He closed the door behind him and waited for me to lock it.

Like I always did, I double checked to make sure it was secure, and the alarm was on.

"I'm too tired for bullshit, Ri. If you've got something to say, just fucking say it." He must have been as exhausted as I was. My patience was paper thin.

"It's nothing." He looked away down the street.

"It's not nothing. Come on, spill." I tucked the keys into my pocket and gave him a light shove in the direction of our places.

He staggered half a step before righting himself. "Hey. What the hell, bro?"

"Just some gentle encouragement. What's going on?" A few lights were still on in town, but apart from that it was just him, me and the occasional passing car. "You thinking about Leah's mouth?"

Her sucking him off right beside me was borderline painful. I had just enough self-control to keep myself from losing my load while driving. I wanted to pull over to the side of the road, bend her over and bury myself in her, to the hilt. If I wasn't working at the time, I would have.

"It's hard to forget," Riley said. "She has a talented mouth."

"Better than mine?" I asked. Not insecure, just curious.

"As good," Riley said.

"Then what's the problem?" I asked. "You ready for more?" By the time she left with my sister and her friends, Leah was unsteady on her feet. From the alcohol, not from her arthritis. I was an asshole, but I didn't take advantage of drunk people.

"I'm wondering where she fits," Riley said. "In town, with us."

I stopped him, my hand on his shoulder. "I'm not leaving you for her. This is you, me *and* her."

"What if she wants more?" His gaze drifted toward where the mountain rose above the town, invisible in the darkness.

"Did she tell you she wants more?" I squeezed his shoulder when he didn't answer straight away.

"She was talking to Josiah Lachance," he said, still not looking at me.

My brow furrowed. Fucking Josiah. That prick lurked around town more than he had a right to. What would it take for him to understand he wasn't welcome?

"Josiah was talking to Leah?" My jaw tightened. I

clenched my teeth together, barely containing the urge to punch a wall. Breaking my hand wouldn't help anything.

"Yeah, outside the grocery store." Riley nodded in roughly that direction. "I saw her follow him out."

"Fuck." I exhaled hard out of my nose and forced my teeth apart. "What were they talking about?"

"I didn't hear." He turned his face toward me. "She said something and he got into his truck and left. I reminded her she belonged to us and she…"

"She what?" I pressed.

"She said we don't own her and if she wanted to be interested in him, or someone else, she would."

I'd be first in line to punch Josiah. From the look on his face, Riley would be right behind me.

"She's stubborn," I managed to say, pushing my anger down into a smaller ball.

"What if she does want him?" Riley asked. "Or some other guy?"

"I'm not giving her up," I said slowly.

"She might decide to return to the city," Riley said.

"Did she say that?" I stared at him.

That didn't make any sense. If she had, he should have told me sooner. What would I have done? Confronted her, definitely. Beyond that…

I tried to ignore the stab of panic. Everyone fucking left, why would she be different? Everyone except Riley. I worried that some day he'd decide this wasn't enough for him. He was smart. He could go to university and do whatever he wanted with his life. Sometimes I wondered why he stayed here. The life he could have if he left—

I shoved the thought away.

"No," Riley admitted. "I think she likes it here as much as we do. But she's a city girl. She might decide a small town like this is too stifling for her. Too, I dunno, small."

"Is that what's eating at you?" I asked. "Is Aurora Hollow too small for you?"

He looked confused. "No. I love it here. I guess I feel like… I dunno, she's tipped everything upside down. I want her, but I don't know which way is up anymore. I don't know if she's going to stick around, or run off with Josiah or some other dickhead. Or leave and never look back."

I hooked my hand around the back of his neck. Brought his face closer to mine. Inhaled the scent of bourbon and leather.

"Since when are you insecure?" I asked, my voice rough.

"I'm not fucking insecure," he growled. "I'm conflicted. There's a difference."

"Sure there is." I brushed my lips over his, once, quickly before letting him go and stepping back.

"Now who's the insecure one?" His eyes shone in the light of a streetlamp behind my shoulder.

I puffed out a breath. "Both of us." I shouldn't care what anyone thought. Shouldn't let it change the way I behaved. Especially when we were more or less alone.

He opened his mouth as if to challenge my words, but then his shoulders slumped. "Yeah. Let's get out of here. Your balls must be blue as hell by now."

"Bluer." I put my hand on his shoulder again and squeezed. The only sign I could give right now of my feelings for him. The only one I'd give if we were alone. Expressing emotions wasn't something us mountain men were known for. The whole gruff lumberjack vibe lived on in us, even though we only chopped wood for winter.

"Poor baby." His tone was lighter now, but not completely devoid of frustration and, in spite of his protests, insecurity. What could I do to alleviate that for him? I had no idea.

My dad was recovering, but he still needed to

rest. I should be insisting he retire, or step back from a lot of the work he'd been doing for the last twenty years. I should be taking that off his plate. But if I did, I wouldn't be there to work with Riley. Could the business afford another staff member to replace me?

I didn't want to contemplate it. I hated the idea of walking away. Riley might fucking hate me if I did.

Yeah, there was nothing I could do to help his insecurity because I had enough of my own I didn't know what to do with.

I did what I do best. I elbowed Riley and said, "Who are you calling baby, asshole?"

He grunted a laugh, shoved his shoulder against me, then headed on down the road.

"You want to throw hands?" I said jokingly. "Is that what you want?"

"I'm not throwing hands with you," he said over his shoulder. "You're bigger and meaner than me."

"Damn right I am." I trotted a couple of steps to catch up to him, and shoved my hands into my pockets. "Wouldn't want to damage your pretty face anyway."

He turned around and walked backwards, grinning at me. Fucker was cuter than he should have been.

"You think I'm pretty?" He tripped over a crack in the sidewalk and almost fell over on his ass. At the last moment, he saved himself by grabbing a sign post beside him.

"Yeah, you're pretty," I said. "Clumsy as fuck, but pretty." I grinned at him.

He flipped me off with both hands and turned to walk the right way. "You're not so bad yourself."

"For a mean asshole." I toyed with the keys in my pocket while stepping carefully over the crack.

"Yeah, for a mean asshole." He walked beside me in silence for a few minutes, while the town settled further into their beds. Lights turned off until the only ones left were in storefronts and the streetlights.

No cars had passed for a while now. Times like this, I felt like we had the whole place to ourselves. The only sounds were our shoes on the sidewalk, and the breeze as it wandered past, making me shiver.

In a few short weeks, it would start to snow. We'd be busier than ever. It might be time to contemplate another couple of staff, even if I was going to stick around. Invest in a couple of snowmobiles. A few more snowboards.

I wanted to kick something. This was the life I

wanted, not running the fucking pub. I shouldn't be looking for more staff for our adventure tours, I should be looking for a manager to take over the Frosty Brew.

I'd get on that right then if my father wouldn't lose his shit. The weight of his expectations was almost crushing at times. It threatened to knock the wind out of me, leaving me gasping for air. Struggling to breathe, like I was drowning. Being pulled away by the current and tipped over the falls. Crashed against the rocks and broken into a million pieces.

Sometimes I envied Riley, not having that kind of connection. Not having anyone forcing him to stay in town. What would I do if I left here? I didn't know. I might shove him and Leah into my car and drive. I didn't care where. Wasn't that how she found this place to start with? Driving until she found somewhere to stop. We could do that. See the whole country if we wanted to. The whole continent. The whole fucking world.

Aurora Hollow was home, but sometimes it felt like a prison sentence. A noose around my neck that I couldn't pull off. If it wasn't for Riley…

I kept those thoughts to myself as we walked past Leah's rental cottage. The place was in darkness. I toyed with the keys again, tempted to slip into her house, into her bed. Into her pussy.

I would, but not tonight. I'd fucked her when she was sober. I wanted her to remember every second of it. My skin against hers. My cock sliding into her while my hands pinned her. I wanted her to watch me come as I lost my release inside her. I wanted that to be seared in her mind forever like it would be seared into mine.

When I claimed her, I'd do it fully. Then she'd understand how much she belonged to us.

29

LEAH

"WHAT ARE YOU DOING?" Connor strode over from his truck, hands tucked into his pockets.

"Painting." I unfolded my easel and set it up a comfortable distance from the zip line platform. From here, I could see over the trees, and the sparkling snake of the river.

"No shit," he said dryly.

I glanced up at him and smirked. "You did ask." I adjusted the easel and turned to shake out my camp chair. "I like the view here." I gestured toward the trees, but my eyes were on him.

It was his turn to smirk. "Of course you do." Arrogant prick.

"Am I going to bother you, sitting over here?" I asked.

"Do you give a shit if you do?" He pulled his hands out of his pockets and crossed them over his chest, looming over me as I lowered myself into my chair.

"I wouldn't want you so distracted someone got hurt," I said honestly.

"Except me," he said with a slight tilt of his head, like he was challenging me to deny it.

"I don't want you to get hurt either." I shifted to get comfortable. "If I'm going to distract you, I'll move further away." Reluctantly, I started to push myself to my feet.

He placed a hand on my shoulder and pressed me back down. "Stay there. I'm not going to be distracted."

Was that a flash of concern I saw in his hazel eyes? The glance down at my legs confirmed that suspicion. He'd seen my discomfort and didn't want me to push myself any further. Although, moving a chair and easel a few metres away wouldn't exacerbate things too much. I was tender today, rather than aching. For now.

Unless you counted my clit, which responded to both his presence and his worry. Even his possessiveness.

I sat back down and leaned to pull a canvas out of the bag beside the easel.

"You going to paint me, Kent?"

"What happened to honey?" I settled the canvas on the easel and reached for my paints.

"I figured a change wouldn't hurt. So, are you?" He watched me squeeze paint onto my palette and pull out my brush.

"I might," I said. "Do you and Riley take turns? Putting people on and off the harness, I mean." Now I was imagining them taking turns with me. One filling me to the brim before the other topping me up even further. Watching each other while they fucked me.

Judging by the way Connor's eyes darkened, his mind went to the same place.

"Yeah. Keeps things interesting. Wouldn't want to forget how to do half my job."

"I'm sure you wouldn't forget." I mixed my colours together, trying to get the right shade of green for the top of the trees.

"Right. I don't forget stuff easily. Have you always painted?" He stepped around so he could watch me put the first brush strokes on the canvas.

"I've always made art." I rolled my shoulders to

loosen them, trying not to show that the question got to me.

"Let me guess, you started with finger painting," he said, as if that was a bad thing.

"Actually, I started by sticking sticks into balls of mud." I glanced at him, then back at the canvas.

"You started by playing with balls?" He laughed softly.

"And sticks," I said. "Don't forget the sticks."

"Never." His voice made me glance up at him again. He seemed to have something specific on his mind, but he blinked a couple of times and pushed it away.

"You and Riley have been tight for a long time?"

"We've been inseparable since forever," he said. "Might as well have been twins. I don't remember a time when I didn't know him. Probably isn't one. Our mothers were friends before we were born. Fathers too."

"You knew Coral Clarke?" I asked gently. As if that hadn't happened a lifetime ago.

"Not really." Connor adjusted his arms. "She lived up the mountain. Came into town for school."

"Do you remember her?" I didn't know why it mattered, but I was curious. So many years later, her death still caused ripples. I saw that in Gavin Clarke and Josiah's haunted eyes. Josiah was the town pariah, Gavin, the town charity.

"I don't know." Connor's eyebrows dipped. "Sometimes I think I do. But I was a kid, so I might be, I don't know, imagining it, because I've heard about it for so long. Like, you hear something often enough you start to believe it, you know?"

I nodded slowly. "I get that. Do you remember when she died?"

His frown deepened. "I remember the town being in an uproar. Everyone was whispering about it, but no one would talk about it out loud. It was like… If they did, it'd be real. And no one wanted it to be real."

"I suppose they wouldn't." That made sense. No one would wanted to accept the death of a little girl, especially as tragically as that. In a small town where everyone knew each other, they all would have known her and her family.

"They probably didn't want to upset the kids in town," I said. "Adults are good at knowing what's best for us, or thinking they do." I rolled my eyes to show that I was speaking sarcastically, even though it was clear enough he'd pick up on it.

He snorted with what sounded like bitterness to match my own.

"That's for fucking sure. They like making decisions and assuming everyone is all right with them. And if we're not, they don't give a shit."

"I'm sure your parents give a shit," I said, guessing that was what he was referring to.

His brow smoothed out and he straightened his body. "Yeah. I have to get to work. Enjoy your…art." He waved a hand toward my easel before turning and stalking away to the platform to greet today's round of zip liners.

"Thanks," I called out to his back.

It seemed I hit a nerve without meaning to. That went both ways, so I turned to the view and focused my attention on painting the forest, the sky and the platform to one side.

On the platform, I painted a single figure facing away from me. Dressed in a khaki shirt and dark jeans, over worn boots. Dark hair and an ass I could bounce a coin off.

As I worked, I got to thinking about what I said about sticking sticks into balls of mud. That was where it started, but it grew from there. While I cleaned my brush, I found myself looking around for fallen branches, pieces of discarded wood that could have been put together to make something unique. A large chunk of bark could have been a turtle shell. A branch which looked like an antler. Another could be a unicorn horn. A fallen log was perfect as the body of a unicorn. As for the legs...

I shook my head and went back to painting. Something I could do while sitting down. I had to ignore the longing to pick up the pieces and stash them in the back of my car. Focus instead on what was in front of me. Connor helping a young woman into the harness. She was laughing, her hand on his shoulder. She seemed to miss his disinterest entirely. He adjusted the harness, showed her where to put her hands and gestured for her to step off the platform. She shrugged and disappeared down the line in a squeal of excitement.

One by one, the tourists climbed into harnesses and stepped off the platform. Some hesitated, looking nervous. A couple stepped back to let others go first, but eventually took their turns.

No one fled back to the buses, which was fortunate because they were gone, waiting for everyone at the other end. Even if they weren't laughing the way they were with Riley and Seth, they still seemed to be having fun. Most talking to Charlie, while Connor was all business.

I finished the rough draft of my painting as the

last of the tourists whizzed away, and Charlie and Connor started packing up.

He said something to her before she nodded and climbed into one of the trucks to drive away.

His hands in his pockets again, he strode over to me, to stand behind me and look at my work.

"It's not finished," I said. "I'll take it to touch it up."

"It's good," he said grudgingly. As if giving me a compliment was almost painful. "You painted me." He pointed to the canvas, but his finger didn't touch the still wet paint.

"What makes you think that's you?" I looked up at him sideways.

"I'd know that ass anywhere." He was all smug now, admiring the image of himself.

"Do I want to know how you know what your own ass looks like?" I asked.

"The gym has mirrors," was his reply.

"So you watch your ass while you work out?" I held back a laugh.

"Look at that ass." He gestured at the painting. "Can you blame me?"

"I guess not," I said. "I'm starting to think I did that part too well. Maybe I need to fix it." I reached for my brush.

He grabbed my wrist. "It's perfect. Leave it."

"Okay." I leaned back, but he still held on, his eyes on mine.

He brought my hand to his mouth and kissed my palm. "Do you know what you do to me, Kent?"

"Paint you too well?" He wasn't talking about that and we both knew it.

He moved my hand to the front of his jeans and pressed my palm there so I could feel his growing erection.

"That's what you do to me." He rubbed my hand up and down, lightly, holding me loose enough that I could pull away if I wanted to. "Are you going to be a good girl and do something about it?"

"I could paint that too," I said sweetly.

"You've decided to be a brat instead?" With his other hand, he undid the front of his jeans and pushed them down until his cock popped free. Holding my wrist more firmly, he pressed my hand to his length until I curled my fingers around it.

He rolled his hips a couple of times, thrusting into my fingers and groaning softly. "Be a good girl and suck my cock."

I looked up at him while I turned around in my chair to face him. One hand on his face, I leaned forward and wrapped my lips around him, taking him all the way into my mouth until he tapped the back of my throat.

"Yeah, just like that." He grabbed my ponytail and held my head as he slid all the way out of my mouth, then thrust back in.

"You take my cock so beautifully. Your mouth was fucking made for me."

I ran the tip of my tongue up and down his length, teasing the tip and tasting his salty pre-cum.

"Mmmm, just like that," he said breathlessly. He rolled his hips faster now, holding me in place while he vigorously fucked my mouth. "Good fucking girl. I'm going to come in your mouth and you're going to swallow every drop. Understood?"

I looked up at him and nodded.

He grunted and thrust a couple more times before pulling his cock out of my mouth.

"I changed my mind. I decided I'm in the mood to make some art." He fisted his length, pumping himself a few times before groaning, a squirt of pearly cum interjecting from his tip, onto my face and hair. He worked himself until every drop was released, then stepped back. A slow, satisfied smile crept onto his face.

"Fucking perfect."

Cum slid down the side of my face, warm and

sticky, dripping off when it reached the bottom of my chin.

"Don't wipe it off." He pulled his phone out of his pocket and took a photo. He turned the device around to show me my face, white with his cum.

"You missed your calling," I said.

I hadn't expected to find that hot, but it was. I was an absolute mess because of him. If anyone could see me now, they'd be in no doubt as to what happened. Freshly fucked and then some.

He grinned. "I can't wait to show Riley. Now, take off those leggings and show me that pussy. I'm feeling hungry."

30

LEAH

"Connor."

He caught the side of my face with his hand before I could look toward the road.

"No one's here. Take them off."

I only hesitated for a moment longer before I hooked my thumbs into the waistband of my leggings and pushed them, and my panties, down to my ankles.

"That's it. Spread those legs for me." He leaned back to get a good look as I parted my knees. "You're fucking soaked. You liked me fucking your mouth, didn't you? Open those lips and show me how wet you are."

I reached down with both hands and pushed the sides of my pussy open. The breeze on my damp skin was cool, but the rest of me was on fire. If he didn't touch me soon, I might combust.

"Gorgeous." He kneeled down on the grass in front of me and gripped my thighs in his large hands before pressing his mouth between my legs. He ran the tip of his tongue down my slit and back up again. "Delicious." He teased my clit with his tongue, drawing it between his lips and sucking.

"Does that feel good?" He looked up at me.

"So good," I said softly. "More, please."

"Polite." He dove back in, devouring me with his lips and tongue, sliding a finger inside, then another. "The next time I put any part of me inside you, it will be my cock. You want that, don't you? Tell me how much you want my cock."

"I want... Your cock." I could barely think straight, much less conjure the words. But it was true, I did want to feel him inside me. And Riley. An image of Josiah popped into my head, his dark eyes looking down at me as he thrust slowly. I wasn't used to wanting anyone like this, or being wanted. A girl could get addicted.

"Good girl," he said. "Of course you do. When the time is right, I'll give it to you." He dipped his head then, focusing on fucking me with his hand and tongue, hooking his fingers around to stroke my G spot.

"Mmm, yes," I breathed.

He slipped his fingers out and placed his hands under my thighs to lift them over his shoulders. I had to put my hands to either side of me on the chair to keep from tipping back, while he devoured me like he hadn't eaten in weeks.

"Connor," I whispered. "I'm going to—"

"Not yet," he said, his voice muffled by my pussy. "I haven't finished yet."

I rolled my head back and stared up at the sky to keep from falling over the edge. My whole body tingled, burned and ached with need. Desperate for release.

"Please," I whispered.

"Not yet." He worked me harder, driving me closer and closer. I had to draw on every drop of self-control to keep from coming.

Right when I was about to shatter, in spite of myself, he pulled away.

"Maybe I should wait until Riley is here."

I glared at him. "If you're not going to—"

He grinned. "You're not going to finish yourself, if I have to…" He reached into the pocket in the back of his jeans and pulled out a length of narrow rope.

I blinked a couple of times and stared at him. "What are you doing?"

He eased my legs down off his shoulders and pulled me forward, gripping both of my wrists with one hand.

"Making sure you don't touch yourself." He wound the rope around my wrists and pulled it tighter.

"I have to pack up my things," I argued.

"I'll pack them up." He tied a neat knot in the rope.

"What about my clothes?" I leaned forward and started trying to tug them back into place.

"Oh no, don't do that." He grabbed my ankle and eased my leggings and panties off over my shoe, then the other one.

"I'm not going into town half-naked," I protested.

He laughed before throwing my clothes into my bag and starting to pack everything away. "Yes, you are."

"You're a prick," I told him. My body was aching and he was happy to torture me?

That made him laugh harder. "Have you just figured that out?"

Careful of the still wet paint, he placed the canvas

in the back seat of his truck, and everything else in the foot well.

"Need a hand getting in?" He looked smug as fuck.

"I'm going to leave a puddle on your seat," I said with my eyes narrowed.

"Good." He strode over to me, scooped me up and placed me on the seat before fixing my seatbelt into place. "You look good like that." He patted the side of the car before closing the door and going back to get my chair.

"Where are we going?" I asked once we were back on the road. "There's going to be people at the other end of the zip line."

"Good, they can watch." He didn't seem even slightly concerned. "In case you hadn't noticed, I have a thing for that. Nothing wrong with it. There's an Internet full of people who like to be watched."

"This should probably be where I tell you that you won't have any trouble finding someone who also likes being watched," I said.

"But you're not going to because...why?" He slid a look over to me before turning his attention back to the road. "Let me guess, Leah fucking Kent has a thing for it too."

"I don't know what I have a thing for," I confessed. "I guess I don't hate this."

I nodded down toward my bound wrists. "Maybe even being half-naked on a public road." No one in the cars passing the other way could tell I was sitting there with a bare, saturated pussy. Watching them fly past was strangely arousing.

"I don't hate it either," he said.

"Shouldn't you be sitting with your pants off?" I reasoned.

"Probably," he agreed. "Next time. You can suck me off while I drive."

"On a mountain road? That sounds dangerous," I said without thinking. "Wait, I just remembered who I'm talking to. Of course that's something you'd do."

"Without doubt." He slowed the car and took the bend. "I'm getting hard thinking about it." The growing tent in the front of his jeans was evidence of that.

"Is there anything you wouldn't do?" I asked.

"I wouldn't eat pig brains." He grimaced. "Or cockroaches. Or those hundred-year-old egg things. I prefer a rush of adrenaline, not a rush of vomit."

I snort-laughed. "That's something we can agree on. I prefer a technicolour canvas to a technicolour yawn."

"This conversation is making my cock deflate," he said.

"We should talk about something else." I shifted in my seat, glad the cover was comfortable against my bare ass.

"Better yet, we don't talk at all." He slowed the car and turned into the car park beside the buses.

I swallowed as we drove by them, aware if anyone could see down into the car, it would be the bus drivers. I carefully kept my hands over my lap, trying my best to cover my bare pussy.

"Good timing," Connor said as he killed the engine. A stream of tourists filed past, heading onto the buses and over to their own vehicles.

"There goes your audience," I remarked.

He grinned over at me. "Charlie and Seth are still here."

He pushed out of the car and waved to Riley before opening my door. "I brought you a present."

His hand on the roof of the car, Riley ducked his head and looked inside. He saw me sitting there and grinned.

"I like this present. How thoughtful of you."

All I could do was smile back.

"I thought you'd like to see her come."

Without stopping to look whether the staff were

watching, Connor grabbed my legs, turned me sideways and knelt down in front of me. As if he hadn't stopped at all, he dove back between my legs with his mouth and hand.

"You're the best." Riley leaned on the door of the truck and watched. "Seth, Charlie, see both of you later." He raised a hand in a wave.

"Later." Seth's voice was so close. I couldn't see him, but if he looked just the right way, he could probably see me. He must have seen Connor kneeling there, feasting on me.

"Don't do anything we wouldn't do." Charlie's voice was just as close, her words ending in a laugh.

"Too late for that," Riley said. He looked back at me and smiled. "Can you untie her hands? I need to see her touch those nipples of hers."

Keeping his mouth in place, Connor slid his fingers out of me and quickly worked the rope loose.

I shook out my hands to get the blood flow back again, while Connor pulled down the front of my shirt and bra, exposing my breasts.

"Touch them." Riley nodded at me.

I rolled my nipples between my thumb and forefinger, savouring the added surge of desire that passed through me.

"Are you close to coming?" Riley asked.

"So close," I said breathlessly.

Connor pushed me harder, driving his hand in and out of me while sucking and biting my clit.

I put my head back as a wave of pleasure washed over me, shattering me into more pieces than there were stars in the sky. Breaking me thoroughly before putting me back together, bit by bit. My vision went dark and nothing existed but bliss, and the press of fabric against my skin.

After the longest time, I came back to earth, gasping and blinking, the wave trickling slowly out the tips of my toes.

"She does that so well," Riley remarked.

"So fucking well," Connor agreed. He pressed his mouth against the inside of my thigh, kissing the skin there. "I didn't want you to miss seeing that."

"I'm glad I didn't," Riley said. "That was fucking everything."

"That wasn't everything," Connor said. "It was just the start."

"Hell yeah it was," Riley agreed. He leaned over and squinted at me, his gaze on my face. "Is that—"

"Yes it is." Connor looked smug. "We started without you, but I didn't want to finish without you." He pulled out his phone and showed Riley the photo he took earlier, when the cum was fresh and wet.

"You're my hero." Riley patted his shoulder.

"There's room for more." Connor stood and stepped out of the way.

"This day just keeps getting better." Riley undid the front of his jeans and pulled his cock out. He wrapped his hand around it and pumped, thickening it, while keeping the tip pointing at me.

"Sit forward. Yeah, just like that." He brought the head of his cock closer to my breasts, rubbing the slit around them and over my nipples. Leaving a trail of pre-cum on my skin.

"We're all artists today," Connor said. "I don't mean bullshit artists."

Riley and I both choked out laughs.

"That's a matter of opinion," I said.

"Just for that." Riley grabbed the back of my head and pushed his cock against my lips. "Open up."

When I opened my mouth, he shoved his cock inside, all the way to the back of my throat. "That's the best way to shut up a smart mouth. Right, Con?"

"She looks good with your dick down her throat," Connor said.

Riley regarded me. "She really does." Holding my head, he fucked my mouth harder, making me gag over and over before he pulled out and came over my breasts. Leaving a string of cum from one nipple to the other.

"She looks good like that too." Connor looked satisfied. He held up his phone. "I'm not going to show this to anyone," he said before taking another photo of me.

"You better not," I growled. This wasn't something I needed the whole world to see.

Connor just smiled and tucked his phone away.

31

LEAH

"THANKS FOR HAVING ME OVER." I tucked a few strands of still-damp hair behind my ear. With any luck, Fiona would assume I had a shower before walking over to her place for dinner. Not that I washed to clean cum off my hair and body.

"We should have had you over sooner, right Sarah?" She smiled at her daughter, who sat on the floor, a colouring book open in front of her.

"Right," Sarah said without glancing up. Her attention was all on getting the green pencil inside the lines.

"She's very focused." Fiona slid an oven mitt off the oven handle and opened it to peek inside. "It's almost ready. I hope you like quiche." Homemade bread rolls were cooling on a rack beside the stove.

The smell was making my mouth water. "I love quiche."

"Grandma and Grandpa once gave me a birthday card that said hogs and quiches on it," Sarah said. "It was funny."

I'd seen cards with the play on the words 'hugs' and 'kisses' before, but I couldn't contain a smile at the expression on her face.

"That's hilarious," I said.

"It is. It had pigs and quiches on it. You know what else would have been funny?" Her eyes widened. "Bacon."

"Maybe the quiche had bacon in it," I suggested.

She tilted her head, thinking that over. "It might. Then it would be hogs, hogs and quiches." She grinned.

I laughed. "I guess it would." Apparently she didn't have a problem with where bacon actually came from. I'd known people who seemed to think it only came from the grocery store. Growing up in a place like this, and enjoying fishing, she'd have had a better understanding of the origins of food.

She pushed herself up to her feet, ran over to her mother and gave her two hugs and a kiss on the cheek. "Hogs, hogs and quiches."

Fiona hugged her back. "Welcome to my crazy life," she laughed.

I smiled softly. My mother and I never had a relationship like Fiona and Sarah did. Seeing it now made me realise even more acutely what I missed out on. If I ever had kids, I'd want them to grow up like this. Happy, content and accepted. Loved.

"Your crazy life is a lot of fun," I said. I couldn't help being a little envious.

"Yes it is," Fiona agreed. She patted Sarah on the back. "Go wash your hands for dinner. Don't take long."

"Okay!" Sarah skipped off toward the bathroom.

Fiona raised her eyebrows at me. "So, tell me about *your* crazy life. You've been busy?"

My face heated. "What have you heard?" Had Charlie or Seth said something? For that matter, had Connor or Riley?

She laughed at the expression on my face. "No one said anything. Why? Do you have a guilty conscience?"

I cleared my throat. "Of course not. You're right, I've been busy. I got some painting done this afternoon." After Connor took me back to get my car, I did a bit more work, touching up the first draft.

"Have they convinced you to paint them naked

yet?" She pulled a bottle of white wine out of the fridge and held it up until I nodded. She poured some into two glasses and handed one to me.

"No." I took a sip. "I'm sure they'd enjoy that, though." They certainly enjoyed painting me. "If they could sit still for long enough."

She laughed and turned to pull the quiche out of the oven. "You might need to do it while they're asleep. They might stay still then."

I hadn't thought far enough ahead to consider sharing a bed with either of them all night. Or literally *sleeping* beside them. Would they want that? And if they did, separately or together?

Three of us in a bed would be a tight fit, but two attractive mountain men on either side of me? That didn't sound like the worst thing in the world.

"I'm not sure if they lie still when they sleep," I admitted. "They probably bungee jump."

She laughed. "That sounds about right. They couldn't keep still when we were at school. It used to drive the teachers crazy. Crazier. Not that I was much better, if I'm honest. I was just quieter about it than they were."

"Are you saying you weren't a perfect angel?" I teased.

She snorted. "Not even close, but I mostly turned out all right." She batted her eyelashes.

"You definitely did," I assured her. "Sarah is proof of that."

"That's it, you can never leave town," Fiona declared. "You're good for my ego."

I laughed. "I'm being honest, that's all." After a beat, I asked, "Do you remember Coral Clarke?"

She frowned as she opened a drawer to pull out a knife and started to slice the quiche.

"Not really. I remember the teacher sitting us down and saying she wasn't coming back. I don't think anyone really understood why. We cried, then we went back to cutting pictures out of old magazines. That seems really cold, thinking back."

Her eyes glazed for a moment before she shrugged and went back to slicing.

"Not if you were too young to understand," I assured her. "I would have done the same thing. All of those things seem, I don't know, abstract at that age. On the other hand, if our ice cream drops off the cone…"

She laughed and placed slices of quiche onto plates before carrying them over to the table. The rack of bread and a tub of butter followed, along with a bowl of salad.

"That's instant childhood trauma, right there." She placed knives and forks to either side of the plates and gestured for me and Sarah to take our seats.

"It's ice cream." Sarah slid into her chair.

"Dropping it on the ground is practically the equivalent to the end of the world." Fiona nodded, fighting back a smile.

"Unless you're a dog," Sarah said. "Or a pig. Then you're happy because you're going to eat it." She stuck out her tongue and mimed lapping ice cream off the ground.

She was too cute.

"Maybe we should go around dropping our ice cream more often, for the dogs and pigs?" I suggested.

Both of them looked playfully horrified at the idea.

"Only if it's strawberry ice cream." Sarah grimaced and started on her quiche.

Fiona shook her head sadly. "Sometimes I wonder where she came from. On the other hand, more strawberry ice cream for me."

"You can have every spoonful," Sarah said. Judging by the way she dug in, she preferred quiche.

I sliced off a section and popped it into my

mouth. "Mmmm, this is good." I could taste the bacon, and the handmade pastry, which melted in my mouth.

"It's nice to cook for someone else," Fiona said. "Too often, Sarah and I heat up something in the microwave. I'm trying to teach her how to cook."

"I kneaded the dough!" Sarah declared, her mouth full of eggy quiche.

"You did a great job." I picked up a roll and broke it open, watching the steam rise from the perfectly cooked bread. "This is delicious."

"I might be a chef when I grow up," Sarah said. "Or a baker."

"You'd be a good baker," Fiona told her. "You like being up before the sun. You could make me cupcakes."

"Yes!" Sarah wriggled in her chair.

I ate quietly, watching them as they bantered back and forth, talking about their Sunday and the school week ahead. The conversation was cozy, comfortable. Like a warm hug.

The whole town was like that. A warm hug with hot, possessive mountain men thrown in for good measure.

While they talked, I thought back to the afternoon. Connor fucking my mouth, then binding and edging me, then finishing me off before Riley fucked my mouth. Knowing Seth and Charlie were close by, knowing what was going on. Did they know I was the one in the truck? They probably guessed. Next time I saw them, I was going to blush like hell.

"Does Miss Ferguson's brother like you?" Sarah asked me.

I tried to contain my surprise at the sudden question, but probably failed. "Why do you ask that?"

She shrugged. "I saw him leaving your house one time. Is he your friend?"

"I guess you could say he is," I said. We hadn't talked about anything beyond that. Did I want to be more than friends? More than fuck buddies? I couldn't deny I was attracted to him and Riley, but my feelings for them were complicated.

"Is he your best friend?" she asked, in that singsong way kids had when they were teasing.

I laughed softly. "I don't know. Maybe. I've made a lot of friends since I moved here. You might all be my best friends." I glanced over at Fiona, who smiled.

"I feel like I've known you forever," she said. "I'm glad I spoke to you that day and told you about next door."

"I'm glad you did too," I said sincerely. Otherwise,

I might have spent a couple of nights in the hotel before moving on. For some reason I couldn't put my finger on, it felt like the universe wanted me here. Like I belonged here. As though these were my people.

Whatever happened with the guys, I was going to do whatever I could to stay here.

"Mom said we could have had a serial killer next door instead," Sarah said, her eyes wide. "You're not a serial killer, are you?" She scrunched up her brow as if trying to picture me doing something horrible like that.

"Definitely not," I said with a laugh. "I like to eat cereal, not kill it."

Sarah giggled. "Me too." After a beat or two she added, "Mom also said she wouldn't have minded the hot mafia twins from her favourite books, to live next door."

"Sarah!" Fiona said with mock outrage.

"What? You did," Sarah insisted. "Remember? You said they could—"

"If you want ice cream for dessert, don't finish that sentence." Fiona waved her fork at her daughter. She rolled her eyes and turned to me. "It's not my fault if book boyfriends are better than real-life ones. Especially the hot mafia ones." She sighed.

"All boys are yucky," Sarah declared.

"Yes. Go on believing that until you're at least… forty," Fiona said jokingly. "Maybe fifty. I am *not* ready for you to grow up and start dating."

"When are you going to start dating?" Sarah asked her.

Fiona almost choked on a piece of bread. When she'd finished coughing, she said, "When you're forty. Until then, I have my books to keep me warm." She slid me a sly look. "Did you know Riley and I exchanged books? He likes a good mafia romance too."

"That explains a lot," I said.

Should I be jealous at the idea of them sharing something like that? I decided I shouldn't. They'd known each other for so long, if something was going to happen between them, it would have by now. Both of them made it more than clear it wouldn't.

Honestly, it was cute. I hadn't known Riley was a reader. Was Connor one too? He seemed more like the kind of guy who would sit down in front of a different action movie every night. Or make furniture out of reclaimed wood, just for fun.

She laughed. "It really does, doesn't it? Those two would make good mafia henchmen. I can see it now."

She held up hand in front of her as if sketching out the scene. "Breaking kneecaps and threatening people during the day, showering women with presents at night."

"I might have to start reading mafia romance," I said.

Although, my reality sounded better than that. Yeah, they claimed they were assholes, but they gave good orgasms. Better than anyone I've ever been with by a long way.

Imaginary guys couldn't do that, could they? Maybe they could, with virtual reality and the right toy, but give me the real thing.

"I can let you borrow some if you want," Fiona offered.

"I'd like that," I said. "I can let you borrow my dinosaur romance in return." I picked up my wine and held it in front of my grin.

"Dinosaur romance?" Sarah echoed. "What—"

"I think it's time for ice cream," Fiona interrupted. She gave me a sidelong look, but smiled as Sarah scrambled out of her chair and raced over to the freezer.

RILEY

"BOOKINGS ARE UP." I looked from my laptop, over to Connor.

He was looking through invoices on his own laptop, a frown on his face.

"Good. We're going to need it to pay all of these." He tapped on the keyboard, putting the invoice details into the accounting app.

"That bad?" I finished answering a potential customer enquiry and pressed send.

He shrugged. "It's the price of expansion. It will be worth it; we just need to get past the teething phase. We've got this."

"Do we?" I scrolled down to the next query, opened it and started to respond.

"Ri." He sounded frustrated. "Ri, look at me.

We've worked too long and hard not to succeed. When we took this over from Dave, we knew it was going to be a challenge. You and me, we don't back down from a challenge. Right?"

"Right. Failure is not an option." He was hot when he got all blunt and bossy like this. Sometimes I provoked him just to see it. Today, though, this was something different. I needed to know he was still on board with me.

"Exactly." He pointed a finger gun at me. "In fact, I was thinking about hiring more staff. We could expand faster if we don't have to deal with shit like this. And we could run more tours."

I nodded slowly. "I'd prefer to be out there than sitting in your kitchen doing this."

But my stomach dropped. I couldn't help reading more into it. If we had more staff, he'd have more time for the pub. And less for me.

"Yeah, sorting invoices sucks." He rolled his shoulders. "If I can hand this off to someone, I'm there for it."

"I don't mind answering questions, but it's not as much fun as rafting. Or zip lining. Or skiing." I want to remind him why we were doing this in the first place. We both liked the freedom of running our own business, and loved the one we chose.

He'd go crazy in the pub all day long. And all night.

"Nothing is as much fun as those, except fucking," he said. "Speaking of fucking, we could ask Leah if she wants to work for us doing some of this." He scrubbed his chin with his hand, looking thoughtful.

"Good idea," I said slowly. "Do you want her work for us so we can fuck her when we want to?"

I deleted a couple of spam emails from our inbox. Then a couple more. Did they really think we'd believe a billionaire wanted to send us money for no reason? Neither of us was born yesterday.

"That too, but not just that," he said easily. "I'm pretty sure she needs the money and she can do this sitting down. Or lying down if she has to."

"Now I want to see if she can answer emails while I fuck her from behind," I said.

"I want to see that too," he agreed. "Her and you. We could see who can answer more emails while I fuck you."

"I'd like to see how many invoices you can record while I fuck you," I said. This conversation was becoming very distracting.

"None. You fuck too well for me to focus on invoices." He adjusted the front of his jeans.

"I think that's the right answer." I adjusted my

own, dark grey, track pants. "We should definitely ask her. We'll have to train her."

"Absolutely," he agreed. "She's a smart girl. She'll figure out exactly what we want pretty quickly."

"Not too quickly," I said. "Otherwise she won't need us around for too long, giving her pointers."

"I'll give her a pointer all right."

"I can't wait to see that." We'd taken it slow so far, but I wanted to go further, and soon. I'd never been known for my patience, and this was becoming painful. I had to bring the conversation back down to earth for now though.

I propped my elbows on the table and rested my face on my hands. "If she comes to work for us, what does that mean?"

He glanced up, his head at an angle. "It means she takes the tedious, but necessary, administration work off our hands?" He clearly couldn't see what I was getting at.

"I mean, what are you going to do with the extra time you have if you're not doing that?" I asked. "Will you be spending more hours at the pub?" That was only a small part of what I really wanted to know.

He straightened his head. "I hadn't given it any thought. We've only been having this conversation for ten minutes."

"Okay, now I've brought it up, what do you think?" My pulse raced a little faster, an edge of anxiety creeping in where it wasn't wanted.

"I might. I don't know. I guess I'll be wherever I'm needed. Why? What are you getting at?" He seemed irritated now.

"What's going to happen to our business when you take over from your father?" I blurted out. "You can't be in two places at once."

He sat back and stared at me. "How long has this been bothering you?"

I scratched the skin under my eye. "A while. I know it's what he wants to happen. Then when he had his heart attack… If you take over from him soon, he can retire."

"Is that what you want?" Connor asked. "You think I should kick his ass out and take over from him now?" His expression was unreadable.

"It's not what I want," I said, my voice low. "Like you said, we worked hard to build this business. It's always been you and me. I don't want anything to happen to him, but he needs you."

"What do you need?" His expression softened. "If we close the business, you can, I don't know, live your own dreams. The adventure tours were my idea. I never asked if it was what you wanted."

"It is what I want," I said quickly. "I don't want to close the business." The idea made my blood boil and my chest ache. It would be like cutting off a limb. Aurora Adventure Tours was my life. It and Connor. If I was honest, Leah was quickly creeping into that same net.

"I don't either," Connor said. He rubbed a hand over the back of his neck. "I see why you've been quiet lately. You think that at some point I have to choose."

"Don't you?" I asked. "What option would you have? Work twenty-five hours a day eight days a week?"

He barked a laugh. "You know that's not humanly possible, right?"

"Who said you were human?" I said, content to lighten the conversation. "You might be some kind of mutant."

He tipped his head back and laughed. "That's not the first time I've been accused of being a mutant, but I'm not superhuman."

He chuckled for a while before blinking and bringing himself back to the present. "You're right, I can't do both," he admitted. "Not when I think the pub needs its own restaurant and hotel. Both businesses need to expand and that's a fuck ton of work. That doesn't mean our business has to close."

"What does it mean then?" I asked. My mouth was suddenly dry. "You're not going to close the pub, or sell it?"

The surprise on his face told me he hadn't considered either of those options. Of course not; it was his father's legacy we were talking about. Not to mention, the heart of the town. Closing the place would devastate Aurora Hollow.

"I was thinking of hiring a manager," he said. "Someone to run the pub. If Leah can come on board, I'll have more time to look at expanding both, while you and I run the tours."

My jaw dropped open like it was on a hinge that suddenly failed.

"Oh."

He grinned. "Yeah, *oh*. Unless you'd prefer to take over the tours and be the boss?"

Now it was my turn to admit I hadn't thought about something so big. Did I want that? To make all the calls? To be in charge of the staff? To be able to make the decisions about any expansion?

I sat back and scrubbed a hand over my face. "I think I like your plan better."

He grinned. "Me too."

"Prick," I said teasingly. "You like getting your way."

"No, I fucking *love* getting my way." His adorable grin made my heart flip. It beat even harder when he added, "But you have to be happy with it too. Otherwise, what's the point?" He raised one shoulder and dropped it slowly. "We're a team. Teams work together."

"You're not going to say 'there's no I in team,' are you?" I grimaced.

"Have I ever been that cringey?" he asked. He looked as disgusted by the suggestion as I was.

"Not yet." I tried to hold back a smile, but failed. I failed even harder when he picked up a pencil and threw it at me.

"Fuck off," he said with a roll of his eyes. "I'll never be that cringey."

"Never say never." I picked up the pencil and threw it back in his direction. It landed on the table, slid across the surface and clattered onto the floor.

"I'll absolutely say never." He leaned and put it back where it belonged. "Dumbass catchphrases like that should be beheaded and set on fire."

"Like teamwork makes the dream work?" I deleted a couple more spam emails before glancing back at him.

"Now who's been cringey?" he asked. "How many of those do you have, exactly?"

"I think the correct answer is too many," I said. "But I'm happy to be a *thought leader* in my chosen field."

"Next time we go rafting, I'm taking away your lifejacket." He reached over to pick up his water bottle, open it and take a sip.

"You wouldn't do that," I said. "You love me too much."

His gaze lingered on mine, saying more than words could.

"Not if you use phrases like *thought leader*," he said. "Or teamwork makes the fucking dream work."

"That is accurate though," I pointed out. "We're a team and we're over here making our dream work."

"I guess so, but don't put it that way." He put his water bottle back down on the table. "Let's get this finished. Then we can head over to Leah's and ask her if she wants a job."

"Work, hand or blow?" I asked.

"Yes, yes, and yes." He flashed me a grin before focusing back on his laptop screen.

33

LEAH

I WAS PUTTING the finishing touches to a sketch of my rental cottage when a truck pulled up in front of it. From the other side of the road, I watched Connor and Riley step out. Both of them mouthwatering in fitted t-shirts that showed off muscular chests and biceps.

Connor's dark jeans looked painted on, while Riley's track pants framed the shape of his cock like a work of art. Maybe I should draw them naked sooner rather than later.

Closing my sketchpad, I pushed myself up out of my chair and grabbed the opposite corners to fold it.

"Hey." Connor trotted across the road to take the chair from me and tuck it under his arm. "What are you doing over here?"

"You two like that question, don't you?" I teased. Every time I sat down to make art, one of them turned up to ask me that.

"We like to know what you're up to," Connor said easily. "Were you drawing a picture of Riley's cock?"

"Only if it looks like a house," I said with a laugh.

"It's almost as big as a house," Riley called out, looking pleased with himself.

I dropped my gaze to his groin. "How does it fit in there then?"

"I ask myself that every day." Riley grinned. "Every time I put my pants on, I think *this* is where the seams are going to burst open. And yet, they don't."

Connor laugh-grunted. "You're an idiot. You're big, but you're not *that* big."

"At least he admits I'm big," Riley said, his eyes still on me.

"I noticed that." I checked for cars before crossing the road.

"Here's where one of you tells me how big I am," Connor said expectantly.

It was my turn to laugh. "You don't need to be told." They were both above average and they knew it. They didn't need me, or each other, to stroke their egos.

"I still like to hear it." Connor gave me a sideways look.

I rolled my eyes. "You're both enormous, okay? I'm sure there's a few jealous elephants out there."

"I would have settled for a horse, but I'll take an elephant." Connor looked smug as fuck. Of course he did.

"Me too." Riley grinned. "Except now I'm starting to think she only likes us for our giant cocks."

I pointed at him. "Just remember, you said that, not me. Is there some reason you two are here this afternoon? Shouldn't you be jumping off a cliff or something?"

"We don't jump off cliffs, we climb up them," Connor said. "Or we will, when we expand to abseiling. That's on the cards for a couple of years from now."

"That's why we're here." Riley's gaze dropped to my sketchpad speculatively, before returning to my face.

"You want me to jump off a cliff?" I asked. That didn't sound appealing. Unless I was attached to a safety harness and a strong rope.

"No, we want you to help us build our business," Connor said.

My good mood faded away. He knew my ability

to be physically active was limited these days. I wouldn't even try abseiling. Hell, I'd stay off rock climbing walls. If I didn't, I'd suffer for it later.

I admit to a stab of bitterness for the things I could no longer do. Things I always wanted to try that now were off-limits. I reminded myself there were a lot of things I could do, but the things I couldn't still pissed me off.

Connor must have seen the expression on my face and understood the reason for it. He put the chair down on the grass and placed his hands on my upper arms, his fingers pressing lightly into my flesh.

"We don't want you to help put people in harnesses or any of that shit. Riley and I were wondering if you wanted to help with the administration side of things. Answering emails, paying invoices and crap like that. You could do it from anywhere you like. Then Riley and I can focus on the tour side and expanding the business."

"You could get a staff discount," Riley offered.

Connor glanced at him. "We're not charging her for any tours."

"One hundred percent discount, who could refuse?" Riley was unruffled.

"Why do you want my help?" I asked, confused.

"There must be plenty of people in town with experience doing that sort of thing."

"Maybe, but we want you," Connor insisted. "Are you going to say you don't need to work? Because I know you do. We'll pay you to do something that won't be a strain on your body. Where else in town is going to offer that?"

"Nowhere, I suppose," I admitted. Not to mention the fact I hated the idea of asking anywhere to let me sit as much as I needed to, or take a day off for a flare-up. With this, I could do both. And if it gave them more time to grow their business, that was a bonus.

"Okay, I'll do it." I nodded firmly. I certainly could use the money. A few other people had bought my paintings and drawings, but it wasn't enough by any means.

"Of course you will." Connor dropped his hands and leaned over to pick up the chair. "We had no doubt."

"I should have held out longer." I followed them to the front door of the cottage. "Thought about it for a day or two. Made both of you sweat."

"Sweetheart, you already make us sweat," Riley said. He pushed open the door and stepped inside.

"You say that now, but we haven't started negotiating my hourly rate." I placed my sketchpad and pencil down on the dining table.

"We'll pay the going rate for administrative work, and all the orgasms you can handle," Connor said. He leaned the chair up against the corner of the room. "And we'll let you suck our cocks as often as you like."

"That's generous," I said with a playful hint of sarcasm. They didn't seem to mind fucking my mouth.

"We thought so." Connor cupped my face with his hands and brushed his lips over mine. "Should I fuck that smart mouth of yours right now?"

"I think you should," Riley said. He stood back and crossed his arms.

"I agree," Connor rumbled. He stroked his thumbs over my cheek bones, leaned in and whispered, "Get on your knees." After a moment he added, "Both of you."

Riley dropped his hands to his thighs with a slap before lowering himself to his knees. He took my hand and pulled me down beside him.

"Take my cock out," Connor insisted. He was looking right at Riley.

Riley glanced at me before hurrying to pull down the zipper of Connor's jeans and tugging them down his hips. Connor's erection sprang free.

"Leah, do you want to watch him suck me?" Connor's voice was already ragged with need.

"Yes," I whispered.

I wanted that so much I could have flooded my panties on the spot. I might as well have; they were drenched as Riley wrapped his hand around the base of Connor's cock and licked his head. The tip of his tongue teasing, licking the bead of pre-cum that had leaked from his slit.

Connor grabbed a fistful of Riley's hair and guided him deeper onto his length.

His eyes smiling, Riley eagerly sucked. At the same time he pumped the other man slowly.

Connor groaned. "Leah's turn." He let go of Riley's hair, letting him slide his mouth off and move aside to make room for me.

I inched over on my knees, opened my mouth and took him inside, his cock already wet and warm from Riley.

Riley moved around behind me, grabbed the straps of my tank top and pushed them down my shoulders. My bra straps followed until my breasts were bare. He pushed my tank top down to my waist and unhooked the clasps of my bra to let it fall away.

He reached around to cup both of my breasts, palming my nipples while I went on sucking and licking, teasing Connor. My nipples tightened under his touch, until they were rock hard, and my pussy more needy.

Slowly, Riley moved his hands down my body, over my stomach to the top of my floral skirt. He pushed the elastic waistband down, letting the fabric fall to my knees, then dragged my tank top down with it.

"Lift your knee." He tapped one of them.

I raised one, then the other, letting him push my clothes aside. I knelt on the floor in only a pair of pale pink panties.

"Take them off," Connor ordered.

I glanced up at him, watching his face as Riley eased them down and helped me out of them. This wasn't the first time I'd been completely naked in front of them, but this time it didn't involve pain or the bath.

This wasn't about healing me.

This was about fucking me.

Still behind me, Riley ran his hands up and down my body, parted my thighs and pushed his hands between them. The tips of his fingers slid up and down my folds, dipping into my wetness and spreading it around my pussy.

"How wet is she?" Connor asked.

"Fucking drenched," Riley said. He pushed a finger inside me, then another.

Connor drew his cock out of my mouth and stood back to watch. "Make her come."

Riley rubbed the side of his fingers up and down my clit, pinching my nipple at the same time.

With both men watching me like that, I was aroused as hell. My body quickly screamed for release, which came hard and fast against Riley's hand. He held me tight, working me through my orgasm and down the other side.

"So fucking gorgeous," Connor whispered. He stepped out of his jeans, grabbed the hem of his shirt and pulled it over his head.

This was the first time I saw him naked. He was all muscle and grooves, interspersed with scars and tattoos in black ink. A dragon down one arm, full sleeve on the other. His cock jutted toward me.

"So fucking ready for you," Riley said. He pulled my upper body back until I was lying over his lap, one hand holding me in place, the other on my breast.

Connor lowered himself to his knees and stepped

between my legs, pushing them apart until his cock was pressed against my entrance.

"Tell me what you want," he demanded.

"I want your cock," I said softly.

"Beg for it," he said.

My tongue slid over my lips. If I didn't feel him inside me soon, I was going to lose my mind.

"Please," I said a little louder. "Please fuck me. I want you inside me."

He gripped my hips, raised them off the floor and pushed his tip inside me. With a grunt, he rammed himself the rest of the way inside, all the way to the hilt.

I cried out and my back arched, but Riley held me in place. Held me tighter when Connor started to thrust, firm and hard, holding back nothing.

"Her pussy feels like fucking heaven," Connor ground out. "So tight. Made for us." He pulled all the way out before slamming back in and thrusting again with strong, even strokes.

Riley pinched my nipple before moving his hand down my stomach and back to my clit, rubbing while Connor thrust into me.

"Come for us," Connor insisted. "I want to feel you come around my cock."

Between the way he was hitting me inside and

Riley's calloused fingers, I had no defence. I came for a second time, harder and faster than the first, my body pressed against Riley's legs.

"Fuck, Leah," Connor grunted as my muscles tightened around him, forcing an orgasm out of him. He thrust a couple more times before losing himself, spilling his release inside me. He groaned and ground himself against me before sagging, panting and swearing under his breath.

"So fucking good." He took a couple of moments to catch his breath, then rolled off me. "Riley."

Riley worked his way out from under me before pulling me up to my knees. He pushed his track pants down and knelt behind me. With careful hands, he parted my legs. His breath was warm on my ass.

He pressed a finger inside my pussy.

"You look good with Connor's cum trickling out of you, but I want it in there when I fuck you." He pushed it in carefully, then gripped my hips and pressed the tip of his cock into my pussy.

"Wait." Connor searched around in the back of his jeans before pulling out his phone. He held it up in front of him and nodded. "I wanted to capture this moment. Go on Riley, fuck our woman."

"With pleasure." Riley pushed himself the rest of

the way inside me and moaned. "You're right, she does feel like fucking heaven." He grabbed my breasts and squeezed them while thrusting slowly and carefully.

The floor was hard on my hands and knees, but I couldn't bring myself to care. I'd never been with two men at the same time, much less with one filming us.

"You should see yourselves," Connor said. "You're fucking hot. You can watch it with Riley's cum inside you."

My face heated, but I might watch out of curiosity. Hoping like hell I looked as good as I felt.

Riley thrust a few more times, frantically, before crying out my name as he came, filling me with even more cum, until it was overflowing, spilling back over his cock and down my thighs. Warm and sticky.

He sagged against my back, holding me with his hands still around my breasts.

"Now you're fucking ours," he whispered. "Let's get you cleaned and comfortable."

He looked worried as he helped me to my feet. As if it was only just occurring to them it might be a bad idea to fuck me on the floor.

I might hurt tomorrow, but today I didn't care. I'd never been so thoroughly fucked.

34

LEAH

"I THOUGHT it would be a bigger mess," I admitted.

"Because it's two men? Or because one is my brother?" Whitney asked. She grinned at me before turning her attention back to the string of lights she was putting up between the pub and Snowdrop Café.

"Because they asked me to help." I held the end of the string, keeping it from tangling while she fastened it in place. "I figured it was because they were disorganised, but they're not." All the invoices were accounted for, and the emails up to date. Even the social media pages and website only needed to be added to as needed, not overhauled.

"You sound impressed." She climbed down from

the ladder and moved it over a metre or so. Lights in one hand, she scrambled back up.

"Probably best if you don't tell them that," I said wryly.

She flashed me a grin and teased more string up from my hands. "I wouldn't dream of it. They wouldn't fit inside any of the buildings in town if their egos were any bigger."

"Do you mind me working for them?" I asked. I moved the string along in my hands to give her more slack.

"Of course not, why would I?" She fastened the next section in place before moving the ladder again. "If it means you'll stick around town for longer, I'm all for it."

"As long as me spending more time with your brother won't make you uncomfortable." What would I do if she was? She'd quickly become one of my closest friends, but my feelings for Connor and Riley were complicated at best.

The physical attraction was undeniable, but the emotional attraction grew quickly. I wasn't sure how I felt about that. At some point, did they expect me to choose between them? Could I? If they had to choose, would they choose me, or each other?

"I might question your life choices and taste in

men, but you could do worse than either of them," she said. "Don't tell them I said that."

"My lips are sealed," I said.

"Of course they are." She stepped back to inspect her work so far. "Thanks for helping with this. The fall festival is one of the best times of the year. This place really comes to life. And we can have pumpkin spice everything."

"I can get behind that." As far as I was concerned, cinnamon and nutmeg were the taste of autumn. The perfect compliment to turning leaves.

I glanced across the street to where Fiona and Holly were putting up another string of lights. They were talking about something, and laughing.

"Can I ask you something?" I turned back to Whitney.

"Of course you can." She picked up the ladder and carried it over to the other side of the café's doorway.

Holding up the string of lights, I followed her carefully. "Riley and Connor, they're close."

"Since forever," she agreed. "I couldn't turn around without tripping over both of them. If you ever saw one, the other was never far away. Half the time they'd eat dinner at our house, and Riley's the other half. Mom never knew how many people to cook for." She laughed softly.

"You'd say they're inseparable?" When she gestured, I held up the lights to make sure they were fastened above the door and not in anyone's way.

"I'd say so. Why?" She glanced back at me before fastening the lights in place and adjusting them before climbing back off the ladder.

"They both seem interested in getting to know me better," I said slowly.

"As in dating?" She crossed her arms and leaned against the side of the café.

"I guess so." I chewed my lip and shrugged. "Have they ever been interested in the same girl at the same time?"

"This is probably a conversation you should have with them," she said. "Are you worried you'll cause trouble between them?"

"The thought crossed my mind. I don't want to be the reason they stop being friends." I came here to Aurora Hollow to find myself, not make trouble. If Riley and Connor had a falling out, it would affect the whole town and their business. I'd leave before that happened. What was I thinking, getting involved in their business deeper than the occasional tagalong on a tour?

"I don't think anything or anyone could stop those two from being friends." She toyed with a silver ring on her finger. "I can't remember the last time either of them was in a relationship, but I've seen them both go home with the same woman. That might be something to think about. Whether you want to be dating two men at the same time." She didn't seem to be judging.

"Would you?" I asked.

She blinked at me a couple of times. "Date more than one guy at a time? I've never thought about it, but why not? If everyone agrees and everyone's happy, where's the harm? Three holes and two hands, remember?" She grinned.

I returned her smile. "I remember."

Yes, Riley and Connor took turns with me, but they seemed to be as into each other as they were into me. They seemed comfortable with each other. Like being together was nothing new for them.

"You could build yourself a harem," Whitney said. "Why not have three or four boyfriends?"

"That sounds like a handful, literally and figuratively," I said.

The image of Josiah and the way he looked at me popped into my head. Even if he was interested, where would he fit into things? Would the other two be able to put their animosity aside and accept him? That might be a hurdle bigger than the mountain itself.

"True, but imagine all the orgasms." Whitney sighed. "I'd be lucky if I'd be able to walk after the first night or two."

Her words hit home, but not in the way she intended. Shuffling along behind her wasn't too strenuous, but if we had too many more lights to put up, I was going to have regrets later.

"Are you okay?" She must have seen the expression on my face. "I just meant all that dick would be a lot, but in a good way."

"I know," I said quickly. "It would. I…" I adjusted my ponytail.

"Don't like dick?" she asked, her expression deadpan.

"What? No. I like dick," I said quickly. "I have ERA, it makes being mobile difficult sometimes." I quickly explained, not wanting to make a fuss, but wanting her to understand my reaction.

"Oh," she said slowly and thoughtfully. "That explains why you look uncomfortable sometimes." Her eyes widened. "Oh, shit, I shouldn't have asked you to help me do this. I'm sorry, I had no idea." She started to take the string of lights from my hands.

I drew them away from her. "It's fine. I want to help. If it becomes too much, I'll say so."

"Would you though?" She gave me a sidelong, disbelieving look. "I know first-hand how stubborn people can be. They'd prefer to push through than admit they're struggling."

She wasn't pulling any punches.

"Okay, I've done it a few times," I admitted. "I'm trying to get better at pacing myself. This is fine though, I can do this."

People all over town had been talking about the fall festival for the last week. Everyone was so excited. I wanted to be a part of that.

"Promise me you'll tell me if it gets too much." She looked at me like I was one of her students, who better do what the teacher says.

"I will," I assured her. "As long as you promise not to treat me like I'm fragile. I'm not going to break into a million pieces just because I'm standing up." It was my turn to give her a firm look.

"Anyone who can put up with my brother for an extended period of time is not fragile," she said with a smile. "Far from it. If you were, he'd eat you alive. Besides, I know him. He doesn't like people like that. My brother has always enjoyed a challenge. Which is ironic, considering he poses one more often than not."

We both laughed.

"Poor Connor." I shook my head. "He's not that bad."

She gave me a speculative look. "No he's not. If I didn't know better, I'd think you were falling for him. Riley too, perhaps?"

"They… They keep life interesting," I said.

She dropped her head back and laughed. "They certainly do that. Like I said, you could do worse than them. Aurora Hollow could use more men… I could finish the sentence there, to be honest, but what I meant is they're good men. They can be absolute assholes at times, but deep down, their hearts are in the right place. Deep, deep down."

"There must be plenty of single men in town trying to get your attention," I said. I'd noticed them looking, even if she hadn't.

"One or two," she conceded. "I might even go out with them sometimes."

I had a feeling there was more to what she was saying. Someone she had her eye on. I wouldn't pry. When she was ready to tell me, if she was, I'd be here to listen.

"We should get finished with this." I nodded toward the lights still held in my hands.

"Yes, we should," she said. "Don't want you standing for longer than necessary. Honestly, I don't want to get up on this ladder more times than necessary either." She made a face that made me smile.

"The things we do for our community," I said tentatively.

Was I assuming too much in including myself in that? What was the old saying? In some places, you had to live there twenty or thirty years before you were considered a local. I'd be in my fifties before that happened.

"Exactly," she said without hesitation. "We wouldn't have it any other way, would we? Just wait until the festival, you're going to love it. We have live bands in the park and in the pub, and one down by the lake, in the little amphitheatre there. BYO blanket or chair. The streets will be lined with vendors selling every kind of food you can imagine. Word of advice, don't eat breakfast on Saturday morning. You'll want to keep some room in your stomach for a bit of everything."

"Noted." I followed her to the next spot when the lights needed to be attached. "That sounds amazing."

"It is," she agreed. "I think it's my favourite event

of the year. Closely followed by Christmas. And the entirety of the summer. And the first snowfall. And the last snowfall."

"So, everything?" I teased.

She laughed. "What can I say? I adore living here. I couldn't imagine being anywhere else. This place will always be home."

"I don't blame you." I handed her the last section of lights. "This town could easily be home for me as well."

The longer I was here, the more I could imagine spending the rest of my life here. Life in the city seemed unappealing and distant. Like that was another life a long time ago. Possibly one lived by someone else. It all seemed like some kind of dream. The kind that became less and less real as time went on.

"Good, because you're one of us now." She fastened the last of the lights and jumped off the ladder. "You know what I forgot is amazing around here? Halloween. There's nothing like Halloween in the hollow."

"I look forward to it," I said sincerely. What would Connor or Riley dress up as? I'd be curious to find out.

35

***

LEAH

"ARE YOU READY TO GO?" Connor asked as he pushed the front door open and looked inside.

"Why do I bother to lock that?" I asked.

He grinned. "I have no idea. To keep honest people out?"

I snort-laughed. "That sounds accurate. Because I can't keep you two out, can I?"

"Why would you want to?" Riley called out from behind Connor.

"I can't think of a single reason." I rolled my eyes playfully but picked up my bag from the table and tucked my phone into my pocket.

"Because there isn't one." Connor took my bag and swung it over his shoulder. "Riley and I are exceptional."

"Hey!" Riley looked at him as if he thought Connor said something offensive. Only the crinkles around his blue eyes showed he was joking.

Connor slid him a look. "Right, I'm exceptional. You're okay." He elbowed Riley playfully as he walked past, heading back out the door.

"I should have taken 'exceptional' when it was offered, shouldn't I?" Riley asked me.

"Probably," I agreed. I pulled the door closed behind me and made sure it was locked. In case any honest people walked by.

"How did all your tours go today?" With the increase in visitors for the festival, they were busy all day. Jacob had insisted he had enough help at the Frosty Brew, leaving us to enjoy the festivities, and the night off.

"No one died," Connor said.

"That's a bonus," I teased.

"It's a bonus for you," Riley said. "Otherwise you'd be spending the rest of the night doing the paperwork."

"Is that what you hired me for?" I fell into step beside him. "So I could clean up your messes?"

"We don't make those kinds of messes," Connor said. He walked close to me, close enough I could feel the heat radiating off his body.

"Right, we make good messes," Riley agreed. "Do we really want to go to the festival tonight?" He looked back over his shoulder at my cottage, a hint of longing in his expression.

"I do," I said. "I've never been to one before."

Hearing Whitney and the others talk about it, I couldn't help being excited. I'd spent a couple of hours this morning with Fiona and Sarah, walking through the food and craft stalls, buying a couple of things here or there.

Holly had a table selling homemade preserves. She'd been nice enough to let me leave a couple of my paintings there, in case any visitors wanted to buy them.

From what Whitney said, the fun really came in the evening and at night. As we walked towards Main Street, I could already see, hear and smell why.

The sound of music came from the park, which was decorated with twinkling lights. The smell from various food cooking on grills, or staying warm in food trucks made my mouth water.

The sky was purple, the stars already visible. A carpet of thousands of them, twinkling with lights of their own.

"This is magical," I said softly.

Groups of people gathered here or there, talking

and laughing. Enjoying each other's company. Kids ran back and forth around them, giggling and playing. No one seemed deterred by the chill in the air.

"You're magical," Riley said, lacing his fingers through mine.

"No one's ever called me magical before," I said.

"I don't know whether to be disappointed in them or relieved to be the first," Riley said. "I think I'll go for both."

"People are dickheads," Connor remarked. "That's their loss."

"Exactly," Riley agreed. "Too bad for them."

I thought about my question to Whitney, but now wasn't the time to bring it up. Right now, I wanted to enjoy the festival and their company. The time for deep and meaningful conversations was later.

"What do you feel like?" Connor leaned toward me, so close his shoulder pressed against mine. "Pizza? Poutine? Burger? Crêpes?"

"Crêpes sound perfect," I said. "With chicken and avocado."

He nodded and headed over to the van to place our order.

"You really never been to a festival like this before?" Riley asked.

"Not like this," I said. "Just small ones at school, where you get to dunk a teacher in the dunk tank."

"We have a dunk tank." Riley gestured over to the park. "We might convince Connor to let us dunk him."

"Fuck off," Connor said over his shoulder. "We can dunk you though."

"You say that like I wouldn't willingly climb in," Riley said. "It's for a good cause." He turned to me and added, "The money is split between charity and town improvement projects. Who could say no to those?"

"Not me, but you're not going to ask me to be dunked, are you?" The evening was too cool to get that kind of wet.

"Not if you don't want to," he said. "But tell me you'll let me win you a teddy bear. I've always wanted to win one for someone I care about. Connor won't let me win one for him." He glanced down at the ground as if suddenly shy.

"If you want to win me a teddy bear, I'd love that," I said. "I might give it to Sarah though."

He looked back up, his brow creased. "No, you have to keep it. That's the point. For you to have a teddy bear that makes you think of me when you look at it."

"You're not forgettable," I assured him. "Okay, a small one then." One that would be cute, sitting on a shelf, or on the mantelpiece.

He grinned. "Deal."

Connor headed back from the food van, carrying three plates. He handed us ours, before starting on his own crêpe.

"This is good," I said around a mouthful of crêpe and chicken. It tasted even better out here with the music, company and deepening sky.

They hummed their agreement and led me across to the park, where amusement rides and games were set up. Tinkling music and shrieks of excitement contrasted with the band, who played off to one side.

A couple of young boys ran past with cotton candy on sticks, waving them like they were Olympic torches.

"Come on." Riley took my empty plate and threw it and his in the trash on the way past. He grabbed my hand and dragged me over to the Strongman Game, where players had to hit a hammer and hope they hit it hard enough to make the bell at the top of the game ring.

"How hard can it be?" He rubbed his hands together, his biceps threatening to break the seams of his dark blue Henley.

"Show them what you've got," Connor told him. He looked as though he was ready to be impressed or amused as fuck, depending on how well Riley did.

Riley slid him a sly grin.

"I don't mean your dick, idiot." Connor rolled his eyes.

"Shame." Riley picked up the hammer and hefted it a couple of times. He turned side on to the game and raised the hammer, slamming it down onto the round target on the base. The hammer connected with a clang, sending the marker flying toward the bell.

It stopped a centimetre from the bell and fell back down.

Riley grunted. "That was for practice." He raised the hammer again, bringing it back down harder than before. This time, the marker hit the bell, making it ring out.

The crowd who gathered to watch him try his luck cheered and patted his back to congratulate him. He muttered his thanks, humble for once, before gesturing toward the display of teddy bears.

"She'll take the biggest one you have," he declared.

"I don't need a huge one," I argued. "Teddy bear," I added quickly.

I had a funny feeling I could protest all I wanted, I was going to get handed an enormous bear.

That was confirmed a moment later when the blue-haired young woman in charge of the game pulled a huge, bright blue teddy bear down from the shelf and handed it to me. She gave me a grin and a wink as if to congratulate me for my company.

I smiled back and held the plush bear close to me. I thought I'd outgrown my teddy bear days a long time ago, but there was something comforting about this one. Something sweet about Riley needing to show off his strength to win it for me.

"I'll have to think of a name," I said.

"Looks like you." Connor looked the bear up and down, then glanced at Riley.

"Big and cuddly?" Riley asked. "I'll take that comparison. Come on, let's go on the Ferris wheel." He grabbed both of our hands and started to pull us along behind him.

"Will they let me on with this?" I nodded towards the bear.

"They better," Riley said. He bought us tickets and led us to the gate as the Ferris wheel slowed to allow us to climb into a car.

Since no one stopped me from taking the bear, I placed it down at my feet and got comfortable on one side of the long bench. Connor sat beside me and Riley opposite us.

"Wait until you see the view from the top," Riley said as the car started to wobble and move.

"I'm surprised you don't have a Ferris wheel tour," I teased.

Connor snorted. "This doesn't go fast enough for us. If it did, I'd be all over it."

"That would be sick," Riley said. "Gravity-defying Ferris wheel."

"I'm starting to think I shouldn't have given you the idea," I said jokingly. "Next thing, you'll have one of those and a rollercoaster that starts at the very top of the mountain and goes all the way down."

"That would rock, but it wouldn't be good for the environment," Connor said. "If we could have one inside the mountain…"

"You'd have to be a billionaire to do that," I said. "By the time it was built, you'd be a millionaire."

A ride inside the mountain probably wasn't good for the environment either.

They both laughed.

"Accurate." Connor shifted over and draped an arm over my shoulder. "Let's enjoy this. Look, we can see the lake from here."

I looked out over the lights of the town, and

beyond to where Lake Aurora reflected the festival lights, the water glittering.

"We'll be skating on that in a few weeks," Riley said. "I fucking love this town. I remember guys from school leaving because they said there was nothing to do, but there's so. Fucking. Much. How could anyone be bored here?"

"And when it rains, you can read mafia romance books," I said.

He stared at me for a moment, before making a face. "Fucking Whitney. Connor, your sister has a big mouth."

Connor's body shook slightly as he laughed. "If you're ashamed of what you read—"

"I'm not," Riley said quickly. "Leah and I would have gotten around to that sooner or later. If you want to borrow any of my books, you're welcome to." He nodded.

"Same here," I told him. "Have you ever read dinosaur romance?"

"What... You know what, never mind." Connor shook his head. "I don't want to know."

Riley grinned and mouthed, "He'd totally read those."

"I can lip-read you know," Connor said dryly.

After a moment he added, "I might try one. A guy gets curious."

"You might even learn something," Riley told him.

Connor flipped him off with both hands.

I laughed softly and looked out over the edge of the car.

I froze. Frowned.

I must be seeing things. He couldn't possibly be here.

I squinted as he turned his face up towards me. My lips dropped apart.

What the hell was my stepbrother, Brooks, doing here?

36

LEAH

THE CAR barely stopped before I pushed the huge teddy bear at Riley and worked my way through the crowds. Heading in the direction I'd seen Brooks standing.

It was definitely him; he'd locked eyes with me before turning and disappearing into the throng.

"Leah!" Connor called out after me. "What the hell?"

I stood on my toes, trying to see where he might have gone. By the time the Ferris wheel slowly made it back down, after stopping to let off others, he could be almost anywhere.

I thought I caught a glimpse of blonde hair through the press of people and started off at a trot.

"Leah!" Connor called out again. "Leah, stop!"

A hand caught my wrist and Connor pulled me back to his body.

"I said *stop*," he growled in my ear.

I looked back at him, ready to argue, but he was sinking to his knees. He gestured to Riley, who put the teddy bear aside and helped me to sit on Connor's shoulders. Holding my legs carefully, Connor rose, pushing me up with him.

"There, whoever you're looking for should be easier to find this way," he said gruffly. "Are you going to tell me who it is?"

"If you promise not to beat the snot out of him," I said. "I thought I saw my stepbrother." I scanned the crowds, my vantage point on his shoulders allowing me to see over the heads of everyone.

"Your stepbrother?" Riley scooped up the teddy bear and held it under his arm. "What's he doing here? I thought you didn't get along?"

"We don't. I don't know why he's here," I said. "Possibly for the same reason everyone else is."

What were the chances his presence was a complete coincidence? I could chalk it up to that, but I didn't believe it.

He didn't look surprised to see me.

"If he's come to win you a teddy bear, I don't promise not to beat the snot out of him," Riley said.

I gave him a sideways glance. "I can guarantee he's not here to win me a teddy bear."

Brooks wouldn't waste his time with games of chance. He also wouldn't waste his time doing anything nice for me. Honestly, I was surprised he didn't try to find a way to get us stuck, so we'd spend the night at the top of the Ferris wheel.

There was no love lost between me and him.

"If he's here to make trouble, I still don't promise," Riley said, stepping closer, like he'd appointed himself my bodyguard.

"Neither do I," Connor said. "I'm not letting him fuck with Leah." He looked up at me. "Any sign of this dickhead?"

I shook my head. "I can't see him anywhere. If he wants something, he'll come out of the woodwork at some point." At the worst possible moment, knowing him. It was like he had a sixth sense for pissing me off.

Connor grunted something before lowering himself back to his knees and letting me climb down from him.

"Thank you." I took his hand and pulled him back to his feet before grazing my lips across his.

"Yeah. Didn't want you running." He gave a half shrug.

"That's very sweet." I wound my arms around his neck and gave him a hug, and a firmer kiss.

"That's me, sweet." He smirked.

I batted his chest with the back of my hand. "Be nice to yourself. You're not a complete asshole."

He wrapped his arms around me, his hands on my ass. "Before I met you, I was an incomplete asshole." He pressed a light kiss to my forehead. "But if you tell anyone I said that, I'll deny it. Connor Ferguson doesn't do sweet."

"My lips are sealed." I mimed zipping them shut and throwing away the key.

"All this talk about sweetness makes me want ice cream," Riley said. He draped his spare arm around my shoulders and embraced us in a group hug, including the massive teddy bear.

"I can't believe I'm hugging a plushie," Connor muttered. The top of the bear was practically in his face.

"You say that like it's the first time ever," Riley teased.

"It's not the first time. The last time, I was five," Connor told him.

"I remember," Riley said. "You had that plush moose. You used to carry him everywhere."

"And you had a plush unicorn, for some reason." Connor smirked.

"Because some of us believed in magic," Riley said with a shrug.

"You don't anymore?" I couldn't remember the last time I believed in magic, so I was in no position to judge.

"I didn't think I did, but then I met you." He kissed my mouth before dropping his arm and handing me back the teddy bear.

"If you keep saying things like that, you won't need ice cream," Connor said.

"I still need ice cream," Riley said. "Let's go before they sell out." He took my hand and led me back toward the food trucks.

I followed behind, but kept an eye out for Brooks. Or someone who looked like him.

The guy I saw might have had a striking resemblance, nothing more. But I knew that wasn't true. I'd seen recognition on his face, even at a distance. It was definitely him. Why had he run like that? Why not stick around to find out why I was here too?

The sooner he turned up, the sooner I'd get those answers.

If he turned up.

"He'll turn up," Connor said, as if reading my

mind. We stood close together, waiting in line for ice cream. "This place is too small to hide for long. If he tries, Riley and I know all the good hiding places."

"And the bad ones too," Riley said. "A couple of the huts further up the mountain are dangerous. As in, about to fall down, or in places where they'd be destroyed by rock slides or avalanches. Not the fun kind of dangerous."

"Sounds like the perfect place for him," Connor said darkly.

"I don't disagree, but I want to know why he's in Aurora Hollow before he meets some nasty, sticky end," I said.

In spite of our differences, I didn't want Brooks to die. We'd only known each other a handful of years. For a while there, I thought, perhaps naïvely, that we could be friends. That was before our parents started pitting him against me. Things soured all too quickly after that.

Once in a while, I wondered what would have happened if we hadn't let them do that to us.

"If you say sticky end again, we're going to skip the ice cream," Connor whispered.

"Oh yeah?" I asked over my shoulder.

"Mmmhmm." He pushed my hair aside and kissed the side of my neck.

A shiver of heat went through my body, down to my core. "You make a compelling argument."

"Of course I do," he murmured against my skin. Grabbing my hand and Riley's, he tugged us out of line. "Come on, I know a place."

He pulled us across the park, and down toward the lake. About halfway between them, he pushed us into a stand of trees. The space between the trunks was enveloped in darkness. A pocket of shadows in the middle of the light, noise and festivities.

I found myself pressed against a tree with a thick, wide trunk and the faint smell of sap.

Connor pressed his body to mine and claimed my mouth with his. His lips tasted mine while his tongue insisted on entry. I opened my mouth to him, my tongue teasing his.

"Save me some." Riley waited until we came up for air before turning my face and slamming his mouth down onto mine. He kissed me deep and hard before breaking away and snaking an arm around the back of Connor's neck pulling him in for a kiss.

The shadows allowed enough light to watch them, their tongues stroking each other's lips, breathing each other's air like they'd done this a million times before.

They were comfortable with each other and that was hot as hell.

Finally, they broke off and Riley kissed me while Connor worked his hands under my shirt and around to my back. He unhooked my bra, letting my breasts fall free. He slid his hands up and down my back before pushing my shirt up off over my head. He grabbed a hold of my bra and pulled it away, letting both garments drop to the leafy ground.

Leaning down, he drew my nipple between his lips and started to suck.

"I fucking love that sound," Riley whispered. "Connor sucking."

"Yeah?" Connor glanced over at him.

"Yeah," Riley said, an edge of challenge creeping into his tone.

Apparently Connor was up to meeting the challenge, because he sank to his knees and pushed down the front of Riley's track pants and boxers.

I made out Riley's cock in Connor's hand before it was between his lips. The only nearby sounds were the wet sucking of his mouth and Riley's groans of pleasure.

"He always had the best fucking mouth," Riley whispered. "The only one just as good is yours." He grabbed a handful of my hair and pulled me over to kiss my mouth.

He tasted sweet and salty, his stubble rough against my face. I wanted, needed more.

Breathless, I broke off long enough to say, "Do you always share?"

"Always," Riley agreed. "We're not going to stop now. You're stuck with both of us."

I glanced down to Connor, to see him bob his head as he went on sucking.

"If you want other guys, we'll work on that," Riley added in a barely controlled whisper. "But you don't have to choose between us and neither are we."

"Good." I grabbed the front of Riley's shirt and kissed him again, while he palmed my breast, making my nipple hard. If my body was any hotter, I'd set the tree behind me on fire.

Connor pulled his mouth off Riley's cock and undid the front of my jeans. He pulled them down and my panties with them, pushing them off my feet until I was naked in the shadows. He pressed a hand between my thighs and grazed it over my pussy.

"So fucking wet," he whispered. "Riley, I need to see you fuck this pussy. Right now."

He shuffled back and pushed himself to his feet, giving Riley room to step in front of me and cup my ass. He picked me up until my legs wrapped around his waist. Lining his cock up to my entrance, he swiped the tip through my wet heat a couple of times before pushing himself inside me, deep and hard.

"Fuck, yeah," Connor whispered.

I froze as a group of people walked past, talking and laughing, but Riley didn't stop or even slow. He rolled his hips, thrusting into me as though they could see us and he was enjoying the audience. He wouldn't have stopped if they turned the lights on their phones toward us, illuminating our every movement.

A small part of me wished they would, but they walked past, oblivious to what was going on amongst the trees.

"So close," Riley whispered with a laugh.

I responded with a low, husky laugh of my own. "You really want to be seen, don't you?"

"I like the risk," was his answer. No surprise there. These two lived for risk. What was life without it?

Riley pressed a hand between us, stroking my clit while he thrust slowly. "So fucking perfect," he whispered. "So fucking ours. You know what I'm picturing right now?""

"What?" I asked, my eyes half closed as I savoured his fingers and his cock.

"I'm picturing your stepbrother watching us," he whispered. "And Josiah, since you seemed curious about him. I'm picturing them with their cocks hard, waiting for their turn with you."

His words pushed me right over the edge. I couldn't have stopped myself from coming if I wanted to. Not even if Connor ordered me not to. I could see exactly what Riley was describing and it was hotter than hell. Josiah and Brooks, fisting their cocks, aching to slide them inside my body.

I have to admit, it wasn't the first time I had that fantasy about Brooks, but Josiah was something new. So fucking complicated but that didn't matter in the moment. All that mattered was the wave of bliss that washed over me, taking me and Riley with it, losing ourselves in each other.

37

LEAH

THE CLEANUP WAS NEVER as fun as the setup, but most of Aurora Hollow turned out to help, making it quicker than it would otherwise have been. I kept an eye out for Brooks, even quietly asking around, but I saw no sign of him. No one could remember seeing anyone who fit his description.

I was starting to think I imagined seeing him at all. He might have been a trick of the light or something like that. Either way, he didn't come knocking on my door or turn up beside me to pick up discarded paper cups, or pull down streamers.

By the middle of Monday afternoon, the town was cleaned up and all the food trucks and amusement rides were gone like they'd never been there. If it wasn't for indents on the grass, they might also have been figments of my imagination.

"Thank goodness that's done." Louisa wiped her hands on her jeans. "Thanks a lot for pitching in. It's very much appreciated."

"You're more than welcome," I said honestly. "I feel like it's the least I can do given how nice every-one's been."

"I heard Holly sold both of the paintings she had at her table." Louisa bent forward to tie up the top of a bag of trash.

"She did," I said. "Early in the day too." I didn't know who she'd sold them to, but I was grateful for the money.

"I'm not surprised one bit," Louisa said. "You're very talented. It won't be long before people are coming up here just to buy a Leah Kent original."

My face heated. I glanced down at my shoes and muttered, "I don't know about that."

She finished tying the bag and stood up straight to rub her back. "I do. I know what people come to Aurora Hollow for. Some come to the atmosphere. Some come for the adventure tours. And some come for things they can't get anywhere else. The craft items, made by local folk. I've seen it a bunch of times. They buy up everything they can, take it to a gallery in the city and put up the price. Sooner or later, the artist figures it out and sells directly to the gallery themselves." She smiled. "Eliminate the middle man, as they say. Middle person is probably more appropriate these days. At any rate, there's been muttering about setting up a gallery here for years. Sooner or later, someone is gonna do that. Maybe it'll be you."

"It's crossed my mind a few times," I admitted. "If I had an investor or two, maybe then…"

I had no illusion I could do it on my own. Physically or financially.

"There might be some rich city folk ready to invest in something like that." She picked up the bag and hefted it higher before carrying it over to the pile ready for trash collection.

I watched her for a moment, lost in thought. Was that really something I could do? Set up my own small gallery here in town? Rent out space to other artists, so they could reach buyers of their own?

The place could have rooms at the back for art classes for people of all ages. That would mean putting down roots here in town. Cementing my place as a member of the community. What would the rest of the town think of that? Living here was one thing, indicating I planned to stay was another.

I decided to put that in the back of my mind for now. I'd barely begun doing the administration work for Riley and Connor. That and my own art deserved the bulk of my attention at the moment.

I caught a hint of black slipping out of the store opposite the pub. I hadn't seen Josiah Lachance for a couple of weeks. Presumably he stayed up the mountain, keeping away from aggressive, prying eyes in town.

Without realising it, I crossed the road and hurried after him.

"Josiah, wait," I called out.

He glanced back over his shoulder. Scowled. "What do you want?"

"I—" What did I want? "I just want to talk. See how you are."

He stopped and squinted at me. "Why do you want to know?"

He reminded me of a wild animal, wary, but eyeing a handful of food. Certain he should run, but something kept him there.

"Because I don't like the way you've been treated," I said. "You deserve to walk around town as much as anyone else."

"Yeah, right." He clearly didn't believe a word I

said. Waiting for the punchline as if this was some kind of sick joke.

I took a couple of careful steps forward. "It's true," I said firmly. "If they can welcome a total outsider, they can welcome you. What happened was—"

"I know what it was," he snapped. "I don't know why you're trying to be nice to me, but fucking *stop*. You don't get bonus points for it. No one's going to give you a gold fucking star. I don't need to be your pet project or whatever the hell is going on in your head." He gestured towards my face, his movement small as if he didn't dare to have his hands any further from his own body than they were. As if being any closer to me might set him on fire.

"I don't see you that way," I said. "Has it been that long since someone was nice to you that you don't recognise it?"

If I wasn't watching closely, I would have missed his flinch. He wasn't a wild animal, he was an abused one. Locked in a tiny cage, given scraps to eat. And for what? Because he dared to bark a warning that wasn't believed? Because he looked away and something terrible happened? Because he was a kid who had a responsibility dropped on his young shoulders?

It wasn't fucking fair.

"Don't. Be. Nice. To. Me." He closed his eyes and shook his head, then opened them again. "Don't talk to me. Unless you want the whole fucking town to hate you, then do yourself a favour and stay away from me."

He turned and hurried away, this time straddling a motorbike and jamming a helmet down on his head. He started the engine, gave me a look over his shoulder before roaring away.

"Josiah… Oh." An older woman came bustling out of the store beside me. She held a bag in her hands. "He left the nails he bought." She held a packet in her hand. "I guess he'll come back for them."

Impulsively, I held my hand for the packet. "If you can tell me where, I'll take them to him."

She looked at me like I was out of my mind, but shrugged. She handed me the packet and gave me directions, which I listened to carefully before thanking her and stepping away.

I didn't know who would be angrier that I was doing this, Connor or Riley, but I wasn't planning to ask their permission. I was doing something nice for someone who needed a break. Okay, and I was curious to see where Josiah lived.

I hurried back to my cottage and slid into the

driver's seat of my car. The bag of nails, I tossed onto the seat beside me. I put the car into drive and headed in the direction the woman told me to go. Driving more slowly than the speed limit, because as soon as I left Aurora Hollow, the road became windy and narrow.

She was right when she said I couldn't miss the way up. Every so often, a track broke off to the left or right, but this was the only sealed road. I passed the spot where the zip line platform was, and kept on going.

To the left, I saw a glimpse of white. The falls. I wanted to slow down and take a look, but I could stop on the way back. Whatever Josiah needed the nails for, it could be important. Better that I get them to him before he realised he needed to go back for them.

I drove past the gate to Aurora Lodge and on to a couple of cottages maybe half a kilometre away. As I pulled into the track leading to them, I spotted Josiah's motorbike, tucked in beside one of the buildings.

"This must be the place," I said to myself.

I parked beside the motorbike and killed the engine. Grabbing the nails, I pushed out of the car and stood.

I froze.

I was barely aware of the packet of nails falling out of my hand and hitting the dirt with a crunch.

"What the fuck are you doing here?" Josiah appeared from around the side of one of the buildings.

I was barely aware of him too.

"I've been here," I whispered.

I knew that cottage right in front of me. Knew exactly where the creek was. The creek I'd been told a million times to stay away from. I always had. Sitting beside it, but keeping a respectful distance. Knowing my father would scold me if I went any closer.

My father?

Oh God.

I didn't know I was falling until I landed on my knees in the dirt.

Footsteps ran towards me, the sound of concern. "What the hell?" Josiah kept his distance, his hands out in front of him.

No. No. No.

None of this could be true. My heart raced faster than the water down the falls. It couldn't be true, but I knew it was. I didn't remember everything, but I remembered enough.

I covered my face with my hands.

They were wrong.

Coral Clarke hadn't died that day.

I'd just come home.

THANK YOU FOR READING! The story concludes in Take Me Slowly part 2.

If you'd love a bonus scene of Riley after his little run in with Leah and her easel, you can find that here.

ABOUT THE AUTHOR

Maggie Alabaster writes reverse harem romance.

She lives in NSW, Australia with one spouse, two daughters, one dog, and countless birds.

Sign up for Maggie's newsletter! Sign Up!

Join Maggie's reader group! Join here!

Follow Maggie on Bookbub! Click here to follow me!

Check out Maggie's website- www.maggiealabaster.com

Pucking Hardened Hearts

Dusk Bay Demons

Puck Drop

Breakaway

Power Play

Brutal Academy

Book 1 Heartless

Book 2 Cruel

Book 3 Vengeful

Court of Blood and Binding

Book 1 Song of Scent and Magic

Book 2 Crown of Mist and Heat

Book 3 Sword of Balm and Shadow

Book 4 Whisper of Frost and Flame

Dark Masque

Book 1 Bait

Book 2 Prey

Book 3 Trap

Saving Abbie

Book 1 Pitch

Book 2 Pound

Book 3 Session

Book 4 Muse

Book 5 Rhythm

Book 6 Encore

Novella Venomous

Saving Abbie books 1-4

Saving Abbie books 4-6 + Venomous

Ruthless Claws

Book 1 Ivory

Book 2 Crimson

Book 3 Elodie

Harmony's Magic

Book 1 Summoned by Fire

Book 2 Summoned by Fate

Book 3 Summoned by Desire

Shifter's Vault

Book 1 Discarded

Book 2 Deceived

Book 3 Disgraced

My Alien Mates

Book 1 Star Warriors

Book 2 Star Defenders

Book 3 Star Protectors

Academy of Modern Magic

Book 1 Digital Magic

Book 2 Virtual Magic

Book 3 Logical Magic

Complete Collection

Summer's Harem

Book 1: Shimmer

Book 2: Glimmer

Book 3: Flicker

Complete collection

Short reads

Taken by the Snowmen

Jingle All the Way

Also by Maggie Alabaster and Erin Yoshikawa

Caught by the Tide

Book 1–Pursued by Shadows

Book 2 Pursued by Darkness

Book 3 Pursued by Monsters